THE ARROGANT ARTIST

BOOK 2 INTERNATIONAL BAD BOYS

JA LOW

JALOWBOOKS

International Bad Boy Set

Copyright @ 2020 JA Low

All rights reserved. No part of this eBook may be reproduced or transmitted in any form, including electronic or mechanical, without written permission from the publisher, except in the case of brief quotations embodied in critical articles or reviews.

This is a work of fiction. Names, characters, businesses, places, events, and incidents are either the products of the author's imagination or used in a fictitious manner. Any resemblance to actual persons, living or dead, or actual events is purely coincidental. JA Low is in no way affiliated with any brands, songs, musicians, or artists mentioned in this book.

This eBook is licensed for your personal enjoyment only. This eBook may not be re-sold or given away to other people. If you would like to share this eBook with another person, please purchase an additional copy for each person you share it with. If you are reading this eBook and did not purchase it, or it was not purchased for your use only, then you should return it to the seller and purchase your own copy.

Thank you for respecting the author's work.

Cover Design @ Outlined with Love

Editor @ Swish Design & Editing

www.swishgrafix.com.au

❦ Created with Vellum

NOTE FROM AUTHOR

This was previously released as Love in Color.

1
EMILY

"You look beautiful tonight." Toby gives me a heartwarming smile as he takes my hand, helping me out of the taxi. He's looking rather handsome too, dressed in a navy suit, his blond hair slicked back. Toby and I have been dating for five years. We met the last year of university. He was doing an international business degree, and I was finishing an art history degree. Toby's now a business analyst for an international finance company. He's been putting in long hours at the office as well as traveling a lot to New York. I'm so proud of him.

I wish I were doing something with my degree like he is. Instead, it's sitting at home gathering dust. I thought at this point in my life I'd be working at the Tate Modern, or one of the Serpentine Galleries, or maybe even in my wildest dreams, the Louvre in Paris. Instead, I'm working in the gift shop at Madame Tussauds selling tourist crap. I haven't had the best of luck with jobs. I've bounced around from one horrendous position to another.

Who knew there would be so many people with art degrees

trying to get a job? I can't even get unpaid work in a gallery, and I can assure you I have tried everything.

Luckily, I have Toby because he encourages me every day never to give up on my dreams, and that one day, I too will be living mine, just like he is.

Toby places a hand at the small of my back as we enter the restaurant. It's some fancy restaurant in the city that he likes to go to for client lunches. I know I can't afford anything on the menu. The restaurant is opulent as we take the first steps inside, where we're greeted by a gorgeous blonde maître d who could be on the cover of *Vogue*.

"Table for two, please," Toby asks the woman.

"Certainly, sir. Follow me." She smiles at him, and we follow the supermodel through the luxurious restaurant. I watch as her high ponytail swings from side to side in a mesmerizing fashion as we make our way through the dimly lit restaurant.

"Table for two." The woman gestures to a small black wooden table with a small votive candle in the middle giving off the smallest amount of light. Toby pulls my chair out for me, always the gentleman, and I take my seat. "Here are your menus. I'll send your server out to you in a moment. Please, take your time." Then she twists on her heels, and she's gone.

"This is gorgeous," I say while looking around the stunning restaurant with its mirrored ceilings and silver chainmail chandeliers which are more like sculptures than the need for light. The dark gray walls look almost like silk with what looks like hand-painted silver flecks through the wallpaper.

"A bottle of champagne, please," Toby orders when he catches the attention of a waitress as she rushes past. The waitress nods and walks away while my heart starts to quicken.

Fancy restaurant. Check.

Champagne. Check.

Five years of dating. Check.

Four years of living together. Check.

This is it!
Tonight is the night!
The night that Toby pops the question.
"Are we celebrating something?" I smile at him.

He seems nervous, jumpy even. A tiny bead of sweat settles across his upper lip. I take another look around the restaurant. Although beautiful, it's not exactly where I imagined being proposed to. I was hoping for something more like on the steps of the Met in New York or outside the Venus de Milo in the Louvre. I've been leaving hints for Toby about engagement rings for the past year, and by now I hope he knows that I'd love an antique ring, one that has a beautiful story attached to it, or even more so I'd love one of his family's heirlooms. I don't need a new ring, and it doesn't even have to be a plain white diamond—I'll take a pink or a canary or even a sapphire—because I'm not traditional in that sense.

"Actually, yes, we're celebrating something." Toby can't look at me. He scans the room impatiently I'm sure willing the hostess to return with the champagne. I wonder if the ring is in the bottom of the glass like they do in the movies.

Remember, Emily, don't drink the entire contents of the glass, you don't want to choke on a two-carat engagement ring.

"Oh, how exciting. What is it?" I talk more when I get nervous, I can't help it.

"Wait until the bottle comes," Toby tells me. This is it. He has a plan, and I must be patient. He has probably been organizing this night for months, and I don't want to ruin it by being too eager. I smile and wait while the butterflies flit around my stomach.

Toby's such a catch, or should I say that's what people tell me. He comes from an extremely wealthy family who may even be related to royalty or something like that. They are blue-blooded with country estates and posh accents while I come from a hard-working, middle-class family. I got into university via a scholarship, whereas I'm pretty sure Toby's family has a wing of the university named after them.

Even though we come from two different worlds, we fell in love. I'm not one of those girls impressed by money. I hate that Toby has to buy everything in our relationship because, let's face it, my meager wage isn't paying for first-class trips to Majorca like we did last summer. He knows it makes me feel uncomfortable, but he simply smiles and tells me that he's lucky because he has a large trust fund, and why wouldn't he want to spoil the woman he loves. I can't argue with that.

The waitress comes back with the expensive bottle of champagne. She pops it and pours us each a glass, then places the bottle back into the champagne stand beside us before rushing away.

Toby holds up his glass. "To the future." Then he clinks his glass against mine.

My heart does a double beat. I take a sip, the bubbles tickle my nose, and the smooth liquid warms my belly.

"So, I wanted to talk to you about something, Emily."

I try and calm myself down by taking a deep breath. I need to act surprised when he asks me to marry him.

"You know how I have been working on projects with our New York office?" I nod. He's been flying back and forth frequently for meetings for the past six months. "Well, they have asked me to take over the New York team for a two-year contract."

Oh. My. God. We're moving to New York.

Yes. Yes. Yes.

This is the fresh start I need.

"Oh, Toby, this is an amazing opportunity. You deserve it so much. I'm so proud of you, baby. You've worked so hard." Giddy excitement fills me as I continue, "There are so many amazing galleries in New York. I bet I can easily find work there."

Toby stiffens, placing his champagne glass on the table, his look now serious.

"Actually, Ems..." there's a long awkward pause, "... I was thinking of going alone."

I just stare at him, my lashes blinking slowly, my brain trying to compute and then catch up to what his words mean.

Alone?

As in one person?

As in just him?

"Oh. Okay. It's a work thing... I understand." I try to hide my disappointment, but the pain is killing me inside. "Long distance is going to be hard." I simply can't afford to fly back and forth between London and New York for the next two years. I have no idea how this is going to work.

There's another long pause, then he says, "I don't want to do a long-distance relationship, Emily."

Again, I just stare at him, my brain not really computing the words he's speaking to me. "You don't want me to come to New York, but you also don't want to do a long-distance relationship." Toby nods. "I don't understand what you..." Then it hits me. "You're breaking up with me?" The question comes out louder than I anticipated, and people at the next table turn to look at us.

"I'm not breaking up with you, just asking for a break."

What the hell?

I'm sure my jaw hits the floor.

"I thought you were going to propose." My voice squeaks, then a sneaky single tear falls down my cheek. No. I will not cry. Toby dislikes emotional women.

I hear someone tsk behind me.

"Emily, I'm sorry." Toby grabs my hands and holds them with his own. "But honestly, babe, you can't be surprised."

What? I don't think I can be any more stunned than I am at this moment.

"Excuse me?" I pull my hands away from his.

"Ems... you've done nothing with your life. You flit around from menial job to menial job, which was cute for a couple of years, but we're getting older now. I want to be proud of the woman I marry."

Oh, holy hell, his words are like a knife to my heart, slicing it in two. I have never felt so worthless than I do right now.

"I think it's best we have some time apart. You sort yourself out. You can stay in my apartment while I'm gone. I'm not an asshole. When I come back, and you're in a better position with your life... I can propose then."

I stare at him, completely dumbfounded.

Does he actually think what he's saying is okay?

"So, what you're saying is... you want to see other people while you're in New York?" His cheeks turn red, and he has the nerve to turn away flustered. My stomach sinks with realization. "Oh..." well, this is awkward, "... what you're really saying is you've already met someone in New York." There's a long pause before he sticks the knife in further and twists.

"I didn't mean for it to happen, Ems."

My body is shaking with humiliation and anger. My hand is itching to pick the champagne glass up and throw it at his face, or better yet, break off the stem and plunge it in his dark heart.

"How long?" I don't really want an answer to that question, but I know it's important to ask how long he's been deceiving me.

Toby lets out a heavy sigh. "Six months."

My eyes widen. "Six... *months!*" My voice rises.

Toby frowns and checks around quickly to make sure no one is noticing our disagreement. His complete and utter disregard for my pain angers me even more—he's more concerned with what strangers think about him than his own girlfriend.

I lower my voice because I don't want to look hysterical. "I wish I knew we were allowed to screw other people while we were dating because maybe then I might have found someone who actually knows how to make me come, instead of having to resort to my vibrator to get me off. Every. Single. Time." It's a low blow, but it's also the truth. Toby only ever cared about *his* needs, *his* pleasure, and ultimately, *his* satisfaction. His face pales.

"Emily, there's no need to act like this. We're both adults."

My fist wants to show him how much of an adult I actually think he is.

"You're a weak piece of shit," I seethe between clenched teeth. "I can't believe I have wasted five years of my life with you. Five. Damn. Years!" I'm angry at myself for falling for the fairy-tale ending. "I'm the best thing that will ever happen to you, Toby. And when you realize it, after the novelty of shagging some American Barbie has worn off, I'm going to be so far gone..." I waggle my finger in his face, "... you're going to regret this day," I tell him as if putting a hex on him.

"You were always overly dramatic, Emily." He rolls his eyes, and damn him right to hell because a look of boredom falls across his face. "I thought we could have an adult discussion about this," he hisses.

"You're breaking my heart, Toby." I look at him in complete and utter disbelief. "You have been cheating on me with someone else for six months."

Hold in the tears, Emily.

Hold them in, I tell myself. *This bastard does not deserve them.*

Trouble is I fail miserably—stupid tear ducts are overactive.

"You know who I am, Emily. You know my family," he whisper-yells at me. "I have a legacy to uphold." My chest begins to tighten as I try to stave off a panic attack. He reaches out and touches my hand. "When I come back, Emily, you and I can be together." *Is he serious?* "You're marriage material, but only when you have a proper job." *The condescending, conniving, contemptuous prick.*

"I pity your American girlfriend. I bet she thinks she's struck it rich with some posh English guy. I wonder if she knows she's not marriage material either." I pull my hand from his, and Toby gives me another frustrated look as he draws his brows together so hard, they form a single line across his forehead.

"My family would never allow me to marry an American."

I've had enough! Picking up my napkin, I throw it at him but wishing it was something much heavier like a crystal vase.

"We. Are. Done. I hope your new girlfriend has a powerful vibrator, she's going to need one." And with that last barb, I walk out of the restaurant with my head held high.

Only trouble is as soon as I'm outside, I burst into tears.

2

EMILY

"That lying sack of shit," Rosie yells, grabbing a bottle of wine from her refrigerator.

"I'd have thrown the glass of champagne in his face," Ava adds.

"He actually thought you would take him back after he fucked some American bimbo for *two years*?" Georgia states.

I love my girls. When they got my SOS as I sobbed out the front of the restaurant, they launched into *Operation Save Emily*, calling me an Uber and making sure Rosie's apartment was stocked with lots of wine and chocolate.

"Five years I've wasted on that man." I throw back the third glass of wine without any regard for how I'll feel tomorrow.

"I can't believe he's been cheating and for so long. No offense, Em... but seriously, the man is a bore," Rosie tells me, and I giggle. "He has the personality of an ironing board."

"It's the accent, that's all," Ava adds. "Americans love the British accent."

"She's probably some boring accountant or something equally as dull," Georgia muses.

"What am I going to do?" The tears start to fall down my

face. "Toby's right, I've done nothing with my degree. I work bullshit jobs. I'm not at all where I thought I saw myself when I graduated university..." I trail off as the girls all rally around me.

"Sweetheart, you're the best human in the world. So what? You don't have your dream job yet. That's okay. We now make a plan for you to find you and your dream job. Between all of us, I'm sure we can find you something," Rosie consoles me.

"Let's have a look at what's around. See if there's anything you would like to do." Ava waves her phone at me.

All I can do right now is nod my head.

"Look at this one," Georgia calls out.

We have spent the past hour searching the local employment advertisements.

"Artist seeks an assistant for the summer to get ready for exhibition. All food and lodgings will be covered as well as a generous wage. Needs to be able to deal with unpredictable hours and travel. Must be able to speak French, has great organization and administration skills, and above all loves art. The job will be based in the South of France. Serious applicants need only apply."

"That sounds fantastic," Rosie squeals.

"The South of France for the summer, Emmy. This is exactly what you need. Spending your days sunning yourself with some hot French artist who's going to want to paint you because you're his muse, and then have hot, dirty sex with you under the stars."

Everyone goes quiet at Ava's comments, and then we all burst out laughing.

"What? A girl can dream, can't she?" She smiles.

Ava, always the romantic.

"The job says only serious applicants need apply. I don't think I'm going to be sunning myself in paradise with some French god." A girl can dream, though.

"Well, lucky you're serious. It would look fantastic on your résumé and who knows what it could lead to," Georgia tells me.

"Fine! Why not. Not like I'll get the job, anyway."

The girls all scream with delight as they make the best résumé in the history of résumés. Well, as good as it's going to get when we've gone through one too many bottles of wine.

"One awesome résumé down," Rosie states.

"Next. We need to move you out of that shithole apartment," Georgia adds.

I don't know where I'd be without my girls.

3

LOUIS

I can't believe I've sold all my paintings. New York has been one of my most successful trips this year. My popularity is growing every day. I never imagined I'd be here living my dream, and that people who live halfway across the world want to purchase my paintings. As much as I have loved being away, I can't wait to see Elisabeth again, to hold her in my arms, to kiss her, to fuck her. It's been a long week apart.

I drop my keys in the bowl beside the front door. The house is quiet. It's early evening, but the summer sun is still out and glowing in through the open windows. She must be down in one of the studios working—the light is amazing at this time of the evening.

A couple of years ago, we built artist studios at the back of our property. We lease them for free to artists as part of the mentor program that Elisabeth set up helping the next generation succeed in this competitive industry.

We have successfully launched the careers of some truly magnificent young artists over the years. It's something I'm very proud of. There are so many talented kids out there and no one to help them succeed. I want to pay it forward like my mentor did for me.

I make my way closer to where one of the studios is located. Light streams from under the door, and music blares from inside. Yves, my brightest artist, needs his music loud when he paints. The aggressive beats are reflected in his art, the tortured soul that simmers right under the surface.

He's had a rough childhood, and art seems to be the only way he can get his anger out, otherwise he explodes, but that emotion has enabled him to produce spectacular works of art that are selling quicker than he can produce them. He's becoming the new 'it' boy of the art circuit.

I open the door to his studio—he'd never hear me knock, so I don't bother anymore. I step inside the whitewashed walls, one-bedroom cabin, and what I see isn't what I was prepared for. There, spread out on her stomach against the white canvas covered in paint is my wife, who's being fucked from behind by Yves. He's moving her around the canvas as he fucks her harder as if she's his own human paintbrush. My wife is moaning, calling out his name, begging for more, begging for it harder.

All I can do is just stand there. I'm caught between the utter betrayal and the beautiful art they are creating together. It's not until my wife opens her eyes mid-fuck that she screams, pushing Yves away.

"Louis, you're home," she states the obvious while reaching out and grabbing her white robe, quickly covering herself.

"Oh, shit! I'm so sorry, L-Louis. I..." Yves stumbles over his words.

"Get the fuck out of my house, you little piece of shit," I bellow at him, which makes him flinch and blink a few times.

"No." My wife grabs Yves' arm, and my eyes widen in shock. "He's staying."

"You think I'm going to allow this little shit to stay in my house after I come home to him fucking my wife?"

Elisabeth's eyes widen, her body stiffens, and she takes a couple of steps toward me. "I'm his muse, Louis. This is art, nothing more. You, of all people, should understand that."

How dare she throw how we met in my face.

"You weren't married to him, Elisabeth."

She was one of my mentor's muses, one of many who used to pose for him.

"Yes, but he loved me." Her eyes narrow at me. "He understood I was your muse. He knew he had to let me go, so you could succeed. You, of all people, know that sometimes an artist's muse isn't always who you want them to be."

I'm stunned that she's somehow trying to validate her cheating this way.

"And that's what you are to him?" I question, pointing at Yves.

"Yes. Have you not seen his paintings? The passion that screams from the canvas."

Then it hits me.

Yves' latest works have changed from anger-filled paintings to softer themes. This new direction is because they are paintings of him fucking my wife every which way. I launch myself at him, landing a punch hard in the jaw while the studio fills with my wife's screams.

"WHAT THE FUCK?" I'm drenched with water.

"I thought you were dead," Daniel, my brother and agent, grumbles. He's standing there with a green bucket in his hand.

"I was sleeping, you asshole." I shake to try and get the water droplets off my face—the last strings of my recurring nightmare still vivid in my mind. Empty bottles clink as I move the wet bedspread away from me.

"Look at you." He points at the mess surrounding me. "There are beer, tequila, and wine bottles everywhere."

"What can I say, I like it all." I shrug.

Daniel scowls at me. "You need to stop this, Louis."

It's the same story over and over again with him—*stop drinking, get over it, start painting again. You have obligations. Blah. Blah. Blah.*

I tend to tune Daniel out when he goes off on one of his tangents. The hidden stash of whiskey helps as well.

"Do you have a death wish?"

I flip him off, searching around trying to find something to numb the pain again.

"Have this..." Daniel hands me a bottle of water.

I look at it as if it's poison, but he shakes the bottle at me, and I take it. Unscrewing the lid, I throw back the clear liquid in one go.

"Louis, it's been four months since Elisabeth left, you need to stop wallowing." I glare at my brother. What would he know, he's never been in love before. In fact, I know he has a different woman in his bed every week if not multiple. He has no idea what it's like to be in love and then have it ripped away from you.

"Don't you want to outsell that cocky son of a bitch?" He knows that statement will get a reaction from me.

"I *am* painting..." I wave my hand around my Parisian apartment where there are multiple unfinished masterpieces.

Daniel lets out a sigh and pinches the bridge of his nose before he speaks, "These paintings are..." he scrunches up his nose, "... not what your fans want."

I stare at the paintings Daniel is pointing to and tell him, "I'm going in a new direction."

Daniel rolls his eyes. "The color palette is interesting," he says with a grimace. So what if it's not my normal color palette. I've changed. Now I see the world in black, white, red, and gray. There's *no* color left in my life anymore. It was all ripped away from me.

"This is me, Daniel." His face softens a little. "If my fans don't like this new direction I'm taking, then find new ones for me. *It's your job*," I yell at him.

"I guess I should be thankful you have painted anything at all while you're stuck in some self-indulgent pity party for one."

"Fuck you!" My anger bubbles to the surface again. "You have no idea what I have been through."

"Yes, I do. I've been the one mopping up your fucking mess ever since you found out about Elisabeth and Yves."

"Never mention their names again," I hiss.

"You're such a fucking pussy, Louis. So... this bitch broke your heart. She cheated on you with your protégé, and she wasn't even sorry about it. Why the hell are you letting her hold this power over you? Huh?"

I'm stunned silent for a few moments, then my anger bubbles to the surface again. I jump up from my bed and rush at Daniel, pushing him up against the wall, but he doesn't fight back.

"Go on, Louis. Hit me. Fucking hit me if it makes you feel any better." He looks down at me, his chest heaving with adrenaline. "Go on," he goads. I release my hands from his pristine suit that I have now crinkled. "Just what I thought. You're a fucking pussy."

I ignore his barb and make my way over to the kitchen, opening the refrigerator to pull out a mini bottle of vodka and knock it back.

"Why are you letting her destroy you?" My head hangs in shame at his words because I know he's right. "She was a bitch, Louis." I whip around and glare at him. "I never said anything to you when you were together..." His words hang in the air.

"What? Spit it out. Don't stop now. I love this confession time."

"Elisabeth propositioned me." My eyes widen, my fingers clench against the marble island bench and turn white. "Not just once, Louis, many times." My heart is beating wildly inside my chest as he continues, "She doesn't like the word, no."

If my brother fucked her, I don't know what I'll do.

"Did you..."

The Arrogant Artist

He looks at me, shocked. "Seriously? You seriously think I'd do that to you?"

I shrug because I don't know anymore. I have no idea who I can trust when it comes to Elisabeth.

"Why do you think I stopped coming around during the holidays?"

Daniel always told me he was busy or was with a woman. Honestly, I thought we were growing apart.

"She wouldn't leave me alone." I should be surprised by Elisabeth's antics, but I'm not. Not anymore. "So, why are you letting a woman like that steal anything more from you, Louis?"

I know he's right, but I can't stop it. I'm on this destructive path. The anger has taken hold of me like a monster on my back, one I can't shake loose. Nor, for some reason, do I want to.

"This is me now, Daniel." I point to the dark canvases around me.

Daniel nods, the fight leaving him. "These will sell. I don't know if we'll be able to make the millions you were making before, but it will be enough to make a decent living."

It's not like I'm crying poor, even though Elisabeth took half of everything from me. She took my home, my studios, and half my money. The real kicker was when she moved *him* into our home. He's no longer living in the studio in the backyard. No. Now he's the man of the house. *My fucking house.* The house that Elisabeth and I were going to bring up our children in. I guess I'm easily replaced.

"Louis, don't you want to show her she picked the wrong guy." I shrug. "Don't you want her to realize that she gave up on you for some two-bit wannabe, Louis Marchant." I look at the unfinished paintings hanging around my apartment and sigh, knowing he's right. "There's only one of you, and Yves is a cheap knock-off."

I look up at my brother, and there's fire in his eyes. He wants me to be the best I can be. My trouble is I don't know what that is anymore. My muse has dried up and gone away, and I don't know if I'm ever going to find her again.

"Just think about what I've said. Okay?" Daniel looks at me. "I'll be back in a couple of days. I have some stuff to sort out back in London."

I wave him goodbye and fall headfirst back onto my bed, where I'm going to stay for the foreseeable future.

I WAKE up to a woman's screams, the bed moves and jolts beside me. I try and push my eyes open, but nothing happens.

"Wake up, you drunk."

The sheets are ripped off me as all of a sudden bright light streams through the window. There's some pissed-off woman mumbling expletives beside me.

"I suggest you lose his number. You can do better," Daniel tells her.

"Yeah, I think so, too," the woman says.

I flip them off as I cover my eyes with my arm—the blinding light is trying to sear my retinas. A hard slap lands across my face waking me again.

"What the fuck?" Jumping up quickly, my body wobbles as my feet hit the concrete floor. My head is pounding like someone is playing a drum solo in my head. My ass falls back to the edge of the bed as I'm way too unsteady on my feet.

"Get the fuck up. I've had enough of this shit. This is an intervention."

Goddammit! My head is throbbing. I'm not in the mood for another one of Daniel's interventions.

He hands me some Advil and a glass of water to wash them down. "Have a shower, you fucking stink."

I lift my arm, and he's right, I do kind of stink. It takes everything I have in me to get myself up off my bed. Moments later, I stumble into the shower alcove, turn the faucet to hot, and let the water cleanse away the sins of last night.

Feeling better, I re-join Daniel in the living room where he's cleaning up the remnants of my wild night.

"Where did she go?" I look around my empty apartment.

"The brunette?" Daniel questions, and I nod. "She left."

Dammit! I was hoping for another round.

What was her name? Stephanie? Chloe? Mariska?

Shaking my head, I don't know, my brain is a little foggy.

"Trying out muses again?"

"She might have been the one," I answer while grabbing a juice from the refrigerator.

"Doubtful. Your canvases are pretty bare."

"We made art on my bed."

Daniel scoffs. "Fucking lame, man."

I shrug, finish my juice, and wish it was laced with vodka.

"Why are you here so early?"

"It's one o'clock in the afternoon, Louis."

I look up at the clock—so it is. It was a wild night.

Daniel shakes his head in displeasure. "I'm here to tell you, that somehow, a small New York gallery wants to host an exhibition of your latest work at the end of summer." My eyebrow rises in surprise at his revelation. "Yeah, I know, I'm a goddamn freaking legend." Daniel chuckles.

"You should be for the amount I pay you."

He ignores me and continues, "Anyway, they are happy to exhibit pretty much anything you have for them, be it this new demonic direction you seem hell-bent on pursuing or the original old-school Louis Marchant."

"Great."

Daniel looks at me, I can tell he's getting frustrated. "Great! That's all you have to say. This gallery is holding out a lifeline. If you do well, then it's a step in the right direction to getting back to where you once were. At the top."

I shrug. Being the best isn't always what it's cracked up to be.

Been there, done that.

"Seriously, I want to fucking punch you right now, you ungrateful fucking dick," Daniel yells. "Wake up, you fool, before it's too late." He's really pissed, but I'm not sure I care. But he's also pacing which means he's not happy with me right now.

"Fine! I give in…" This makes him stop pacing and talking. "This is what they get." I point at the unfinished paintings in the room. "I have no control over what I paint any more, no more than the weatherman can control the rain. If that's what they want, then I'll do it."

Daniel smiles. "Good." He doesn't fight me on it, at all, and that's a concern. "Because I've just hired you an assistant."

My eyes widen in shock. "No."

"Yes. Your assistant will organize everything in your life, so all you have to worry about is painting."

"No, Daniel."

"Sorry, Louis, this part is non-negotiable. I'm setting your assistant up at your place in the country."

"No. Absolutely not. That's my sacred space. No one is allowed there. Only my staff and me."

"Well, lucky they'll be your staff." I don't think I'm going to win this argument.

"This assistant better not get in my fucking way, Daniel."

"I promise you that won't happen. And if it makes you feel better, I'll liaise directly with your assistant, so you won't even notice she's there. I'll confine your aide to the office."

My eyes narrow at him. I'm not happy that some stranger is going to be invading *my* personal space.

"We need Louis Marchant back. I don't care if you paint a million and one demon paintings all summer. I don't care if every single one of your paintings are black. We need to fill this gallery. We need you back at the top of your game."

"They'll get what they get."

"Fine! I'm happy with that." That was easy, too easy. "But..." and here we go, there's more, "... you need to get back out in public."

"No."

"Your public image has taken a considerable nosedive these past four months." I roll my eyes, Daniel's being overly dramatic. "The images of you stumbling out of clubs with a different woman on your arm every night doesn't look great. Image is everything, Louis."

"Fuck what they think."

"Most of the people with the money are conservative."

"Well, fuck them, too. I don't need their self-righteous money."

"You look like a fucking dick at the moment. Whereas Elisabeth and Yves are absolutely killing it socially, attending all the events, looking happy and in love, not like some desperado drunk who doesn't know where his next dime is coming from."

His words are like a dagger to my heart. *Looking happy and in love.* Fuck those traitorous bastards. I open the refrigerator and pull out a beer. I'm way too sober to deal with this shit right now. Daniel's disappointed stare is weighing heavily on him as he collapses into a chair.

"You need to up your social media game... you don't have Elisabeth anymore to do it." I take another swig of my beer, seething at Daniel's words, yet saying nothing in reply. "He has a million followers on Instagram already." Like that's meant to mean something to me. "You only have three hundred fifty thousand." Again, like that means something. "There are pictures of them at all the hottest parties around the world." So what? Elisabeth never says no to an invite anywhere. "Photos with celebrities. Endorsements from different brands. And what do you have?" He looks at me clutching my beer, my normally clean-shaven face covered in a patchy beard, my disheveled appearance matching exactly how I feel.

"People are clamoring for them... like they used to for you."

I finish my beer and grab another.

Daniel lets out a frustrated growl and breaks eye contact while he lowers his head. "You're lucky you are fucking family because otherwise, I'd have dropped your ungrateful ass ages ago if you were a normal client. Get your act together, Louis. This depressive bullshit is just fucking crap." And with that, he walks out slamming the door behind him.

4

EMILY

"Hi, is this Emily Chapman?"

"Yes, it is." Did I give my number to someone and not realize? It's been a week since Toby broke up with me, and I've been staying with Rosie and have spent most of that time in a wine-induced haze.

"You applied for the art assistant's position." My stomach instantly starts to churn. Oh my God, we applied for that while we were all drunk, and I had completely forgotten about it.

"Yes, I did."

"Your résumé is impressive."

It is?

Shit! What did we write?

"And I was wondering if we could organize an interview time."

Oh my God!

I'M SO NERVOUS, I really need this job. I don't care how much they pay me or if I have to look after some temperamental artist, I'll take it. Of course, that's if they offer it to me. This could be my chance to finally work in the art industry. Yes, it will be as a personal assistant, probably getting coffee and other menial tasks, but I don't care. At least I'll finally be doing something in the art scene. The fact that it's based in the South of France isn't that bad either. I need to get out of London and away from my old life. I need a fresh start, and this will be the perfect recharge. I'll come back with a tan and a new spring in my step, armed with this newfound-art experience which is going to open so many doors for me here in London. I must get this job, so I do everything to look and present the best I can for this interview.

Taking a deep breath, I press the bell of the Mayfair Terrace. My heart is thumping loudly in my chest, and my palms are sweaty. *You've got this, Emily,* I tell myself. *This job is yours.*

The door opens, and I'm little taken aback by the man standing in front of me. I look to the side to check if I have the right number because the man is gorgeous. He looks like he's stepped off the pages of *GQ*. Jet-black hair slicked back and the most intense blue eyes. They're almost turquoise like the Mediterranean Sea I swam in last summer with Toby, bright blue pools that a woman could get lost in.

Like you're doing right now, Emily.

The navy suit he's wearing is cut to perfection over his large frame. I know how much that suit cost because Toby has the same one, but he never looked this good in it.

Control your hormones, Emily. This is a job interview.

"You must be Emily," he says with a deep, timbered voice that reverberates over my body. He offers me a tanned hand to shake. I take it. It's warm and large—

so, so large. "I'm Daniel DuPont..." there's a hint of a French accent as he says his name, "... the artist's agent." I nod in understanding. "Come in." He holds open the door for me as I enter the luxury terrace, then he ushers me along the white hallway. I'm mesmerized by the artwork that lines the walls, especially the beautiful multi-colored striped canvas. He notices that I have stopped walking and am currently staring at the painting.

"Is that an original Louis Marchant?" I ask in awe. He grins, showing me his perfect white teeth and the cutest little dimple on one cheek.

"Yes, it is." He gives me a curious look.

"It's magnificent. He's such a talent. I went to his exhibition years ago when it was in London. I think I had just started at university, and he was becoming known to the art world. I stood there for hours losing myself in the color, the passion that filled each of his pieces."

"Have you seen any of his latest work?"

"The darker ones?" He nods. "Yes, online."

"And what did you think?" Daniel stares at me, and I get lost in his blue eyes for a moment.

"I like them."

"Really? Why?"

"Because life isn't always rainbows. Sometimes it's raw, angry, and messed up."

He's silent for a couple of moments.

Damn, maybe I have overstepped with my comment.

Good one, Emily.

"And you speak French?" He switches to French, and I converse easily with him as we move into the living room. I grew up speaking French, my mother was an artist, so I guess I follow in her footsteps. She was very bohemian, eccentric, but oh so beautiful. She made sure we spoke French at home. But when she left, I was the only one who continued speaking it in private. It felt like I was still connected to her in some way. I understand now why my brother and sister stopped speaking French, they were older and understood more about why our parents had split up, but for me, it was a confusing time.

Eventually, as I got older, I was told how she had left my father for another man. An artist she was working with here in London. They fell in love, and she moved to France to be with him, and that was the last time we ever heard from her. My father, of course, was devastated and declared everything to do with my mother to be banned from our home. My father passed away the last year of high school, and as devastated as I was losing him, there was a sense of relief that I could pursue my private love of art without hurting him. Of course, my siblings aren't happy about my choice, but they have their own goals to worry about, so they don't have time to worry about me.

"Your French is perfect," Daniel comments. My cheeks flare with color at his compliment. "You're hired," he tells me.

I stare at him in shock, more because I have only been here for no more than five minutes. He hasn't even asked me any questions.

"Are you sure?" *Why are you putting doubt in his mind, Emily?*

He chuckles. "I have a good feeling about you, Miss Chapman." His baby blues stare at me intently while I internally sigh. "I think you'll keep my client in check." *Um, okay.* "He's having a rough time at the moment," Daniel says softly.

"I understand." *More than he knows.*

"Will you be able to start soon?"

"Yes. I have to move out of my current place, so I should be ready to go in a couple of days."

Daniel nods.

I still have some things that I haven't had time to pick up from Toby's yet. I've been putting it off not wanting to run into him, but I guess the time has come.

"My client is difficult at the moment, and I need to warn you of that. Surly, to say the least."

Think of your résumé, Emily. Right now, you can't be picky.

"Artists can be temperamental." I give him a confident smile. He doesn't realize I grew up with a temperamental artist. Some days my mother was happy and others she'd sink into a deep depression, and no matter what I did, I could never pull her out of it. I guess accidentally becoming pregnant to a man you never loved, then marrying him and producing more children than you ever wanted, which in turn trapped Mum more into a life she hated with a man who didn't understand art nor did he ever want to, could make you depressed.

"This artist is quite temperamental at the moment." Those baby blues look at me with concern. "Just know you can leave at any moment if you can't handle it. You'll still be paid your salary for the summer in exchange for not talking about your time with the artist."

Not really a great selling point. Daniel's not painting a rosy picture, but I can't be fussy. I wonder who this temperamental artist is?

"May I ask who it is?"

"If I told you, you might not take the job, and honestly, I need the help right now." He's giving me puppy dog eyes. Damn, this beautiful man. "But I promise you... you can talk to me any time of the day or night." Now that's kind of a selling point right there. "I understand the quirks of this artist." I guess that's kind of reassuring, but there's a part of me that's a little hesitant about my new boss seeing as I'll be so far away.

But that con is totally outweighed by all the pros.

I AM ON A HIGH. I have a job. A real job for some mysterious, famous artist in the South of France. They are going to pay me an extremely generous wage, all my living expenses are taken care of, so that means I can save most of my wage, and by the time I arrive back in London after the summer, I'll have a healthy savings account and enough money to get my own place.

My happy mood is short-lived as I make my way to Toby's apartment to collect the last of my things. I turn my key in the front door like I have done a million times before, but this time it makes me feel sick. The door creaks open, and the familiar scents tickle my nose, smells that used to remind me of home, but now turn my stomach.

"Hey." Toby surprises me.

It's early, he should normally be at the office, but instead, he's standing in front of me. I haven't run into him since we broke up. He looks the same—same blond hair, dressed in a navy polo and jeans—but now when I look at him, there's nothing—no butterflies, no flutters, no nothing. All I feel is numbness, anger, and a big dose of regret for wasting so much time with a man who thinks so little of me.

"I'm not staying long, just packing up the rest of my things."

"Oh, okay." Toby seems shocked.

Did he seriously think I'm here for him?

I make my way to our bedroom and pull the empty suitcases from the shelves and start filling them. Toby follows after me watching me pack in silence, but then something clicks in him, and he says, "Em, we need to talk."

I shake my head, continuing to pack. "We have nothing to talk about."

He reaches out, his hands stop my furious packing. "Please."

I pull myself away. I don't like the feeling of Toby touching me anymore.

"We don't have anything to talk about, Toby. You have been cheating on me for six months with some girl in New York. What do you think that's going to do to me?"

"I'm sorry, Em. I didn't mean to."

"I know. It's hard when your dick accidentally falls into a stranger's vagina." He looks stunned at my remark. I have never called him out on his bullshit, always too worried that I'd lose him if I did. Guess what? I did end up losing him in the end, so maybe I should have called him out earlier, and maybe now I wouldn't be where I am.

"I still love you, Emmy."

Goddamn! I think I'm going to be physically ill.

"Stop!" I hold up my hand. "Stop lying, Toby." He frowns. "It doesn't matter, you're moving to New York, and I'm moving to the South of France."

"You're what?" His voice rises.

"Yeah... that's right. I'm working for an internationally acclaimed artist," I answer and make sure I give it a good dose of rubbing it in.

"That's amazing. I'm so proud of you."

No. He doesn't get to be proud of me for doing this.

"I should really thank you for breaking my heart. Otherwise, I probably wouldn't have taken a chance like I have." That's the truth. Maybe fate has other plans, and I needed to lose everything to put me back onto the right path.

"I didn't mean to hurt you, Em."

I roll my eyes. "But you did. And the worst thing is, Toby, you have changed the fabric of me." Toby grimaces and touches the back of his neck. "You left a scar on my heart because you lied and deceived me. You changed me, and not in a good way. I pity the next guy who comes into my life because he's going to have a really hard shell to get through now."

Toby's face falls, the reality of his actions hitting him hard. Well, I can only hope.

"Em, I'm sorry."

Damn those stupid tear ducts losing control again.

Why is there not an off switch?

"I was good to you, Toby. I was the perfect girlfriend. I let you have your freedom. I never nagged at you. I never checked up on you. I trusted you." Now the tears really fall. "I trusted you, and you fucked up that trust."

Toby looks apologetic as my words hit him. "I wish I'd done things differently, but I didn't."

Me, too. I wish he'd broken up with me six months ago instead of lying to me all this time.

"How am I going to trust another man now?" His cheeks redden as he drops his chin to his chest. "You have ruined my next relationship before it's even started because you were a selfish asshole." I grab more of my clothes and throw them into the suitcase with so much force it pushes it slightly across the bed.

"You're right." Well, I wasn't expecting that. "I'm an asshole. You were the perfect girlfriend. You did trust me. You let me be me. You never asked more of me. You loved me just the way I am. And I let..." he tries to hold back his emotions by pausing and then continuing, "... I let other people convince me I deserved better. That I deserved someone of equal stature."

Wow! Okay. That hurts. He thinks I'm beneath him.

"I know I'm going to regret letting you go, Emily, but I have to."

"Why, because you're in love with someone else?" He can't look at me. "Oh, shit, you are." My stomach sinks, so I keep packing. Why am I even talking to him? It's not helping me at all.

"I wouldn't have cheated if I didn't think there might be a future with this woman."

Make him stop.

Please, make him stop.

"So, what you're saying is you never saw a future with me?"

I know I don't want to hear the answer to this, but I can't help asking anyway.

"No."

"Because I don't come from the right circles."

"No, because you lost your ambition and settled into a routine. You were happy to watch me succeed, but you never made an effort to make yourself successful." Seriously, I'm ready to throat punch him into the middle of next week. "You could have been something, Emily."

"Toby, I was something. I am something. I was the woman who loved you with every fiber of her being, but that wasn't enough, was it?"

"How could I take you to work dinners and tell them my girlfriend works in the gift shop of a tacky tourist site?"

"You love someone for who they are, not what they do."

"You were always so damn romantic, Emily. That's not how the real world works."

"Lucky, because I don't want to live in your fucked-up world."

I push the last items of my clothing into my bag and leave.

Putting that chapter of my life far behind me.

5
EMILY

Daniel met me at Marseille Provence Airport and drove me through the city, then out into the countryside. I have always wanted to come to the South of France. It was where my mother disappeared to and the last known address I have of hers.

I can see now why she gave up dreary England for this place—it's beautiful.

There are fields of lavender and sunflowers that paint the picturesque landscape, and crumbling stone buildings with colorful wooden shutters stand in the quaint little villages.

We drive out through more open fields and turn into a driveway, the long winding lane taking us to the end, where the most magnificent stone building stands before me. Daniel pulls up and stops at the main entrance, then he opens the car door and takes my luggage from the trunk of the car.

"This is…" Honestly, words cannot describe the beauty of this place.

"It's beautiful, isn't it?"

I nod, taking it all in. He opens the creaky sky-blue wooden door, and I follow him through the home-castle or whatever you want to call it.

"There's a pool out the back that you can enjoy on your time off. The chef and housekeeper will start work tomorrow."

Okay! This person must be pretty well off if they can afford a full-time chef and housekeeper. *Who on earth is this mystery artist?*

"You have the house to yourself tonight... thought you'd want to settle in before the madness starts tomorrow." That dimple pops as he flashes those baby blues at me. "There's a little village not far from here if you would like something to eat. You can take one of the bikes, or I can send the driver back to take you."

"I can ride into town, it's not that far." The new me needs to start exercising, especially if I'm going to be eating my body weight in cheese and wine while living here. "And Daniel? Thank you so much for this opportunity."

He smiles. "Don't thank me yet, you haven't met your new boss." He gives me a wink, ushering me into the luxurious home.

He keeps warning me.

And I keep wondering what the hell I have gotten myself into.

I really hope my new boss isn't a complete dick because that's going to make the summer suck.

"Here is your room." Daniel opens the wooden door to my bedroom.

"Oh my..." I rush over to the balcony doors and open them, and there, right in front of me, is the gleaming azure pool, and just behind that, the rolling green hills. Purple streaks of lavender fill the horizon. I can hear birds chirping, the buzzing of the bees hovering around the pink roses that are climbing up the rock wall of the home, and the sweet perfume teases my nose.

This is paradise.

Daniel's standing behind me. "It's beautiful, isn't it?" His warm breath touches my shoulders sending goosebumps over my skin.

"It truly is." I try to remain calm, but honestly, I wouldn't mind if Daniel spun me around and pinned me to one of the stone walls, showing me what real paradise is.

Oh my God, I need to stop it.

It's been two weeks since I broke up with Toby. It's way too early to be thinking about sleeping with someone else.

That didn't stop Toby, the little devil on my shoulder whispers to me.

"In the study downstairs, I'll set up a laptop and a cell phone for you." His professionalism pulls me from my dirty thoughts. He's just doing his job. Daniel's not here to fuck you against the brick wall. *Concentrate, Emily.*

"I'll be emailing you the schedule. You need to make sure the artist keeps to it. We don't have long until this exhibition in New York, and there's a lot riding on it."

I can't believe I'll be going to New York.

Suck it, Toby, I didn't need you to get there after all.

I can work out a plan, organize, and schedule tasks. *Who doesn't like a good schedule that runs to plan?*

"You'll also need to look after the social media accounts. The last person who looked after it left abruptly, and it hasn't been maintained well in the last four months. We need to get this artist back out there again. The artist has no clue about social media, so I'll be looking to you to take the lead on this."

I nod. I know I can take awesome selfies, loving my filters and hashtags. I'm all over that.

"Also, the artist has disappeared from the social scene, too, and I really need visibility again. Start building the buzz for the New York exhibition, remind everyone who the artist is, and that he's still number one."

This mystery talk is driving me crazy. I have no idea if the artist is male or female.

"So, say yes to any and all invitations, and if you're really unsure, just give me a call."

I nod in agreement. So far, the job sounds great apart from the cranky artist, but now I can cope with that.

"Any questions? I know I've just laid it all on you at once." He smiles.

"Just one. Who is it?"

"Follow me, the artwork downstairs will give it away."

Oh, now I'm intrigued.

"You're dying to know, aren't you?" The deep chuckle that leaves his throat gives me chills.

We make our way downstairs past the foyer, then walk into the living and dining areas here I stop to stare at the walls.

"No." I cover my mouth. He can't be serious? I'm *not* Louis Marchant's new assistant.

"You see why I didn't want to tell you."

I walk up to one of the paintings and just stare at the bold colors beaming back at me. "Is that?" My hand wants to touch the mark going across the entire painting.

"Yes, he sliced the canvas. I repaired it for him."

I heard the story about what had happened when his wife ran away with his protégé.

"Is he okay?"

Daniel shakes his head. "Honestly, no. Come... let me show you." Following him past the kitchen down a corridor and then out a glass door, there's what appears to be a storage shed. Daniel unlocks the door and flicks on the light. It's filled with paintings, but these are all black, white, gray, and red. The strokes look angry and violent.

"This is where we are now." He points to the paintings. "He's lost, and I don't know how to help him anymore." I can see the strain on his face as he talks about his client.

"They are still beautiful, though." I run my fingers over the thick, dried paint.

"But Marchant's fans don't want brooding, they want love and light."

"Sometimes life doesn't happen that way. These paintings, they show you what happens when someone rips your heart out. They show a person's pain, and sometimes pain can be beautiful."

"Sounds like you're speaking from experience."

"Yeah, I am."

His eyes narrow in on me. "Is that the reason for you having to move out of your home?"

I simply nod. "I thought my partner was proposing to me, but instead, he was breaking up with me to move to New York because he fell in love with someone else." Daniel's eyes widen, and his eyebrow raises slightly. I didn't mean to unleash my dirty laundry onto him, but somehow it all just blurted out. "I guess at this moment, Marchant's paintings resonate with me." I scan the walls of the dark images that hang before my eyes.

"That man will regret leaving you."

"I think it's for the best, he wasn't the man for me."

"Well, I think you're exactly what Louis needs," Daniel tells me.

DANIEL LEFT HOURS AGO. It's a beautiful early summer's night, the sun is slowly setting, the breeze is warm, so I rode the bike into town to grab some items for dinner. Great idea in theory, I realized pretty quickly that I hadn't ridden a bike for years, and it was a long way. Thankfully, the road was flat because that was my only saving grace.

Finally, my heartbeat has returned to normal as I set myself up by the glistening pool. My dinner consists of crusty baguettes, cheese, and some cold cuts and, of course, a nice bottle of wine. It's quiet out here. There's not a soul out amongst the fields that surround the property, but I like the serenity. I could get used to this pace of life.

I cut off another chunk of camembert and lather it onto the crusty slice of bread. Taking a bite of the deliciousness, it nearly sends me into an orgasm. I unlock my cell and take a picture of my spread and upload it to Instagram. Got to make everyone think I'm having the time of my life and not moping about with a broken heart. I share the photograph of my beautiful meal with the backdrop of the setting sun over the lavender fields and hashtag the shit out of it. #livingmybestlife #blessed #thisisthelife #summerjob #donthateme #singlelife

Once I post the image, the timeline refreshes—I didn't realize I was still following Toby. Staring back at me on my feed is a picture of him with a blonde, kissing on a carriage ride in Central Park. He looks happy. They both do. The image is a direct arrow to my already broken heart. I take a big gulp of my wine to ease my nerves, then scroll to the next image, and it's a picture of the two of them together at the airport. She's kissing his cheek. The caption reads, *I've missed my girl, so great to finally be together.*

"Wanker," I curse at my phone, then I proceed to neck the bottle of wine. I stare at the image of the girl on the screen, who has been sleeping with my boyfriend all these months. Of course, the alcohol makes me start comparing myself to her.

We're total opposites. She's tall, tanned, blonde, big-boobed, and a totally fake Barbie doll, who's wearing designer clothing. Her hair is perfect with makeup applied like a damn professional.

Then there's me. A short ass with strawberry blonde hair and skin that looks like it hasn't seen sun since birth. I have pancake tits that might just make a handful if I'm lucky. I hardly wear makeup, and my clothes are more high-street than designer.

Now I'm on a roll. I take another swig from my bottle of wine and click on her name and start scrolling through her images. Thank God it's not on private. So many photographs of the two of them together doing all these touristy things in New York, smiling, looking happy and carefree when, in reality, they're cheating assholes.

I keep scrolling like I'm going to stop now. Then I see the images of them in Aruba. He fucking took her on holiday while I was at home missing my boyfriend.

What a fucking scumbag.

Wanker.

Asshole.

"Fuck you, Toby Masters. Fuck you!" I curse at my phone.

My night turns kind of blurry after that as I finish the bottle of wine and devour the ridiculous amount of cheese and cold cuts for one tiny human. I'm drunk. And it's hot. I keep staring at the glistening blue pool before me, tempting me to take a dip in its cool water.

As I said, I'm drunk, so deciding to jump in under the moonlight seems like the best plan ever. I can't be bothered going upstairs to grab my swimsuit, so I strip off to my underwear and jump into the pool, letting the cool water sober me up and refresh me, maybe even baptize me because it feels amazing against my hot skin.

This is the last time that I'm ever going to think about that douche canoe, Toby Masters, and his Barbie doll ever again. I'm in the South of France, motherfuckers, and working for an uber-awesome artist.

This beats selling magnets to tourists back in London.

My body finally turns into a prune after spending time lazily swimming in the cool water, and I feel like I've shed my old life like dead skin. I'm ready to welcome a new future, a future which I have no idea where it will lead me, but it has to be better than where I have come from.

I slowly step out of the pool, unsteadily making my way up the stairs. Luckily, the early summer breeze is still warm as I stand in my underwear, which is completely see-through now, wondering where the towels are located.

It's only then I notice a man standing in front of me.

I scream with surprise because I thought I was alone.

6

LOUIS

I should be looking away as the water drips over her near-naked body. It's the gentlemanly thing to do—*as if you're a gentleman, Louis*—but I can't. Not when her innocently white underwear is completely see-through.

This is apparently my new assistant, and I'm drunk. Not like that's a surprise to anyone. The bottle of tequila sits loosely in my hand, but I watch her in utter fascination as she emerges from the pool like some majestic siren of the sea. My fingers grip the bottleneck tighter as I wonder what she'd taste like. Is she as innocent as she looks?

The thin material clings to her lithe body, water droplets falling over her chest, running over her hard nipples. I bite my lip as the blood begins to travel south.

Her breasts are small and pert with the most perfect blush-pink nipples, the color reminding me of the roses that grow along the wall beside the pool. They release the sweetest of perfume in the summer. *Would she smell as sweet?*

I follow another droplet down her stomach until it disappears into her underwear. I silently groan as I notice a dark line underneath the sheer material, a line I want to run my tongue along as my head is buried between her creamy thighs. Those long fingers of hers gripping my hair, urging me to suck her bud harder, almost pulling my hair from my scalp as she thrashes about underneath me, taking every last bit of her orgasm from her sated body. My dick twitches, hardening with each dirty thought that crosses my depraved mind.

Her face turns to me. Bright green eyes hold me captive with their surprised gaze, her hair the color of spun gold that frames her petite face. Her eyes widen, and she lets out a scream pulling me back to reality.

"What the hell do you think you're doing?" My words come out harsh as my body is tense from need—a need that must be sated.

"I... I..." The woman stumbles over her excuse as she tries to hide her near-naked body.

Closing my eyes, I suck in a deep breath, count to three in my mind, and turn on my heel, placing the bottle of tequila onto the table beside her empty bottle of wine and leftover cheeses. Making my way over to the cupboards beside the pool, I pull out one of the white pool towels and throw it at her. It hits her in the face, and immediately I know it's pissed her off.

"Dry yourself off." My lip curls as I try to control the urges that are racing through my body. Those green eyes flare with fire, her creamy cheeks are burning red with humiliation as she wraps her body in the fluffy white towel.

"I..." Her words start off on a whisper. "They said no one would be home." But end more in a snarky tone. She glares at me, angry that I have dared interrupt her alone time in my own fucking house.

"This is my house. I can come and go as I please," I defend myself. My words are curt, I'm drunk, and my body is humming with tension. I need to move away from her. Now. Before I grab her and fuck her wildly by the edge of the pool. I never knew how much pent-up tension I had until I came home to a near-naked woman in my pool.

"Yes, of course." She stands up straighter. "I just... Daniel said..." My eyes narrow, hearing her talk about my brother makes my heart beat faster.

Did he touch her?

I bet he was flirtatious with her?

Did he bring her here for him?

Does she want him?

Why do I care?

What the hell is wrong with me?

"Did he tell you it was okay to swim naked in my pool?" I stare at her, my lip curling in a snarl. Those emerald eyes flare with anger once again. Good, it's better than the puppy-dog eyes I normally get from women.

"He told me to make myself at home." Her words are short, clipped, and I'm fairly sure she's furious.

"I guess you did that." I look her up and down. "Were you waiting for him to return? Were you hoping to seduce him? 'Cause you're not one of the first employees to have tried that with him." Her mouth opens in shock at my statement, but I notice how pink her cheeks have turned. Of course, she thinks Daniel is handsome, most women do.

We are total opposites. He's all dark features with a bright personality, whereas I have light features and a dark personality. We are complete opposites even though we're related.

"Of course not." Those eyes are shooting red-hot daggers at me, and honestly, I'm enjoying seeing her so angry.

"Then was this little setup for me?" Her cheeks redden again. I know what I do to women, the appeal I have on them. "Did he ask you to seduce me?"

"Of course not," she quickly answers, her eyes wide in shock.

"Did he offer you a nice little bonus to help fuck me back into greatness?"

"What? No!"

"Good, because this little display is pathetic." My words hit their target. Her shoulders sink for a nanosecond, and I feel like a despicable human being for saying them. An apology is on the tip of my tongue, but it's been so long since I've had to apologize for my behavior that the words stick in my throat.

She takes a couple of steps toward me, her back straight again. "And yet, it was enough to be able to make *you* rise to the occasion." Her eyes flick to my jeans, the very hard indent of my dick giving it all away.

My nostrils flare with anger. I look back up at her, and she has a satisfied smirk right across her face.

"Clean yourself up. It's embarrassing." My words don't make a dent in her armor. Instead, she gives me a salute. I guess the polite version of 'fuck you' if there ever was one.

Turning on her heels, she grabs her cell off the table, leaving the wine and cheese there. Who does she think is going to clean up this mess? Certainly not me. She saunters away as if she hasn't a care in the world. Once she's out of sight, I pull out my cell and call Daniel.

"What the fuck?" I scream down the line before he even gets a chance to answer properly.

"Where the hell are you?"

"I'm at home."

"You're not in Paris? Your bags were gone when I arrived at the apartment."

"No shit. Did you seriously think I was going to let you leave some stranger in my home for the night?" I stomp through the house, and then one by one, I angrily take the stairs to my suite.

"I vetted her. She's trustworthy," Daniel argues.

"So trustworthy that I found her naked in my pool."

He goes silent.

I pull it away from my ear to make sure he's still there, then he bursts out laughing.

"Fuck you, asshole. This isn't funny." But he won't stop laughing for some reason, so I wait a couple of moments for him to calm the fuck down. "You finished?"

"Yes." He chuckles a little longer. "So... she was naked, hey?"

I let out a deep sigh. "Her underwear was see-through." Daniel lets out a tiny groan. "Seriously?" Of course, he thinks she's hot, any man would.

"Louis, you can't tell me the girl isn't beautiful?" His question requires no comment. "Fine!" He chuckles. "I'll take that as a yes."

"Daniel..." My voice deepens with anger.

"No, Louis, you listen to me... Emily graduated with an art history degree. She speaks fluent French, and she's perfect for the job. The fact that she is also stunningly beautiful, that's just a bonus."

"I'm not going to sleep with her. I don't need my brother finding me women. I don't have any trouble finding my own."

"Good, because I didn't hire her for you to sleep with. She's there as your assistant, and *only* to assist you with your art. Nothing more," I grumble at his comments. "Maybe when the summer is over, I might ask her out if you're not interested."

My body stills. "You?"

"Yes. She's gorgeous, loves art, and she passed my knowledge test easily. She's funny and intelligent. She's the kind of girl I've been searching for."

Daniel hired her for him?

"I'm glad my predicament could be of service for your dating life." I groan, making him laugh.

"It's not like you're interested. So when you're done with her, she can come and help me. I really *do* need an assistant."

What the hell has gotten into Daniel?

"Whatever," I grumble.

"Emily will be of great assistance. This one tiny transgression shouldn't be held against her. I did tell her she had the place to herself. You were not supposed to be there until tomorrow when I brought you."

"It's my house."

"I know, but she didn't know you would barge into the house."

"She was swimming naked in my pool."

"In. Her. Underwear. It's probably a beautiful night down there. Don't tell me you don't just strip off and jump into the pool." Silence falls between us because he's right, I most definitely do. "Just forget about tonight and start new in the morning. She's... had a rough time recently." My interest is now piqued. "No, I'm not going to tell you about it either. You're going have to have to make an effort with this woman and find out yourself."

"I don't need to make an effort to get to know her. She's just my assistant."

Daniel sighs. "Be nice."

"I'm always nice."

"Old Louis, yes. New Louis, no." He laughs.

"Then she'll just have to deal with the new one, and if she can't, she can go back to where she came from."

There's an exhausted sigh from my brother before he says, "Just let her do her job and don't be a dick."

"Whatever! She better do her job, or she's gone. I don't care how much you want in her panties."

"I'll see you tomorrow," Daniel tells me as I hang up on him, throwing my phone onto my bed.

I lay on my bed and stare at the ceiling, my mind a jumble of images. My body is restless. My dick needs to be sucked, and most definitely not by my new assistant no matter how much those perfect pink lips are begging to be wrapped around my cock.

No. I need some no-strings-attached fun.

I turn and look at my cell and an idea brews.

I think my assistant needs a little welcome party to get her used to the Louis Marchant experience.

7
EMILY

L ouis Marchant is an asshole.

An arrogantly hot asshole.

Shut up, hormones, this does not concern you.

I'm still fuming about my run-in with him as I get out of the shower.

How dare he think I'm here to seduce him? What kind of woman does he think I am?

You were standing there pretty much naked in his home. *Shut up, conscience, no one asked you.* Ugh, this isn't the best start to your new job or life, Emily.

I put on my black sleep shorts and pink singlet with a little more vigor than I normally would. This is all Toby's fault, running around New York taking selfies with his blonde bimbo as if the last five years didn't mean a thing to him, that I didn't mean a thing to him.

A hiccup of an emotion clogs my throat for a moment, and I close my eyes to try and shut down the pain.

Enough, Emily! You're a grown-ass woman.

As much as you want to blame Toby for tonight, this wasn't his fault. You had a bottle of wine and thought you were alone, so you could enjoy the pool. If it's anyone's fault, it's *his*, Louis Marchant. He wasn't even supposed to be here tonight. Daniel told me he'd be arriving tomorrow.

Why the hell is he here?

Does he not trust me?

I'm a trustworthy person.

Would you trust some stranger in your home? *Shut up, brain, I don't like your logic. It's making too much sense.* Fine, okay, I'm a stranger in his home while he's away. I get the man has trust issues, who wouldn't after all he's been through. It was just a terrible introduction. The man was probably drunk, after all, he was carrying a bottle of something in his hand, and he did sway a little.

I've read the gossip magazines—Louis Marchant is an alcoholic.

I let out a heavy sigh. Tomorrow's a new day. I have to forget about what happened tonight and hope that Louis is drunk enough that he won't remember anything about tonight. *Fingers crossed.*

I'm going to be the best assistant Louis Marchant has ever had. Anything he throws at me, I'll take with a smile on my face. He can't rattle me with his grumpy demeanor or his mean words—they're going to flow over me like water off a duck's back.

Standing up a little straighter, I give myself the ultimate pep talk. Tomorrow, I'm going to wake up with a smile on my face, a spring in my step, and do the best job I know how. I'm going to be so professional that Louis Marchant will have nothing to ever complain about. Ever again.

I'M WOKEN BY MUSIC—*EXTREMELY loud music*—so deafeningly loud that my room is rattling. Rubbing my eyes, I pick up my phone and glance at the screen—it's 2:37 a.m.

Outside, over the garish music, I can also hear splashing and giggling.

What the hell is going on?

Kicking off my covers, I make my way over to the French doors. Opening them, I'm hit by a sonic boom of sound and what looks like a rap video being filmed below me. I peer over the edge of the balcony into the pool area. There are women everywhere—gorgeous women sitting around in next to nothing.

Have I stumbled into fashion week or something because everyone looks like a damn supermodel, prancing around the pool as if they're walking the runway?

A champagne cork pops, although I can't hear it, and the girls all do this high-pitch squeal at the sound. Their fake laughter is like nails down a chalkboard to my ears.

How on earth did all these people get into the house?

Should I call Daniel?

Should I call the police?

Who shuts down parties like this?

Panic grips me because I'm totally screwing up this assistant thing by having no idea what to do. It's then I notice Louis lazing on a daybed, lounging back and looking like a king. Women are pandering to him, desperately trying to gain his attention.

The guy's a douche, ladies. Have some self-respect.

I realize he's staring right at me with his penetrating glare.

Is he trying to intimidate me?

Is this some kind of payback for my late-night swim in his pool?

Is he seriously this childish?

I'm not looking away, Louis Marchant. You can try and push me to the edge, but I'm not going anywhere. You have no idea how desperate I am to keep this job, so give it your best shot, asshole, because I'm *not* leaving. I simply raise a brow. Daring him. Pushing him to give me his best shot. He looks away for a moment, his hand motioning for someone to come to him. One of the bikini-clad women comes into view. I can't hear what they are saying above the obnoxious music, but I don't have to know what words are exchanged because their actions are making it pretty clear. The woman moves herself between his legs and the next thing I know, her head is bobbing up and down.

Is she seriously giving him a blow job in the middle of the party?

Louis' eyes catch mine again as his fingers tangle in her hair, forcing himself deeper down her throat. Well, one thing's for sure, she's taking it like a champ. My cheeks heat at the images playing out in front of me.

Louis' eyes don't leave mine while he gives me a 'fuck you' smirk as he enjoys his blow job. What a fucking asshole. He's trying to fuck with me. Well, two can play at that game, Mr. Marchant.

I quickly turn away and run back into my room searching my desk for exactly what I need. Ripping a page out of my notebook, I scribble on the piece of paper in a large, black felt-tip pen and walk back to the balcony. The performance has slowed —what a shame. I lift the piece of paper with the number 3.5 written across the page—my score for the bullshit blow job he's getting. His eyes widen, anger flashes across his face, then he yells something at the girl, pushing her off him. I watch as he tucks himself back into his board shorts and storms off.

Emily - 1

Louis - 0

8

EMILY

"Good morning, mademoiselle." The male voice surprises me as I enter the kitchen. A gorgeous man dressed in a white chef's outfit greets me. Seriously, is every man in France good looking?

"Oh, hi." I'm beyond tired and feeling a little flustered. Louis' party went until the early hours of the morning. I am sure the sun was up. After his attempt to give me a show by the pool failed, I tried to go back to bed to grab some sleep, but it was to no avail. I wanted to start fresh on day one of my new job, but due to the private porn performance some woman decided to give early in the morning, sleep wasn't an option. Having to listen to some woman fake an orgasm, and badly at that, at five in the morning was certainly not how I wanted to start my day.

Louis - 1
Emily - 1

"I'm Gabriel, Louis' chef." His chocolate eyes looking me over leisurely.

"Nice to meet you." I hold out my hand.

He ignores it, coming around the kitchen counter to stand in front of me.

"That's not how we greet each other in France." A sly smirk falls across his lips as he steps closer and kisses my cheeks twice and, of course, a slight blush creeps over my face. "What would you like for breakfast?" he asks, his dimples popping in.

"I can just grab something. You don't have to—" He doesn't let me finish as he waves his hand in the typical French way.

"It's my job to serve you." The French words roll off his tongue, seductively.

"Only if you're sure?" I feel bad. I'm not used to this level of richness and people serving me.

"Of course. I'm just about to pull out some freshly baked croissants from the oven." My stomach decides at that moment to make itself known. *Awkward.* We both burst out laughing. "And I have coffee, too."

"I'm going to need that after last night." Gabriel looks up at me with a frown, the tone of my voice obviously giving it away. "Mr. Marchant turned up last night, unannounced."

Gabriel's eyes widen, then he chuckles. "Ah, let me guess... Louis threw a party, did he not?" I nod. He hands me a beautifully brewed cup of coffee. "Don't worry, you'll get used to it." He shrugs.

"This is a common occurrence?" Gabriel nods as he busies himself in the kitchen. "So, I need to invest in some good earplugs, then?"

"Maybe buy a set of those noise-canceling headphones instead. I have a pair." Gabriel laughs as he pulls the buttery croissants from the oven.

OF COURSE, the croissants are delicious. If I am not careful, I'm going to put on a whole lot of weight if I keep devouring this type of buttery goodness every morning. Thankfully, Gabriel has also made a fruit bowl for me, so I don't feel too bad for the extra croissant I've consumed.

We're sitting chatting, laughing at a story he's telling me when we hear someone clear their throat behind us.

Gabriel instantly jumps to attention and moves away from me.

Louis is standing in the kitchen doorway, a different woman hanging from his arm than the one I remember giving him a blow job. His face is like thunder as he looks between Gabriel and me.

"Good morning," I say cheerily. Kill him with kindness I say, but those blue eyes narrow in on me, and silence filters through the kitchen.

"Louis, I'm starving," the woman beside him whines.

We all cringe at the sound of her nasal voice.

"The croissants are amazing. I had two." I rub my stomach, and she looks at me as if I'm crazy with her condescending eyes checking me up and down.

"Do you have any idea how much fat is in one of those?" she states with an American accent.

"Um, no." I'm starting to feel awfully embarrassed at this woman's tone, she's making me feel small and insignificant just with a few words.

"I didn't think so. It looks like you don't worry about those sorts of things." Her eyes trail over me again slowly, and her top lip lifts slightly in disgust.

Gabriel drops a plate at her harsh comment and quickly starts to clean up the mess.

I'm stunned. I've never met anyone so mean in my life. I can feel the stirrings of utter humiliation creeping through my veins, my whole body is heating, my neck is probably red, and my ears feel like they are on fire.

I will not let this woman intimidate me.

Sitting up straighter, I look at her. "And I also see you don't worry about being his sloppy seconds."

Her jaw drops while she rapidly blinks trying to regain her composure. She's shocked that someone like me would dare fight back with someone like her.

I look over her shoulder, and Louis has a bemused smirk on his face. When his eyes meet mine, his lips quickly form a thin line.

"Gabriel, Stephanie will be taking her breakfast to go," Louis tells his chef.

The girl flinches.

"My name is Sophia." Her voice goes up a couple of octaves by the fact that Louis has forgotten her name.

I don't hide my smile.

"Sorry, my English isn't so great," he says in perfect English.

Sophia's face softens a little. *Seriously?* She reaches out and lightly touches his chest as she stares up at him adoringly. Is this chick for real?

Gabriel and I give each other a look of 'what the fuck.'

"I had fun last night," she purrs, but there's no doubt Louis' body stiffens at her words. "You were *amazing*." She says the word with extra enthusiasm, while also trying to be seductive.

Louis says nothing. Sophia's hand moves from his chest down his stomach until her hand squeezes his dick. "You want another round, big guy?"

Louis swallows hard and tries to extract her fingers from his crotch. "No, thanks. Once was enough." His words are curt, and I can tell straight away that they have cut Sophia. Her whole demeanor changes instantly. *As I said, Louis is an asshole.* "There's a car waiting outside for you, the driver will take you anywhere you want to go."

Wow! What a dick. I'm pretty much speechless at this stage while Sophia is being served some karma.

"Seriously? You're kicking me out?" Her unpleasant voice booms through the kitchen— I'm sure my ears are bleeding.

"Yes," he says coolly. "Gabriel, I'd love a coffee." Louis basically ignores her, which Sophia doesn't appreciate. At all. She tugs on his T-shirt, forcing him to look at her.

"You're an asshole." Sophia pokes him in the chest with her overly manicured fingernail—they are so long she might actually stab him.

How does she wipe herself with those nails? I mean that would have to hurt. She probably has a manservant to do something so menial as wiping her ass.

"You understood it was a one-night thing," Louis tells her.

"But I let you put it in my ass."

Oh. My. God. What the fuck! Silence falls across the kitchen.

I choke on the sip of coffee that I, unfortunately, took at the very moment those words came from Sophia's mouth. I'm trying not to push it back up through my nostrils, but I'm not sure I can stop it.

Gabriel halts in the middle of brewing Louis' coffee, the dark liquid falling over the side of the espresso cup as he stares in amazement at the truly obnoxious woman standing in front of us.

Louis looks like he wishes the ground would swallow him whole.

She taps her high-heeled foot impatiently waiting for Louis to respond.

Louis looks to Gabriel and me for help, his blue eyes pleading for some kind of intervention.

"She let you do butt stuff on the first night, you know she's a keeper," I say in French to Louis, my little revenge for him being a dick last night. Obviously, my French surprises him, and the blonde sends daggers my way.

"I don't pay you to sit around and eat croissants. Do your job," Louis demands in French.

Oh, so this is how he's going to play me on the first day.

Okay. I'm up for it. I jump out of my chair and smile. "Sophia, if you would like to follow me. I have your I-fucked-Louis-Marchant-and-all-I-got-was-this-lousy-T-shirt ready for you. It comes in a range of colors and styles." I give her my brightest smile, and Gabriel sniggers behind me while Louis curses me in French.

"You really are a bitch," Sophia snarls.

"Don't you dare speak to my assistant like that," Louis' voice rises. "Now... it's time for you to leave." He points to the exit.

Sophia throws a slew of curses at him, then dramatically turns on her heels and saunters off. Louis scrubs his face in frustration while Gabriel and I burst out laughing. I can honestly say I've never seen anything like that before.

Louis glares at both of us. "I'll be in my studio. You can deliver my coffee in there." With that, he too dramatically exits stage left.

Gabriel and I burst out laughing again.

"Well, that was craaazzzyyy," I say, drawing out the word.

"I'd love to say that was a one-off, but it's not." Gabriel busies himself making the coffee again.

"I can't believe she said that."

"Women will say and do a lot of things to keep Louis' attention." He shrugs.

"Ugh. So, I'm going to have to deal with bitchy women on a daily basis, then?"

"Depends on his mood." *Fucking great.* "It's become a recurring theme over the past four months. It's like he's trying to prove to himself that he can still pull women or something." A typical male response to being cheated on, I guess.

"Why, because his ex ran off with a younger man?"

Gabriel lets out a heavy sigh. "Don't let him catch you

talking about his ex. Anyone who mentions her or him has to deal with his wrath. Their names are never to be spoken here." That's good to know, but it's not like I'd ever bring them up. But still, if by accident I did, I don't want him to yell at me any more than he already has.

"His ex was a real..." Gabriel looks around to make sure we're truly alone, "... bitch."

My eyes widen, I need to know more. "Really?"

"I lived with them for many years. Yves wasn't the first artist she slept with behind Louis' back. There were a lot of men she tried to seduce. She's beautiful, and she knows it." I nod in agreement. I've seen pictures of her, and she's stunning. "She even tried to sleep with me."

I let out a shocked gasp, he nods furiously. "Did you?"

"What? Of course not. Louis gave me a chance and put me through culinary school. I owe him a lot. There's no way in the world I'd ever do that, but not all employees were so..." he trails off. Gabriel doesn't need to finish the sentence. I get the gist.

"And he never knew?"

Gabriel shakes his head. "I tried to... subtly tell him, but he was in love. The woman had him wrapped around her finger, and she could always convince him the rumors were started by jealous people. People who wanted to see him not succeed." *Wow! She sounds like a piece of work.* "Here." He hands me Louis' coffee.

"What do you want me to do with this?"

"Take it to him." Gabriel gives me a look. I'm his assistant, so this does fall under my job description. "His studio is at the other end of the garden, past the pool."

"Good luck," Gabriel states.

Great. Just great!

After a couple of wrong turns, I eventually find his studio. I lightly knock on the door, but no one answers. *Should I just walk in?* I know how artists are when they're in their space. They generally don't like to be disturbed, but he did ask for his coffee. I push on the wooden door, and it creaks as it opens for me. I step up the step and into Louis' secret world.

Everywhere you look there are thousands of paint splatters around the room—even the wooden floor is covered. My eyes are drawn to the canvases hanging around the room, the dark broodiness of them, the deep, dark red anger in some, slashes and scratches on others as if he has literally torn his art to pieces searching for some kind of catharsis. I'm so mesmerized by his magic that I don't notice the bucket on the floor and trip, the ceramic cup of coffee launching itself across the room and then all over Louis. The scalding liquid is leaving a dark stain all over his gray T-shirt. Louis yells as his T-shirt soaks the hot liquid, and it starts to burn his skin. I fall with a thud and a crash against the wooden floor, scraping my skin. Shit! That hurt.

"Fuck, fuck, fuck," he screams.

I look up from my position on the floor, and he's pulling off his T-shirt and patting his stomach, cursing in every language he can.

"I'm so sorry..." I scramble up off the floor. "You need cold water to stop it burning." I rush over to the sink, frantically looking for something that I can soak in water. Finding an old rag, I turn the tap on, then rush back and place the cool cloth onto his taut stomach. The muscles tense as I touch him, but then he quickly recoils back from my touch.

"Don't touch me," he yells. "You've done enough."

He's angry.

I totally understand it.

I would be as well.

He's probably got third-degree burns over his chest, on that incredibly sculpted body. Wow! Who knew artists looked like that? The ones I've met have either been old, or they're as skinny as a rake. But Louis Marchant, with his Mediterranean tan and a body that's chiseled from the finest marble, it's hard not to look and appreciate it. His body is art in itself.

"Just get the hell out, you've done enough."

My stomach sinks when his face goes red with anger while he's dabbing at the red marks on his stomach. He's going to fire me for sure now. It's not like I've made a good impression on him or anything.

Twenty-four hours—that's a new record for getting fired.

"I'm sorry, I didn't mean to…" The look on his face tells me he isn't in the mood to hear my apology. I turn on my heel and rush out of his studio, the tears threatening to fall down my cheeks.

"Are you okay? Hey, what happened?" Daniel surprises me, catching me as I rush inside, the tears now falling uncontrollably.

"I…"

"Did he touch you? Did he hurt you?" His eyes look at my cut-up knees, the blood running down my shins.

"Oh, God, no." Daniel's face is clouded in concern. "I tripped over a bucket on the floor and spilled a cup of hot coffee all over Louis. I guess when I landed, I ripped the skin off my knees."

Daniel stills, his head tilts to the side. "You spilled coffee on him?" I nod, trying to put on a professional face. This has to be the worst first day at a job I've ever had, and I have had a few. His hand comes out and wipes the tears from my cheeks with his thumbs, and my stomach somersaults when he touches me.

"Yes. It was an accident."

"I don't know if I'd be upset if it wasn't. He can be a dick." Daniel makes me smile. "Gabriel told me about the party last night, I'm sorry. I had no idea he was coming here until I got back to Paris."

"No, it's fine. This is his house. If he wants to party, then I just have to deal with it."

"You don't have to. I know what he's like when he parties, he gets out of control. You can always call me, and I can arrange a hotel room for you to stay in. You should be able to feel safe here." I give him a small smile because Daniel is a nice guy, and I wish he were my boss. He kind of is, but I mean, I wish I got to go to work with Daniel every day instead of some self-destructive egotistical artist.

"I'll let you know if that ever happens."

He gives me a nod and marches off toward Louis' studio.

I wish I could be a fly on the wall for that conversation.

9

LOUIS

Motherfucker, that hurts.
It hurts so damn much.
Is my skin peeling?

"What the hell is going on?" Daniel surprises me as he enters the studio, looking pissed off, which is nothing unusual. "Why is your assistant in tears?" I can hear the accusation in his voice. His eyes widening as he notices me shirtless. "You didn't—"

I don't let him finish his words. "Are you fucking serious? You think I'd ever force myself onto a woman?" My chest is heaving with adrenaline. "She poured fucking coffee over me." I pull the rag away from my stomach, which is bright red from the scalding liquid.

Daniel doesn't react. *Dick.*

"Why was she bleeding?" That bit of information gains my attention. "Her knees... they were bleeding."

How did that happen? Oh! then I remember. "She tripped over, hence the coffee all over me, but I didn't notice she was hurt. I was preoccupied trying not to get third-degree burns."

Daniel eyes me again, suspiciously. "What are you doing here?" I keep dabbing the cool material against my skin.

"I wanted to make sure you were behaving." Daniel arches a brow at me.

Dammit! He knows about the party. Fucking Gabriel.

"You know what? Fuck you! If I want to party in my own goddamn house, I'll have one." Throwing the rag at him, I hit him square in the jaw. "I never wanted an assistant, especially not a totally incompetent one like *her*. She can't even serve me a coffee without fucking it up. You hired her because she's beautiful, not because she's any good at the job." A smile falls across his face.

"I knew you noticed her."

I stalk angrily toward him. "I don't give a shit if she's a fucking Victoria's Secret model, she is still fucking useless."

"Your studio is a mess. There's shit everywhere. I nearly tripped over a bucket when I came in."

I roll my eyes at my brother like a petulant child. "This is my space. Everything is where I need it to be."

"Give her a chance before you write her off," Daniel tells me.

"I don't *need* an assistant. I've told you this." Grabbing a spare T-shirt from my pile, I slip it on, my skin still a little delicate as the cotton touches it. I grab the bottle of tequila from the shelf and take a sip.

Daniel's eyes narrow at me, the disappointment coming off him in waves, but he doesn't say anything.

"Okay then, tell me this… are you going to be in control of your social media? Are you going to answer the million and one messages you get on Facebook, Instagram, and Twitter?" I grunt, I know he knows the answer to these questions. "Are you going to sort through your mail? Answer your emails? Check your voicemail?" *I don't like where this is headed.* "Exactly, you want to be able to paint, even if it's this demonic shit." He waves his hand at my creations. "So, trust me when I say you need help. Remember, Elisabeth did all this for you."

"I told you not to mention her name," I growl at my brother. He's really working my very last nerve.

"Oh, for fuck's sake, grow up, Louis. You need to get back into the real world and stop living in this self-centered bubble you seem to be sheltering in because of this shit? It's getting old." I ignore him. "The longer you keep going on this destructive path, the longer *they* win." I take another swig of tequila between his rants. "As much as I hate to say it, the woman was a brilliant brand maker." I sneer at Daniel. "I don't want to compare the two of you, but Yves is everywhere. She's turned him into the biggest celebrity the art scene is witnessing right now." That little bit of information jabs at me like a knife to the heart.

"But that isn't me." I take another swig of tequila.

"I know, but his art is selling and for a *lot* of money." I frown at my brother. "I know, I know, it's not about the money, it's about the art." He mocks. "But your art has given you a great life, Louis."

"And it took it away as well."

Daniel places his hand on my shoulder. "You could have been anyone, and Elisabeth would still have done what she did." I hate that he's right, I know she's an opportunist. I may have sunk into an alcoholic funk, but I've heard the chatter, the rumors, the gossip. I now know Yves wasn't the first man she slept with while we were married. She was simply less discreet with him. Maybe she could see his star qualities, and that's why she didn't care that she got caught. I loved her with every inch of my soul. Giving someone that much control over you is dangerous.

I probably would have forgiven her, that's how much in love I was with her.

As long as she still loved me. As long as she was still in my life. Even if I didn't have all of her, just a piece would have been enough for me. I'm an addict, a junkie, and she's my drug of choice. I still crave her. I still wake in the middle of the night reaching for her, remembering what it was like to have her love shine directly into me. I detest that her love has been replaced with anger, bitterness, and hurt. I abhor that she's changed me into someone even I don't know anymore. I hate that she's taken the colors from my world.

This behavior isn't healthy, I know this, but I don't know how to stop. The obsessive feelings I have seeing the two of them together is overwhelming. Daniel doesn't realize I still check up on Elisabeth online. I obsess over the images I see of the two of them. I hate the way she still lights up my screen even though her light is directed elsewhere. I'm sick, that has to be the only explanation why I torture myself like this daily. Looking at their happy faces, I wonder what I did wrong. Why was I not enough for her? What the hell do I do now?

"Louis," Daniel calls for my attention. "I'm worried about you."

I know I'm an asshole. I know I am hurting everyone around me, but I just can't stop the anger that's taken me over like a raging bull.

"Don't be," I warn as I take another swig of my tequila.

"You can't keep burying yourself in tequila and women."

"The fuck I can't."

Daniel lets out an exhausted sigh. "I'm on your side, Louis."

"Good. Now leave me the fuck alone. I have masterpieces to produce."

Daniel stands there for a couple more moments in silence. "Give her a chance. You two are more alike than you realize."

I take another swig of tequila, the liquid warming my insides, making my thoughts slow, blanking out the images of Elisabeth and Yves together which continuously loop in my mind.

"As long as she stays out of my way, then we'll be fine," I grumble, picking up one of my paintbrushes and sticking it into the pot of black paint. I angrily start smearing it across the canvas in no particular pattern.

"Fine! I'll go check on Emily and see if she's okay. Let's hope she isn't packing her bags."

"If she can't handle me, then fire her." My hand moves rapidly across the canvas smearing black paint like there's no tomorrow.

Daniel doesn't answer me.

When I eventually turn around, he's left.

I slump into my chair with my bottle in my hand, exhausted where I sit and drink until the day blacks out just like my painting.

10

EMILY

Gabriel is helping me with my cuts which are quite deep and still bleeding. I'm sitting on the kitchen bench as he dabs the antiseptic liquid onto my knees.

"I'm sorry about him." Daniel's voice filters through the room.

Gabriel steps away, looking a little anxious.

Daniel walks around and inspects my knees, and a frown falls across his beautiful face. "Are you okay?" I can hear the concern laced in his voice.

"I'm a klutz. I am so sorry I burned Mr. Marchant."

"You're not the first person to have thrown a drink on him."

I smile, but I do feel bad about it.

"I'll get him another coffee," Gabriel adds, quickly moving away.

"Make it a pot. He's found a bottle of tequila." My eyes widen. "Don't worry, you won't see him for the rest of the day. He's in one of his moods, but it makes for good art." I can hear the sadness in Daniel's voice, and it upsets me that he can't help his brother. "Do you mind if we go have a chat in the office, I'd like to organize his schedule." He holds out his hand and helps me down from the counter.

We make our way to the office off the living room. "Please take a seat." I choose one of the tan leather armchairs and sink back into the buttery soft leather, running my hand over the beautiful material. These must have cost a fortune.

"May I just say I'm utterly mortified about my first twenty-four hours on the job." Daniel looks at me curiously. "I promise you... nothing like this will happen again." He needs to know I'm serious about this job.

A smile forms on Daniel's face when he says, "It's been an interesting start, that's for sure."

My cheeks bloom with a blush remembering Louis finding me nearly naked in his pool. "He told you..." Oh crap! Daniel knows about the whole pool incident.

He nods, smiling at me.

"I wasn't trying to seduce him." The words tumble out of my mouth, and I can't stop them.

"Never said you were."

"He thought last night..." I nervously play with my hands. "I mean... I understand what he saw, but... I'm not one of *those* girls."

"One of those girls?"

"Yeah, an art groupie."

Daniel bursts out laughing. "Art groupie? I've never heard of such a thing."

"Really? I went to university with them. Just like women who try and bag a footballer or a celebrity, these girls want to sleep with the brightest star on the art scene." I can see Daniel is finding this all very amusing. I really need to shut up, but when I'm nervous, I babble and say the wrong things at the wrong time, making it even more awkward than it already is.

"I never thought you were one of *those* women. Louis wasn't meant to have been here, but as you might suspect, he has trust issues, especially with women." I nod my head in agreement, and I totally understand why. Betrayal from the closest person to you will do that. "You did nothing wrong. The number of times I have jumped into that pool in my underwear, well..."

Hot damn! Now I'm thinking about Daniel in his underwear, and my face burns even brighter.

"Look, Louis is difficult at the best of times, but with his divorce finalized last week, and..." Daniel takes a deep breath and lets out a heavy sigh when he continues, "... with him just giving her whatever she wanted, he's not in a good place." *That doesn't seem fair since she's the one who betrayed him.* "I'm not asking you to cut him some slack..." he trails off, "... but cut him some slack," I add.

Daniel chuckles. "Yeah. I'm hoping things improve." I can see it on his face that he isn't so sure, though. "Anyway, let's discuss your job, and then I have to get back to Paris to look after my other artists."

DANIEL LEFT HOURS AGO, and I have been going through all of Louis' private messages on his social media pages. The amount of body parts I have seen is mind-boggling. Who thinks sending a stranger images of your most intimate parts is a good idea? The desperation of these women offering Louis themselves is actually quite sad.

There's a knock at the office door. Looking out the window, I notice how dark it's become. I have been working in here for hours.

"Sorry to disturb you..." Gabriel smiles, "... I just thought I'd let you know that I took some food to Louis in the studio. He was passed out, but I know when he wakes, he'll be hungry." A frown falls across my brow—he's passed out drunk already. That's not good. "And I've left you some dinner, it's in the oven."

"Thank you so much."

"I'm glad Daniel hired you. I think you're going to be good for him." Gabriel's comment makes me smile.

"As long as I don't spill hot coffee on him."

He chuckles. "He deserved it after this morning." I smile. "Good night, Emily."

"Good night, Gabriel."

"Emily." Gabriel pops his head back into the office, and I look up at him. "What that woman said to you today... she's wrong. I think you look perfect the way you are." Aw, bless him. He really didn't need to say that. Not going to lie her words did sting, but I also I wasn't the one doing the walk of shame either.

"You just want me to keep eating your croissants."

"Of course." He smirks.

"Thank you, Gabriel. I appreciate it." He gives me a salute and disappears.

A little while later, my stomach rumbles, and I take it as my cue to grab something to eat. I shut the laptop down, roll my shoulders back, and shift my neck from side to side. I'm not used to being hunched over a computer all day, but it beats standing on my feet for nine hours at Madame Tussauds. Walking back into the kitchen, I pull out the roast chicken and vegetables Gabriel left in the oven for me. Grabbing myself a soda from the fridge, I decide to sit outside in the garden. It's another beautiful night. The pool looks inviting, but tonight I won't be jumping in. I've learned that lesson. I take a seat and notice the light is on in Louis' studio.

Should I check on him? No. I'm not his babysitter. *But then again, I am his assistant, and shouldn't I be assisting?* Ugh, my conscience gets the better of me. I'll check on him after dinner.

I take the first bite of my chicken, and it's amazing.

It doesn't take me long to finish my dinner as the sun sets. I take my dishes back to the kitchen, wash them, and head on over to Louis' studio before I go to my room for the evening.

When I knock on the door, there's music playing, but he probably can't hear me. So, I open the door slowly and make my way inside.

Oh shit! I'm glued to the spot.

Louis is sitting on a paint-splattered sofa, his tanned hand fisting himself with his eyes closed and primal grunting falling from his lips.

Then the floorboards creak.

Shit! I'm busted.

11

LOUIS

I've watched the day turn from yellow to orange then to black, and still I'm staring at the canvas and yet, there's still no creativity. The tequila certainly isn't helping as I passed out for a little while. But when I came to with my head pounding, my eyes bloodshot, and everything that I had been trying to drown out floods back in damn technicolor.

Thankfully, Gabriel dropped something for me to eat before he finished for the day to help soak up the alcohol. I pull out my cell, and I know what I'm doing is a slippery slope, but I'm desperate, desperate for my daily hit. I unlock it and pull up *her* account.

God, she's beautiful.

I stare at her face, trying to remember what her skin felt like, how her body felt, hoping and praying that through the screen, she can bring back some of my magic that she took away when she left me. There's a photograph of her at the beach dressed in the skimpiest of bikinis, her large breasts almost spilling out of the black fabric. Her skin is sun-kissed, and I know she has an all-over tan because she hates the lines.

My dick twitches to life thinking about her curves, remembering every inch of her glorious body. I pull out my dick. This is what I need—I want to feel dirty jerking off to an image of my ex-wife, or maybe I just want to feel something, anything, and if this is the only way, then dammit, I'm going to do it.

My hand slides over me as I try and remember the way she felt against my skin, her smell, her warmth. The scent of roses filters through the window, changing the image of my ex to my assistant emerging from the pool. My dick instantly turns hard. Recently, it has taken me a while to get an erection as the ache filling me takes over.

My mind conjures up images of Emily in her simple white cotton underwear. I imagine licking the stray droplets of water off her creamy white skin. Then down between her breasts, across those dusty pink nipples where my teeth sink into her flesh, while I watch her head fall back in ecstasy.

My hand moves quicker along my dick.

Now, this is all kinds of fucked-up. The scenario currently running through my mind isn't right, but it just won't stop. The image of her dropping to her knees and taking me in her mouth, just like she saw that girl do to me last night. I'd wrap my hand around her wet hair and make sure she takes me all in, choking on me, bringing tears to her eyes, but knowing she loves every minute of it as she hums in appreciation like a good girl does.

There's something about her that gets under my skin. She is equal parts fragile and strong. Situations where she looks like she's seconds away from bolting, instead, she's dishing it right back to me.

Last night? That was a dick move—the party, letting a girl give me head in front of Emily—but I was frustrated, I was angry, and I was turned on. I don't know why this woman makes me so angry and frustratingly horny at the same time. She has me confused and messed up.

Not going to lie, having her watch me last night was one of

the hottest things I've ever seen, but then she comes out with a fucking scorecard. Pushing me. Daring me. I wanted to stalk up to her room and spank her creamy white ass until it was the same color pink as her fucking nipples.

My fist chokes my cock harder. I'm brutally jerking myself, angry that I am letting this girl mess with my head. She's my assistant, an employee, and no one special. Yet, when I look at her, I see color again. The outer edges of my dark world have the faintest glow of light surrounding them. The problem here is it pisses me off even more because I know what it means.

I'm going to fight it.

I'm going to fight it so hard because she's not what I want.

I continue to choke my dick to images of her running through my mind, and that's when a floorboard creaks in my studio. My head whips around, pulling me from my fucked-up fantasy.

Reality hits me with a fucking sledgehammer as I see the woman playing in my mind staring back at me but in the flesh. Those emerald eyes sparkling with shock, embarrassment, and a tiny, ever so tiny, portion of curiosity.

Is she the kind of woman who likes watching her partner jerk off over her?

No. I bet this English rose has to have the lights out, and the sheets pulled up high when she sleeps with someone. I bet she doesn't know how to let go, to fuck with abandonment.

Why do I want to show her? You have to still be drunk, Louis. These thoughts are not normal.

Her pink mouth is wide open, those apple cheeks are flushed the perfect pink, reminding me of her hardening nipples that are poking through her white T-shirt. It looks like she might like what she sees. This isn't good—my hand won't stop pleasuring myself. Why should it? She's the one who has interrupted me, interrupted my alone time, maybe next time she'll know to knock when she enters my studio.

I'm close, so fucking close, I can't stop now.

Slowly, Emily retreats back out the door she came through.

I LOOK up at the ceiling feeling like an utter bastard.

This isn't me.

I tuck myself away. I'm sure this borders on sexual harassment, and she'll probably sue me. Maybe she did it on purpose? Thinking it would be a perfect payday for her knowing she has enough witnesses on her side. I angrily pull open the studio door and see her running across the grass.

"Emily, stop!" I yell.

I'm half expecting her to flip me off, curse at me, keep running, but she doesn't. I jog quickly over toward her, her cheeks are flushed, her green eyes wide with fear, and she's unable to look at me. Shit! As I slow down to stand in front of her, I notice her arms are wrapped around her as if she's trying to protect herself from me. Is she scared of me? I know I'm an asshole, but shit! I run my hands through my hair. I've never had a woman be scared of me before.

"Emily." Her name falls from my lips slowly, so I don't spook her.

"Mr. Marchant." Now is not the time to be thinking that sounds hot coming from her lips. "I'm so sorry. I knocked, but the music was on loud." She's still looking at the ground when she continues, "I just thought maybe you needed something..." Her eyes widen as she realizes how suggestive that sounded. "I mean... shit," she curses, which makes me smile. "I mean... to see if you needed anything professionally speaking, not..." She waves her hands in the direction of my crotch.

"Not?" Now, I'm teasing.

She's flustered, which makes me want to keep teasing her. "I just didn't want you to think I was trying to seduce you." Her back straightens as she pushes her embarrassment to the side. "I'm *not* trying to seduce you." She almost shouts the words at me making me burst out laughing.

She frowns. "What's so funny?"

"That you think *you* could seduce *me*." Her eyes widen in surprise. "You know who I am, do you not?"

Emily's face turns red, and it's not from embarrassment but more like anger.

"I know exactly who you are."

"Then you know that you..." my eyes look her up and down before I go on, "... aren't my type."

She sucks in an audible breath. "Good to know because I don't make a habit of sleeping with washed-up artists." Emily's eyes widen, and she quickly covers her mouth, shocked at what she's just said.

She should be, I'm her fucking boss.

My gaze narrows in on her. "You think I'm washed up?"

She shakes her head as words seem to fail her at this moment.

A long silence falls between us.

"But I am." The truth falls from my lips. "Look at me. I'm a drunk."

Emily looks up at me, her face softening a little.

"I've lost my muse."

Why am I telling her this? Her face softens even more at that confession. Daniel seems to think she knows art, so I'm hoping she understands exactly what that means. "I can't paint anymore. I mean I can paint, just not like I used to. Not like everyone wants me to." I've utterly embarrassed myself now, ripping open my wound to a stranger who's standing in front of me.

Emily's hand comes out and rests on my arm. "Sometimes, you need to seek the darkness to find the light."

Her words resonate with me. That's where I am at the

moment, in the darkness, but I don't know if I'll ever see the light again or even if I want to.

"I'm so far in the darkness, Emily, I can't get out."

She frowns. "Maybe it won't happen today or tomorrow, but one day soon, you'll push through."

"It's been four months, and I'm still hurt, and most definitely as angry as the day it all happened. She left me for a better, newer, younger version of this 'washed-up' artist."

"Louis..." she says my name on a whisper, and I hear the pity behind the word.

"No. I don't want your fucking pity." I pull my arm away from her. I don't like that look on her face. It's full of sympathy, and I don't want that from her. I want to see those cheeks flushed again, I want her anger, I want her angry emerald glare.

I need it.

I crave it.

"Next time knock because if I see you again when my dick is in my hand, I'm going to assume you want it." Emily takes a step back from me, putting distance between us.

Yeah, that was a little *too* far, Marchant.

I turn on my heel and storm off back toward the main house before I say anything else. I grab a bottle of wine from the cupboard in the kitchen and stomp up to my room.

I need to close this chasm that's opened up in my chest from telling Emily things I shouldn't have.

12

EMILY

"Do you do *any* work?" Louis storms into the kitchen, catching Gabriel and me laughing together over breakfast.

Louis has become moodier this week since his late-night confession. He showed me a vulnerable side to him that night by showing me how hurt he truly is over Elisabeth and Yves. And he was right, I did pity him because I realized I wasn't that upset over Toby anymore, that I wasn't missing him or pining after him. I don't even think my heart is broken anymore, and that's kind of sad when you think about it.

Maybe I never loved Toby?

Certainly not like Louis loved Elisabeth.

Maybe I should be losing my shit and going all Godzilla on everyone. Maybe that's what true love is. I can't even remember what Toby smells like, and even his voice is fading from my memory. After five years, shouldn't those things stay with you? I mean, it's only been three weeks since we broke up. It's not very long, yet it feels like Toby is so in the past that he isn't even relevant anymore.

"Seeing as it's only seven in the morning, and I'm currently eating my breakfast, then *no*."

Those blue eyes narrow. *I've got him there.*

"You don't seem to be doing *any* work." Louis' glare has now moved to Gabriel, and he starts again, "Every morning I see you flirting with Emily when you should be bringing me my damn coffee." With that little tirade, he storms out of the kitchen, and as he leaves, Gabriel pokes out his tongue, and I laugh.

"He's in a great mood today," Gabriel grumbles as he moves around the kitchen

"Yeah. You might want to warn the staff. I received a Google alert about the people who shall not be named, that they were honored in Beverly Hills for some bullshit art thing last night."

Gabriel rolls his eyes, preparing the asshole's coffee. Since my fateful coffee incident, Gabriel has been the one taking him his morning coffee in his studio, neither of us trusting me with the hot liquid.

"He hates those sorts of things," Gabriel adds.

"Yeah, he might, but it still sucks seeing your ex with her new boy-toy being honored by them." Gabriel nods in agreement. "I need to come up with something to take the focus off them on Instagram and bring it back to Louis. I can only take so many photos of his artwork. Judging by the female fan club, they want pictures of him, preferably in the nude." I sigh. He has no idea the amount of porn I get to see daily via his social media accounts.

"Good luck with that." Gabriel smiles.

"Maybe I should take his coffee to him today. Try and get some action shots."

"Shouldn't I come with you?"

"Oh geez, one mistake, and it's being held over me. I can do it. It's technically my job."

Gabriel hesitantly gives me the mug of coffee, and I give him a big thankful smile.

Slowly, I make my way to his studio. I haven't been there in over a week since I caught him jerking off. Not going to lie, the man is an asshole, and if I could poke him with white-hot iron pokers, I would, but it was the hottest thing I have ever seen. I may have, on more than one occasion, used my little vibrating friend to help me finish myself off over that spank-bank material.

Yes, I know, I'm going to hell for that.

I knock on the door loudly and wait patiently. Nothing. So, I do it again, this time harder, hurting my knuckles in the process.

Still nothing.

Shit!

I push open the door, but the studio is quiet. I make sure to look down and not trip over anything on my way through. If I spill another mug of coffee on him, I'm fired for sure.

"Hello," I call out, hoping not to catch him in a compromising position. Again.

"Oh, it's *you*," he growls.

Okey-dokey, it looks like his mood hasn't gotten any better. That tone of voice he's taking with me stings a bit.

"I have your coffee." He turns and looks at me, then takes the offending mug out of my hands. "I guess you *can* do your job, after all." I let that barb go over me and channel my mantra of 'I will not kill my boss' take over.

"Yes. It's amazing what you can achieve when there aren't any hazards on the floor." Those blue eyes flare over his coffee cup, but he doesn't say anything. "Actually, I need to grab some new pictures for your social media. Your fans are wanting more of you." I give him an enthusiastic smile hoping it's not going to turn into an argument.

"No."

"Yes," I reply back.

He raises an eyebrow, surprised that I dare to disagree with him.

"*No*," he says the word more forcibly this time.

"Yes. And I can do this ping-pong match of words all day if you like. It's no problem for me, but I'll get what I want." He lets out a frustrated sigh. "Can you pretend to be painting, and I'll take a couple of snaps now. You won't even know I'm here." I shake the phone in my hand.

"I do not *pretend* to paint."

Oh my God, I internally roll my eyes at him so hard I'm sure they are lodged in the back of my skull. "Well, then just paint, and I'll snap away."

Louis doesn't move, he simply sips his coffee, slowly, in silence, as if he doesn't have a care in the world.

I will not kill my boss. I say this mantra over and over trying to keep calm.

I don't cope well with silence, and I'll always want to put an end to it. "So, what have you been working on?" I try to take a look at his canvas but can't really see past him.

"Nothing of importance."

Ugh, this man is infuriating. He takes another sip of his coffee, slowly.

Okay, two can play this game. I pick up my cell and take a snapshot of him sipping his coffee.

"What the hell? Emily!" He glares at me.

"I need a candid picture, and now I've got it. I can leave you in peace. Thanks." I give him a smile and waltz out of the studio, and on the way out, I can hear him cursing in the background while I do a little happy dance.

There's more than one way to skin a cat.

13

EMILY

Tonight is Louis' first social event since I started working with him a month ago. I'm quite nervous because I'm not sure what to expect. Well, I know what to expect from Louis—no doubt he'll be a dick, probably drinking too much, maybe trying to bring home some kind of skanky woman—it will be no different to any other night at Casa la Groupies.

I pleaded with Daniel to come with me because I don't trust Louis, but he had business in Dubai or something, which is kind of convenient but couldn't be helped. As Louis' assistant, I have to keep an eye on him, make sure he doesn't mess up by making the front page of a gossip magazine again for all the wrong reasons. Basically, I am babysitting a full-grown man, and I'm hoping, no praying, that I'll be able to control him.

I even asked Gabriel if he wanted to be my plus one for the evening. Unfortunately, I couldn't even pay him to accompany me. So, I'm all on my own tonight. I can do this. I'm overthinking it. It's going to be fine. How much trouble can Louis seriously get into at a private party?

What the hell am I saying? That man can get into plenty.

The party is at some rich guy's home. I'm not sure what the party is for as nothing was mentioned in the invitation. Maybe they're celebrating being rich or some other indulgent rubbish. Daniel assured me there would be influential art collectors there tonight, and he believes it will be a good way to reintroduce Louis back into society, slowly.

"What the hell are you wearing?" Louis glares at me as I make my way down the stairs.

"What?" I look down at my dress. I've chosen a chambray shirt dress with a cute pair of cream wedges. My strawberry blonde hair is pulled up in a messy bun, and my makeup is natural. I think I look cute. Louis is dressed in a pair of dark denim jeans and a white shirt, the sleeves rolled up showing off his tanned arms. He looks effortlessly casual. Damn him.

"You look like you're wearing a tent."

I look down at myself again. *I guess I could put a belt with it.* What the hell am I thinking? I don't give a stuff what a man thinks about my clothes. I feel good. Toby used to do that to me all the time, and I'd immediately change into something that made *him* feel good.

"What does it matter to you?" I pull the strap of my bag up over my shoulder.

"Because you work for me."

"Exactly, I work for you. I most certainly don't dress for you." I ignore his asshole stare.

"You represent me and this…" he waves his hands in the air, "… isn't how I want to be represented."

"I'll remember this conversation when you're obnoxiously drunk tonight because people are going to be talking more about that than what your assistant is wearing."

He lets out a frustrated huff, turns on his toes, and stomps out to his car.

Emily - 2

Louis - 1

WE ARRIVE at the luxury home, which juts out and hangs along the rugged coastline. The driveway is filled with every man's dream car. There are millions of dollars' worth of ostentatious wealth laid out before us. I can see Louis hesitate in the car. For some reason, he looks a little nervous.

"We don't have to stay long," I tell him.

He turns to me and gives me a sad smile, then opens the door to get out of the car. Of course, ever the gentleman, he lets me get my own door. *He's such a gentleman,* I think to myself.

I straighten out my dress, then quickly try to catch up to Louis who's striding into the party ahead of me.

"Louis, you made it," a tanned silver fox greets him, kissing Louis' cheeks. He looks genuinely happy to see him.

See, Emily, tonight is going to be all right.

"And you brought a date."

"No," we both answer in unison.

"She's my assistant," Louis clarifies.

"A very beautiful one." The silver fox reaches out and kisses my hand, honey-colored eyes looking at me approvingly.

Um, no, thank you, and I look to Louis for help.

"Hands off, Phillipe," Louis warns.

I relax a little. It seems Louis understood I was in an uncomfortable position.

"We don't fuck the help, remember?"

I turn and look at him, eyes wide, fists clenched. *What the hell?*

Phillipe chuckles, his honey eyes bouncing between us. "I don't fuck my help, that doesn't mean I can't fuck yours."

I'm standing right here. They do realize that, don't they?

I'm seconds away from turning on my heel and telling them all to go fuck themselves. I am not some piece of meat to be leered at and passed around.

Then a beautiful brunette slinks over to the silver fox, linking her arm with his like a beautiful leech.

"Louis darling, nice to see you again," she purrs, hungrily looking him over.

"Selena." Louis nods in her direction but doesn't seem interested.

"Mon trésor, this is... sorry, I didn't catch your name?" Phillipe asks me.

Oh, so now you want to know my name?

"Emily," Louis tells him.

"This is Emily. She's Louis' assistant. Isn't she a beauty?"

Is this guy serious?

The brunette looks me over, a smile forming on her face while I feel awfully uncomfortable.

"Oh, yes... look at her creamy skin, mon chou. It looks delicious."

Panic filters over my body. What's going on? I turn to Louis again, seeking his help.

"Selena..." Louis' voice deepens, and his eyes narrow in warning "She's not part of the scene, Phillipe." Louis looks at Phillipe, and the silver fox chuckles.

"Fine. We get it. She's off the menu. You're no fun anymore, Louis," Phillipe teases. "I guess we'll have to find some other fresh meat to play with, mon amour." He turns and nuzzles Selena's neck. "I'm sorry, princess, Daddy couldn't deliver tonight." *What the fuck?*

"Unless Louis wants to?" She looks at him while seductively sucking on her ruby red lips, but before Louis can answer her indecent proposal, they are distracted by some new guests. Louis puts his hand at the small of my back and moves me away from the kinky couple.

"They like to share," he states. I'm slightly confused, and he must read that on my face. "Seriously, Emily, are you that sheltered?" I didn't think I was, but judging by his question, maybe

I am. "Phillipe and Selena are swingers. They like sharing." My mouth forms an O. "I need a fucking drink." Louis storms off toward the open bar, and I follow after him.

Shit! Has Louis been invited to a sex party? I hope not because that's going to make my job all the more harder. *Wrong use of words there, Emily.*

I'm not having fun. Not like I should be—I am here to work. Louis told me to stay in this seat and that he'd be back. But that was, I look at my watch, thirty minutes ago, and I don't see him anywhere.

I jump up off of my chair and start looking for my fucking alcoholic boss. The party is pumping, there are maybe about a hundred people in attendance. There's a ton of older men with younger women. I wonder if they're all swingers, or if it's just the host? I haven't seen any sex happening just lots of chatting. Maybe that happens later. Maybe they are checking each other out trying to work out who they want to sleep with. Okay, this is way out of my comfort zone even trying to figure it out.

I look around the room, and the girls all appear like the same versions of each other—big boobs, Botox face, plumped lips, tight dresses, long nails, and hair extensions.

I continue walking around the party, pushing my way through the guests, deflecting the advances of a couple of older, creepy guys. I'm now pretty sure this is a sex party, and I am most certainly *not* on anyone's menu. If I don't find Louis soon and something happens, Daniel is going to fire me.

My job is to clean up his reputation and being seen at some rich man's sex party probably isn't what Daniel had in mind.

I wonder if Daniel knew?

I scan the area again but still nothing. He's not inside. I know this because I stumbled upon the sex part of this party upstairs. I need to bleach my eyes when I get home. Now that inside has been thoroughly checked, I need to go outside into the expansive gardens. If he's asleep behind some bush, I'm going to kill him.

Begrudgingly, I make my way to the gardens. Grabbing my cell, I flick the torchlight setting on so I can find my way in the darkness. I search for a good ten minutes until I round a corner and find a white ass with pants around their ankles. I move the light up the body, and tanned legs are wrapped around the waist. I move higher, and the light catches their faces.

"What the fuck?" Selena screams, trying to shield her eyes from the bright torchlight.

"What the fuck, Emily?" Louis screams as he continues to pump into Selena.

Shit!

I turn on my heel and move away quickly.

Ugh, such a fucking asshole.

He's fucking his friend's girlfriend in the bushes, and here I was thinking he was in trouble. I was worried I was going to find him in a pool of his own vomit. I'm a damn idiot.

I stomp back into the party, push my way through the people, and walk out to the driveway where all the cars are located. I find our driver and our car parked about one hundred feet up the road and make my way to the car.

"Oh, Miss Emily." Yanis, our driver, looks at me startled. "Are you ready to go?"

I open the door and slam it shut. "No. Louis hasn't finished screwing some woman in the bushes yet. I guess when he's done, we can go." Yanis nods but doesn't say a word while I busy myself on my cell and wait.

An hour later, Louis opens the car door, his blue eyes are wild with fury. "I've been looking for you."

"Well, now you've found me." I barely look up from my cell, texting my girlfriends like crazy. I also may have Googled 'ten ways to kill your boss and not get busted' because why not.

"I thought something had..." He doesn't finish his words as he angrily rakes his fingers through his hair.

"I'm fine. Have you finished? Or are you simply taking a break so you can go back for round two? I'd like to know so I can plan my night."

Rage seethes behind Louis' eyes. "I never go back for seconds. No one is worth it."

He's one hundred percent a dick.

"Yanis, looks like we're ready to go. Louis has finished fucking for tonight."

Louis slams the car door, and I hear him cursing as he rounds the other side. He opens his door and slumps into his seat, then slams that door shut. I can smell her perfume on him, and it makes me want to gag. He pulls open the mini-fridge in front of us and pulls out a bottle of vodka. Taking off the lid, he throws back the bottle taking a hefty sip. Then he surprises me by handing me the bottle.

"I don't know where those lips have been. Eww." I turn my nose up at the vodka.

"Places that you'll never get to experience." He takes another swig directly from the bottle.

"Good. I'd rather stay disease-free, thank you very much." I fold my arms across my chest.

"You're the most infuriating woman I have ever met."

He takes another gulp of his precious vodka.

"The feeling is most definitely mutual."

Louis huffs beside me, cradling his vodka like it's some sort of precious artwork.

It's a long, silent trip home.

14

EMILY

"How did it go?" Daniel calls me the next morning. "It went okay." Honestly, I'm not sure what to tell him.

"Looks like he behaved. There's nothing in the press this morning."

Phew, I have to say that makes me feel better.

"Yeah, I guess he did."

Daniel doesn't buy it and then asks, "What did he do?"

"You could have warned me it was a sex party."

"What?"

"The host is a swinger."

"Oh my God, Emily... I had no idea." I can hear it in his voice that he's telling the truth. "Were you okay at the party? Fuck! I should have been there. I didn't mean to put you in that kind of situation."

"Daniel, you didn't know. I was okay. I waited in the car with Yanis while Louis finished up."

"Finished up?"

"Yes. I found him in the garden behind the bushes with the

host's partner. Apparently, it's all above board... the host was fine about it. I thought it was best I give Louis his space."

"Fuck." I can hear the frustration in Daniel's voice. "I'll talk to him. He shouldn't have left you, not... dammit! Not in a place like that."

"Daniel, it's fine. I'm fine. I can look after myself. Please, we don't need to make a big deal about it."

"But—"

"No. Seriously. It's fine. Eye-opening, but okay."

Daniel's not convinced, but I don't need him rocking the boat with Louis. After last night, I haven't seen him yet, and honestly, I'm not sure I want to.

"You're doing a great job. I know he's a difficult man to live and work with, but you're handling him fantastically. I know Louis isn't surrounding himself with the greatest of people right now, but I'm hoping it's a phase."

"Isn't he a little old to be having phases?" I ask, honestly.

"Yeah, he is." Daniel lets out a sigh. "But I don't know what else to do with him."

"Maybe he needs to get away from France for a bit. It holds so many memories for him here. Maybe he needs a change of scenery."

"Are you trying to score a holiday?" He chuckles. "I mean, you do deserve one, especially after last night."

"I hear the Seychelles are nice this time of year," I tease.

"Why yes, that does sound nice, but I get what you're saying. Maybe he needs to get away from it all... away from the bad influences."

"Maybe he needs a shock to the system to get back to being the great artist we all know he is again."

"Leave it with me, I'll see what I can do."

"He's destroying it." Gabriel runs into my office, his face is panic-stricken.

"What are you talking about?"

"Louis, he's destroying his studio."

Shit! I jump up and rush out to where I can hear crashing. I pull open the wooden door, and there he is bare-chested and in ripped jeans, tearing into his canvases, paint up-turned everywhere, and he's pulling everything apart.

"Nothing. I have fucking nothing," he shouts while he pulls the dark canvases off their stands.

"Louis," I call out to him, but he's lost in a haze of what looks to be tequila induced. I make my way through all the broken canvases, brushes, and paint tins.

Louis is staring at the now blank wall.

"I feel nothing when I'm in here."

"Maybe you should try and paint somewhere else."

"No," he yells as he turns. "You don't understand."

"Yes, I do." He ignores me and continues to kick shit around—his temper is out of control.

"I may not be some kind of art genius, but I used to paint," I tell him. "But I haven't painted in five years."

Those blue eyes widen, and it stops him in his tracks.

"Yes, but you don't have anyone missing your paintings, not like me," he says coldly. "I have the weight of the art world on my shoulders, all waiting with bated breath for my next masterpiece, which will never come because that bitch took it when she left me." A glass smashes against the wall, then another one and then another.

I let out a sigh.

I have come to the realization that Louis doesn't want to be helped. He's happy wallowing in his misery, and he doesn't deserve company. If he wants to waste his best years on self-destruction and self-righteous behavior, then he can go ahead because when he finally wakes up, he's going to have no one left around him who cares. He's going to wonder where everyone went who looked out for him.

I walk out, pull the door shut as the sounds of crashing echo through the studio.

"I'm exhausted," I tell Gabriel who's standing outside the studio looking worried. "Let him trash it all. If that's what he needs to do to get whatever it is going on with him out, then so be it. He needs to start making the right decisions, but he doesn't want to. He's not ready. So, until then, we put up with him acting like a damn toddler and having a tantrum until he hits rock bottom.

Gabriel nods sadly, and we both make our way back to the house with the sound of smashing and loud bangs being heard from behind us.

I HEAR a crash inside the house which wakes me up. I look over at the time. It's 1:23 a.m.

"Motherfuckers." I hear shouting from downstairs and suck in a deep breath.

Louis spent the day destroying everything, and now he's come up to the main house to continue his rampage.

"I made you," he screams, and then there's another crash.

I turn the corner and find Louis stumbling around, not really able to function.

"I made him." He's waving his cell phone in the air. "I found him. I made him. *Me!*" He throws his phone across the tiled floor, and it smashes, small parts of the phone shatter as it hits the wall on the other side of the room. I watch in slow motion as Louis' fist connects with the wall.

Shit! That's his livelihood, those hands.

"Louis," I call his name, but he does it again.

I rush toward him and cry out, "Stop! Louis. Please stop."

Tears well in my eyes as I look down at his bloodied and bruised hands. He also looks down at them and seems confused as if he isn't sure how they got that way.

"Let me get the first-aid kit."

He stumbles and falls onto the leather sofa in the living room. I rush quickly to my office and grab the first-aid kit, but by the time I come back out, Louis is asleep. I sit down beside him, slowly and carefully fixing his hands. He doesn't stir. He doesn't even flinch—Louis is that drunk as I clean his wounds. I feel for him because tonight I really saw his pain and how deep it runs.

"I wish I knew how to help you," I whisper. Seeing someone who you looked up to become a shell of who they once were, is hard. Louis is an asshole, but he's a talented asshole. I wish I had one-tenth as much talent as he does. I hate that he's wasting it over a woman who doesn't give two shits about him.

"You can't."

Louis surprises me, making me jump. I thought he was asleep. Those bloodshot blue eyes open and focus on me. I still have his hands in mine trying to tend to his wounds as his fingers curl around mine and squeeze tightly.

"I want to help, Louis." I look down at him, and for the first time, I see him utterly vulnerable.

He reaches out, his palm touching my cheek. "You're so beautiful."

I swallow his compliment down, hating that it affects me. His thumb caresses the apple of my cheek, and I lean into his touch. It's been six weeks since Toby left me, and I miss the touch of a man. The pads of his fingers are rough, coarse from years of holding a paintbrush. His hand moves and wraps around the base of my skull, his fingertips digging into my hair. "You're pure sunshine, and I'm nothing but darkness."

I frown at his words—he's still drunk.

"I'd destroy your sunshine with my darkness, Emily."

"Or, I could light up your darkness."

He smiles at me, and it's the first genuine smile he has ever given me.

His fingers dig and pull my hair harder. "I wish that were true."

Butterflies do somersaults in my stomach as this moment seems, well, intimate. Then, before I have a chance, his hand tightens, he pulls my face to his, and he kisses me. Freezing me to the spot, my eyes widen. His soft lips press against mine, while thick fingers tug on my hair. His hard body presses against mine, and a tiny whimper falls from my lips, which opens them to him. He takes his chance and hungrily takes me. Those once-soft lips are now hard with desire. His kiss is all-consuming. He takes and takes, clouding my mind with lust—a lust that's so deep I can feel it in my toes. I've never wanted someone as much as I want Louis Marchant in this moment.

Then, I still, tasting the alcohol on his breath.

What the hell am I doing?

I push myself away from him. His chest is heaving, those blue eyes are bright with desire, and my lips are swollen from his hungry kisses.

He's drunk.

He's probably horny, and I'm the closest convenient woman. I untangle myself from him and abruptly stand.

"It's late. You should rest." And with that, I quickly make my way back to my bedroom, regret hanging around me like a dark cloud.

15

LOUIS

I fucking destroyed my studio, but at this very moment, I don't care because amongst the rubble, I created something, something I never thought I'd do again. I put my brush down and stare at the image in front of me that I've been working on all day.

As soon as I woke up this morning on the couch in the living room, I had to come to my studio and paint. I lost myself in my art for the first time in God knows how long and without a drink. I painted this fucking sober. Bright yellow lips stare back at me. The fact that I have used color in months other than, as Daniel would say, my demonic shit, is haunting me. No. Actually, what's haunting me is whose lips I have painted. I can still feel them against my own. Her soft breath. Her warm body pressed against mine. I shouldn't have done it. I know this, but in that moment when she was tending to my wounds, her soft fingers gently working over my broken skin, something broke inside of me.

I don't remember the last time someone cared for me. This woman doesn't even like me, and yet there she was trying to put my battered hands back together again. She whispered a question to me, not realizing that I wasn't in a drunken stupor, and as soon as she touched me, it sobered me up. I closed my eyes because she was too close, and I didn't trust myself with her.

Emily has no idea that it's images of her that I see when I touch myself. The images of her are the only things that seem to help me over the edge. I was right when I said she was pure sunshine because she is. Prancing around my fucking house in her sundresses, looking all innocent and shit, it drives me crazy.

Her creamy white skin just begs for my lips to touch and my hands to caress it. That golden-spun hair I want to wrap around my hand and control her, especially as she's choking on my dick. I close my eyes at that image and take a deep breath.

I'm glad she stopped things last night because I would have fucked her, and I think she'd have let me too if reality hadn't hit her. I wouldn't have respected her in the morning. I'd have been an asshole to her again. Hurt her. Dimmed her sunshine with my darkness.

I'm no good for someone as beautiful as her.

I'm a fucking mess.

A washed-up artist, she called me, and it's the damn truth.

I look around at the bullshit of an excuse I call art, and then back to what I've just completed, and there's no comparison. I stare at the sunshine lips that I've just painted, and that's when it hits me.

No.

No fucking way.

No.

God-fucking-dammit, just no.

Not her.

Elisabeth's words filter through the chaos that's happening in my mind. *"You, of all people, know that sometimes an artist's muse isn't always who you want them to be."*

I open the cupboard beside me and pull out the bottle of tequila.

Fuck this!

I let the darkness take me over again.

I WAKE up to someone nudging me.

"Louis, wake up," the unfamiliar female voice states. "Gabriel's made you breakfast." I groan, my empty stomach is somersaulting. "I think you need it."

Then I'm hit with bright light, it's too intense, and it instantly gives me a headache.

"Fuck off," I yell, pulling a pillow over my head.

Moments later, it's been taken from me.

"Get. Up." I feel the person tugging on my arm. "Oh, God, you stink." The person makes gagging sounds as my covers are pulled off me.

"Who the fuck do you think you are?" I scream.

"I'm Emily, your assistant. I'm helping you to become a fully-fledged human being in the *real* world again."

I let out a groan.

I was trying to forget about her.

"I'm your boss, and I say leave me the fuck alone." There's silence for a couple of moments, and maybe she's listening to me, but I'm wrong.

"I have a job to do, and if you fire me over doing it, then you're breaking a million and one laws." I still. *What the hell?* "So, if you don't want to lose the other half of your money to another woman, I suggest you get the hell out of this bed you have been wallowing in for the past couple of days and have a shower."

I'm shocked. I thought she was a wallflower, not a ball buster. The covers are ripped off me.

"Louis," she squeals.

I rub my head and kick my feet over the edge of the bed, the room is spinning, so it takes me a couple of moments to gain my bearings.

"What?" I grumble.

"You're naked."

I look down at my dick who decides he wants to salute the morning because he has a mind of his own. "Yeah, because I was asleep, remember?"

Her eyes are wide and her cheeks flushed, but she is still staring at my dick.

"It's just a dick, Emily." She's flustered, but so far, she's made no effect in a comeback. "Granted, you probably haven't seen one this big before."

Her mouth forms a perfect O, and I like that I have stunned her quiet. It helps my headache.

"Will you *go have a shower*?" she says the words with bite, but she's still looking at my dick.

"Wanna join me?"

"Excuse *me*?" Her voice rises.

"The way you keep looking at my dick makes me think you wouldn't mind, you know... helping me."

"Gabriel has b-breakfast ready for y-you when you're finished up h-here," she splutters over her words, and now her neck is a nice shade of crimson.

"I might be awhile. You know... this *is* a lot to handle." I grab my dick.

Emily huffs and turns on her heels.

For some reason, I feel lighter this morning, which is a first in a long time.

16

EMILY

"*It's just a dick, Emily.*" I play the images of Louis Marchant naked in all his glory over and over in my mind. I now know a dick is not a dick, seeing his for the first time. Why on earth did his wife leave him? That man is glorious. What would you even do with something like that? That man hit the genetic lottery—good looking, French, artistic, rich, and mightily well hung.

He thinks I'm an English prude compared to his self-confident Francophile ways. I acted totally fine. *I think.*

"Morning." His voice makes me jump as I'm still lost in deep thought about his gloriousness. I can't hide the blush on my cheeks when I turn around and see him freshly showered. He looks different this morning and not because he has clothes on either. It's like the dark cloud that has been hanging over him has shifted slightly.

"You shaved." I realize his scrappy beard is missing. He doesn't look like the washed-up artist with a drinking problem that I've seen for the past six weeks that I've been here. He now looks like the man I remember seeing in the art magazines and on the Internet. *It's not like I stalked him or anything.* He's wearing faded jeans with fashionable holes and a bright white polo with bare feet. He smells clean like sandalwood and earth.

"Eat." Gabriel places his breakfast in front of him which is surprisingly English—bacon and eggs.

Louis sits on the chair beside me and starts his breakfast eagerly, which shouldn't surprise me as he's hardly eaten anything in forty-eight hours.

We think Louis has hit rock-bottom these past couple of days, destroying his studio and most of his recent work in the process. It probably hasn't helped that while his life has spiraled out of control, his ex and her man are the toast of the town. As much as I think my boss is a dick, and he is, I do feel for him—a *teeny tiny bit.*

He obviously loved his wife more than anything in the world, and her betrayal has ripped at his core. Maybe that's what true love does to you. While Louis imploded over the last forty-eight hours, it got me thinking about Toby and why I wasn't destroying the house over losing him. It's been nearly two months since Toby dropped his bomb. Except for a couple of nights, I haven't really thought about him, and we were together for five years. Other than maybe a bruised ego, I don't know if I'm as heartbroken as I thought I was. Although, out of stupidity, I still check his Instagram, and it still makes me want to puke with all the happy photographs of him and his girlfriend, but the ache I had in my chest seems to have gone. Maybe it's the French air, or maybe I'm just too busy looking after my drunken pain-in-the-ass boss that I haven't had time to think about my feelings for Toby.

Was I really in love with him? This is a question I have been asking myself. Or was it just convenient? Like we got into a routine, and that was all there was to it. Maybe we were never real soulmates. I mean if we were, he wouldn't have cheated, right? *Food for thought, Emily. Food for thought.*

Gabriel places two glasses of freshly squeezed orange juice

in front of me pulling me from my thoughts and disappears from the kitchen. Louis has been vicious with his words the last couple of days I have spent with him on his bender.

"You owe Gabriel an apology. Actually, you owe all the staff a massive one. Maybe a nice bonus would make up for all the shit you have pulled these last couple of days."

"Excuse me?" Louis quirks an eyebrow and looks at me as if I have lost my mind.

"You may be looking all…" I wave my hand in front of him.

"All what?" He glares at me.

"Normal now," I say. "But that doesn't make up for how you have acted over the past forty-eight hours."

"I don't remember."

"Shall I play you the footage?"

"You recorded me?" Louis looks at me stunned as anger laces his words.

"Yeah, I'm going to use it to blackmail you."

"What?" he roars.

"Oh, calm down, will you? Jesus, you have no sense of humor. No. I took the footage because I knew you wouldn't remember, and I knew you wouldn't believe how much of a dick you have been if I just told you. So, I wanted proof to show you."

Louis takes a large gulp of his orange juice. "Do I really want to see this?"

"I think you should." He takes one last sip and nods, so I pull out my cell, bring up the footage, and show him. He stares at it in stunned silence, and when the mini clip is over, he clears his throat. "Um… can you excuse me for a moment?" Louis hands back my cell and walks away from the kitchen.

I give him a couple of moments, then I hear his footsteps as he walks back into the kitchen and goes to the fridge to pull out the vodka. Our eyes meet, and he hesitates, then puts the vodka back in the fridge and rests his elbows on the island bench, his head falling into his hands.

I'm proud of him in this moment because forty-eight hours ago, he'd have taken that bottle and disappeared for the day.

"I'm an embarrassment."

Well, I'm not going to sugar-coat it for him because he is. "Not so great seeing yourself like that, is it?"

Those blue eyes look up at me. "I don't want to be like that anymore."

"Okay."

"Okay? That's all you've got to say."

"Okay, that's good," I add, which makes him smile.

"I was waiting for a tirade of words from you. So, I'm a little taken aback that you've given me a simple 'okay.'"

Leaning forward, I place my elbows on the island bench too. "I don't think I can make you feel any worse than you do right now." He just stares at me. "But I have a plan." Louis raises his eyebrows. "I thought we could go for a bike ride today." He continues to just stare at me, those long lashes blinking slowly.

"You want me..." he points from himself to me, "... to go for a bike ride with you?"

I plaster on my best customer service smile and nod my head enthusiastically.

"No."

"No?"

"Don't give me those eyes, Emily." I'm not sure what eyes he's talking about. I don't think I am giving him anything other than advice.

"You're fluttering those eyelashes at me. I can see what you're doing." His words make me smile because I was totally doing that to him.

"Why not?" I ask.

With a confused stare, he says, "Why would I not let you flutter your eyelashes at me?"

"No. I mean why won't you go on a bike ride with me?"

"Because… I'm an artist," he says rather snobbishly as if that's some sort of reason not to go.

"Exactly. You should be out with nature getting inspired."

Louis scowls at me. "I'm a busy man," he adds quickly. Then he moves away from the kitchen, heading back through the house and outside.

"No, you're not."

His strides are so much longer than mine, I'm almost jogging trying to catch up to him. Louis stops abruptly in the middle of the yard, and I walk straight into him.

"Sorry," I mumble.

He turns around and looks down at me, fire burning behind those blue eyes. "Excuse me? What did you say?" I don't think Louis Marchant is used to people challenging him.

"I said sorry because you stopped abruptly, and I ran into you."

"Before that?" He waves his hand angrily at me.

"Oh, when you said you were busy, and I disagreed with you."

For some reason, my words render him speechless. I notice a vein on his neck begins to tick. Looks like I've pissed him off. Again.

"Do you know who I am?" Louis thumps his chest.

"Yeah, I do." Those eyes narrow in on me as if to say that doesn't answer the question, so I continue, "I actually went to your art exhibition in London years ago, when I was in university…" he tilts his head at my change of subject, "… and it was magnificent. You inspired me. The colors. The way they danced across the canvas. I went home and painted some of my best work after that exhibition. So, yes, Mr. Marchant, I know who you are."

Louis stares at me for a couple of seconds, then turns on his heel and heads toward his studio, the one he's destroyed.

"But I also know you're not that busy because you have spent the past forty-eight hours in an alcoholic orgy daze."

My words stop him in his tracks as his hand reaches the doorknob of his studio.

"You know those women mean nothing to me." Of all the things I thought he'd say to me, that wasn't one of them.

"Okay." Because, you know? Like I care. Not like I haven't thought about that kiss we had a while ago or anything. I mean, he's probably forgotten all about it, and he's replaced my touch with a million others since then.

Louis lets out a frustrated huff and opens the door to his studio, then stops.

"You've destroyed most of it in a fit of rage."

"I know." His words are quiet and sullen. As he walks through the devastation, he picks up empty paint tins and looks at the slashed canvases. "The problem is... I feel nothing when I come in here. *Nothing.*"

"What do you mean?" I'm hoping he'll tell me more, so I can help.

He turns to face me. "All I see is nothingness."

"What did you used to see?"

Louis frowns as if trying to conjure up something that seems so foreign to him now. "Everything. The world was full of color—" He stops, his attention pulled away by something. He bends down and picks up the canvas. It's a new painting, one I haven't seen before. There's a set of bright yellow lips painted on the canvas.

"Life felt extraordinary." His finger runs over the lips, and it's like he's lost in thought as if remembering a memory of them. "I used to feel free."

"And you don't feel free anymore?"

Louis shakes his head, then places the unmarked canvas down on one of the tables. "No, I feel trapped by all of this." He waves his hand around the studio. "I don't know who or what I am anymore."

That comment shoots directly into my chest because I realize he's given his ex so much power over him.

"Then we need to get away from all of this." Those blue eyes stare at me in confusion. "Forget about painting. Forget about the exhibition. Forget about being Louis Marchant, the artist, and let's find out who Louis Marchant, the man, is."

He eyes me suspiciously. "And I'll find all this by going on a bike ride with you?"

His question makes me laugh. "Probably not, but it will get you outside in the fresh air and away from this bubble you have cocooned yourself in." Silence falls between us for a couple of moments, then he lets out a heavy sigh.

"Fine."

I jump up and down with glee.

"But be warned, I'm not going to like it."

"That's okay. Gabriel has already organized a picnic lunch for us."

Louis' dumbfounded for a second or two. "You knew I'd say yes?"

I just smile. "The bikes are waiting for us out front."

17

EMILY

We've been riding around the local area for what feels like hours, I'm sunburned, my thighs are burning, my butt is numb, and I'm sweating like a pig, but Louis has a smile on his face, and the tension from this morning seems to have lifted a little.

"You look like you could use a break," he calls out to me.

"Nope, I'm fine," I reply, even though, in reality, I am ready to die.

"There's a field coming up on the left, we can rest there. There's a big old tree you can sit under for shade. You're as red as a lobster."

Damn English skin.

It's not much longer until a beautiful green tree stands atop a hill in the field. We pull our bikes off the road. Louis takes the picnic basket from my bike, and we trek to the tree. I look around, and there's nothing but sunflowers, lavender fields, and rolling green hills.

"Um... are there any public bathrooms around here?" I scan the horizon.

"Sorry, you're going to have to find a bush."

I look at him in horror.

A bush!

"There aren't any snakes or anything, is there?"

Louis chuckles. "No. You'll be fine. I'll set up."

I frown as I scan my surroundings again. I don't really see anywhere private to relieve myself, but I'm busting from drinking so much water on our ride. I make my way over to where I see a grouping of bushes and squat.

Ah, that feels good even if my legs are shaking like I've done a million squats all in a row! I make my way back to where Louis has set up the picnic for us.

"Your ass is so white it's like a spotlight helping sailors come ashore."

I pick up a bread roll and throw it at him, and he bursts out laughing.

"Screw you." I pout, plonking myself down on the tartan picnic rug. "You shouldn't have been looking," I huff, popping a grape into my mouth.

"Believe me, I didn't mean to, but I thought there was a Lunar eclipse, and the moon had come out."

I shove him hard, and he falls into the grass, laughing. I've never seen this side of Louis before—the jovial, fun side—and it's nice. He picks himself up and brushes off the grass. I grab one of the sandwiches that Gabriel made for us, my stomach's almost ready to eat itself. We both eat in silence taking in the serenity, listening to the bird calls as they fly past.

"So why did you take this job?" Louis asks, breaking the silence.

I dust the few crumbs off my legs and fiddle with the non-existent lint on my leggings. "My boyfriend moved to New York to be with another woman."

Louis looks at me, his long black lashes blink slowly. "How long were you together?"

"Five years. When he broke it off, I thought he was proposing. He took me to a fancy restaurant, told me he got a promotion, but that he didn't want me to go to New York with him. He broke up with me because I lacked ambition. Those were the exact words he used, and that he needed a woman on his arm who he could be proud of." That stabbing pain in my heart is still there when I think about how much Toby hurt me that night.

"He sounds like a jerk."

"He was. Although I guess in some ways, he was right. I kind of just plodded along from one crappy job to the next, not caring too much about anything."

"Well, this one is pretty crappy, too."

I look up and see the genuine smile on his face. "It's not *all* bad. I'm in the South of France, eating delicious French food, looking at a magnificent view of the countryside with one of my favorite artists. I think it's not *too* crappy at all."

Louis' mouth slackens, and I see a small shake of his head in disbelief. "I'm one of your favorite artists?"

"Is that all you heard? Did you need your ego stroked?" I laugh, which makes him smile.

"Yes, please. It's been a while."

"Fine. This is a one-time thing, though. Yes, I love your colorful art." I feel him stiffen beside me, so I turn and see he's picking a baguette apart. "But I like your newer stuff, too." This catches his attention, and he looks up. "I like that you're capturing love from a different point of view. That it's not always sunshine and rainbows, that it's raw, dark, and intense." I have his attention now, his full attention, and if I'm honest, it's a little breathtaking.

"You like the dark side of love?"

"At the moment, yes." I shrug. "But if I'm honest, I am not sure if I was ever truly in love with Toby."

"Why do you say that?"

I fidget a little more rolling a napkin around in my hands.

"Because I'm not having an alcoholic bender because my heart is broken." I look up into his blue eyes, but he looks away quickly.

"I don't think that the way I have been acting is a good indicator of love. I think it's probably more... an obsession." His honesty surprises me, so I turn a little to look at him.

"You're obsessed with her?"

Those words have me concerned, and the look on my face must say it all.

"I'm not crazy," he states while he continues to pick at the piece of bread he's holding. "She's always been there for me, especially with my painting encouraging me, inspiring me. It's like she was my anchor, and now that she has set me free, I'm drifting in a sea of paint. I feel like the only thing that could save me is my anchor, but..." Louis' shoulders slump, "... she's not there anymore."

I reach out and place my hand on his shoulder, to which he tenses under my touch. "It wasn't her that made you a great artist, Louis." He turns and looks at me, a frown marring his perfect face. "It's you." I take my hand away and fold it back into my lap. "I think you're giving her way too much credit. She may have supported you, encouraged you, but she didn't paint for you. She wasn't the one envisioning your work. Each brush stroke along the canvas, that was all you. Just like a great novelist, someone else may have given them an idea, but they didn't write the book."

Louis' eyes widen at my words as if they are sinking in. He lays back and stretches his arms above his head, his white polo rising showing off his tanned, toned skin. I put a piece of fruit in my mouth, and we fall into a pleasant silence as we watch the world travel by.

. . .

WE BOTH MUST DOZE off for a long while after filling our bellies with food and getting way too much sun and a ton of exercise because I wake up and realize I'm snuggled into something hard. It takes me a couple of moments to work out where I am, and that I'm staring at Louis' white polo shirt, which I was just drooling all over.

Oh my God!

I sit up quickly, and Louis chuckles beside me.

"You looked so peaceful."

I wipe the side of my mouth. "I'm so sorry..." I move away from him, "... that was utterly unprofessional." Louis frowns as I shimmy further away from him.

I probably look like a mess—I can feel my hair has a bird's nest going on, so I try to run my fingers through it and then start to pack up the leftovers from our picnic lunch.

"Emily." Louis reaches out, touching my hand. I look up into his bright blue eyes. "It's okay. We just fell asleep together. Nothing happened." I nod, but I am feeling very flustered. "I'm not angry," he says softly. I nod again, words escaping me right now. He frowns again and pulls his hand away. "I'm sorry, Emily." He helps me pack the picnic basket.

"Why are you sorry?"

"I've been a bastard to you since the moment you arrived." I'm not sure where he's going with this conversation, but I continue to listen. "And I can see now that my actions have hurt you. That I scare you."

"You don't scare me."

Why does he think that?

"Because something as innocent as falling asleep beside me has you cowering away from me."

Oh.

"I didn't think it was very professional, that's all." I find I can't look at him when I speak.

"I've hardly been professional myself."

I shrug because I'm not going to lie to him.

"I want to start over." My eyes widen in surprise. "Hi, I'm Louis Marchant. You might know me as your *favorite* artist." He holds out his hand to me making me laugh, but I take it.

"Hi, I'm Emily Chapman. And you might know me as your *best* assistant *ever*."

His hand stays in mine as he tips his head back, laughing.

18

LOUIS

"We should take a photo," Emily tells me.

"You want to show off to your friends that you're with your *favorite* artist?" I joke.

She rolls her eyes. "You're never going to let me live that down, are you?" She shuffles through her backpack pulling her cell phone out.

"Yeah, probably not," I say, liking her honesty, the way she's so open without even realizing it. Every emotion, good or bad, is written across her face in bright neon colors for everyone to see.

"I think a picture of you in a field of lavender will be social media gold." She waves her phone in front of me asking permission without actually saying the words.

"You want to post a picture of me to your Instagram?" I feel a little concerned about this. Is she an undercover groupie?

"Not to mine. To yours."

"Why?"

"Because it's my job."

Shit, of course, it is. I'm an idiot for thinking anything else.

You're also an egomaniac thinking she wanted a photograph with you.

"No." I continue to pack up our picnic.

"Um... yes," she shoots right back.

"No. I'm not going to go stand in front of a lavender field looking like a fool." I shove the leftovers into the bag quickly.

"You're standing here right now acting like one, might as well add a pretty background."

I stop what I'm doing. She's being snarky. The vein in my neck twitches with anxiety.

She lets out a long, exhausted sigh. "You need to show the world you're a functioning artist."

"And lavender fields represent that?"

She rolls her eyes, jumping up and scanning our surroundings. "There are sunflowers over there if that's more suitable." She points off in the distance.

"I don't care about the background. I don't get why taking a picture of me in some field represents my art."

Emily moves a couple of steps toward me. "It's about showing the world that you don't give a toss that your ex-wife is running around the world with your ex-protégé. It's showing her that she now has no control over you. It's also showing your fans, your critics, even you, that you don't need her to be successful again."

"And sunflowers and lavender will do this?" I'm still not convinced, but I give her an A-plus for her enthusiasm.

"Do you want your ex back?" she asks.

"*No.*" Okay, that answer surprises me, and it must surprise Emily as well.

"Really?" Her mouth falls open, and she shakes her head. "Could have fooled me."

"I didn't think... it was the first thing that came out of my mouth."

"I say that's progress." She nods enthusiastically and smiles at me.

"Maybe." I'm unsure why that 'no' was so strong.

"Okay, then we need to create an image of the *new* you."

"With lavender and sunflowers?"

"Oh my God, Louis, stop obsessing over the flowers. I want you to look like you're having fun. That you're happy and content. That's all. The flowers are simply the backdrop."

"And you think this will help?"

She nods. "The last photos posted on your account are depressing." She hands me her cell phone, and I flip through the images. They are pathetic, stupid memes about love sucking, betrayal, and pretty much a lot of dark shit. As I scroll further, I see the images of *her* and *him* on my account.

"Delete all the pictures of them from my account, please." I hand the phone back to her.

She nods but doesn't say any more.

"If you think me taking some stupid photos here will help with my image, then fine, I'll do it. I guess I need to do something to salvage my career."

Her eyes widen, a smile lights up her face, and those two dimples pop in urging me to touch them, but I stop myself.

"See, I told you they wouldn't look cheesy." Emily hands me her cell.

The photographs are good—the light, the composition, the dimensions. She has a picture of me walking through the lavender with a bottle of wine in my hand. Another one of me riding my bike through sunflowers. And another with me lying on the picnic rug, my sunglasses on looking up at the sky. The main thing about these pictures is that I look relaxed and happy. She uses the hashtags #livinglife #happiness #inspiration when she posts them. The cell phone starts pinging with numerous likes and comments.

"What are they saying?" My ego gets the better of me, I have to know.

"Nothing but well wishes. Fans telling you how good you look... how happy you seem." She looks up at me and smiles.

"Guess I'm good at faking it."

"Guess you are." As she turns away, I see a little sadness in her eyes, but she quickly covers it with a smile and starts packing the rest of the gear.

"Hey, Emily, come here." She looks at me weirdly, but I wave her over. "Selfie time." I give her a wink, then put my arm around her shoulders and hold out her cell and snap a picture of us.

"Don't post that."

"Why?" I look up from the picture on the phone.

"Women don't want to see that." My eyes narrow, and my eyebrows draw together. "On *your* social media," she quickly adds.

"Oh, this isn't going on my account. It's going on yours."

"What? No!" she screams, trying to grab her cell from me. But I'm so much taller than her, and my legs are so much longer eating up the grass as I run away while furiously typing up a status.

She eventually catches me and swipes the cell from my fingers making me laugh. "What did you do?" She scrolls through her pictures, her face giving away nothing. "Dreams do come true. Hanging out with my favorite artist in the world." #livinglife #dreamscometrue #bestdayever #hotartist #hessingleladies," she reads the words out loud. "Oh my God, you're such an idiot." She giggles as she lightly hits my arm.

"If I have to do it, so do you." I raise a brow at her. "Show your dickhead of an ex that you're not pining away for him either."

A smirk crosses her face. "Brilliant plan. If he can take pictures of him and American Barbie on a romantic carriage ride around Central Park days after leaving me, then I can get my photo taken with a hot guy, right?" The words are out before she realizes what she's said.

"A hot guy," I repeat her words.

Emily stomps her feet and growls, walking away from me.

"You think I'm hot," I tease her.

"Ego the size of Mount Everest much," she calls back.

"It's not the only big thing I have."

She stops, turns slowly, and looks at me, raising her eyebrows.

Yes, I'm talking about my dick.

"I saw you checking it out this morning." Emily's face goes bright red, and she tries to sputter out an answer, but it gets caught in her throat. "It's okay. I don't mind if you look."

"You can't say those things to your assistant," she tells me as I walk past her toward our bikes.

"And assistants shouldn't be looking at their boss' dicks either, but you don't hear me complaining."

More cursing and grumbling come from behind me as I put the picnic basket on my bike and tie it down. Emily refuses to look at me. She's so flustered, her cheeks are pink, and her ears are bright red. I like that I have affected her so much. This isn't how I thought my day would end up, but I'm glad it has. Getting out of the studio is exactly what I needed, and she knew it. A day not thinking about art, not thinking about anything other than good food and great company has put me in a happy mood.

Maybe I do need to get out more?

Explore the world around me again. Join the land of the living and stop living in the past.

When we finally get home, Emily goes straight to her room to take a bath. She's exhausted from our bike ride, but I'm exhilarated. After a quick shower, I head down to my studio, and that's when the devastation hits me again.

Fucking hell! What have I done?

I start cleaning up the studio. It's a slow process, and it takes me hours until I have it back to some form of normality. A pile of rubbish now sits outside of the studio. I look around at the bare bones of the room, and in some strange way, it feels cathartic. The sunshine lips take pride of place in the middle of the studio for inspiration. The sunshine set amongst the darkness of my other paintings, the ones I didn't fully destroy.

It's late by the time I leave my sanctuary and slowly make my way through the gardens toward my home in the darkness. I take a moment to look up and see that it's a full moon, the silvery ball set amongst the black sky. Tiny bubbles of inspiration pop beneath my skin as I continue walking with the light guiding me. I notice the balcony doors to Emily's room are open, and I catch the movement behind them. I stop and look up as she walks out onto the balcony, her golden hair falling over her creamy shoulders. She's dressed in a thin black singlet, and she looks so young, much younger than I think she is.

"No!" She raises her voice—her phone is to her ear. "I haven't slept with him. It was just a kiss. It didn't mean anything. He was drunk."

I think she's talking about me.

"He's my boss."

Yeah, she's talking about me. I know I was drunk when I kissed her, but it just meant that my inhibitions were lowered, that the control I have around her wasn't as strong. At night, I can't forget about the kiss, but during the days, I have to. It's not right, especially after today. We're in a better place now, and I know I shouldn't be eavesdropping on her conversation. I've done enough shit to hurt her since she's started, but she's talking loudly, and I'm just walking back to my room, so it's not really my fault that I can hear her or that I'm walking slowly.

"Yes, I know he's hot." She waves her hands around. "Yes, I know the kiss was amazing."

Amazing, hey? Good to know. I thought it was incredible too. "But I'm not interested, Rosie." Oh, that was a shot I probably didn't need to my ego. "I need this job, you know that."

That's right, the dickhead ex who thought she wasn't good enough to date, what a fucking fool he turned out to be. Emily is amazing. How could you not want a ray of sunshine like her in your life?

Good question, Louis? *You haven't exactly been appreciative of her sunny disposition since she started months ago.* No, but today is a fresh start, we shook on it.

"Rosie, I have a job to do, and that does not include *doing* Louis Marchant."

Well, it could if she wanted to.

No. She's right. I'm her boss.

"Yes, he messaged me. Can you believe that?" *Who's she talking about now? Who messaged her?* "All because he saw the picture of Louis and me."

Oh, she must mean her ex. What an idiot. I bet he realizes what he's missing now. I knew he'd be watching her waiting to see what she does with her life. That little prick thinks he can fuck around on her, and then once he's finished playing the field, he can come back to her. You're too late, someone is going to come along and sweep her off her feet. That asshole should have appreciated her sooner.

"Of course, I ignored it," she says, then there's a small pause, and she continues, "I know. I'm proud of myself, too."

I can hear the pride in her voice at how she's handled the situation with her ex—good on her.

"I miss you guys, too." I hear the sadness in her voice coming through. "Say hi to Ava and Georgia, too. When I get back, we're going to go crazy. I better go, I'm shattered."

Whatever her friend says next makes her laugh, and I like hearing it. I need to remind myself to make her laugh more.

She says her goodbyes and holds her cell in her hand. Emily looks out across the dark horizon.

Can she see me here? I hope not. I'll look like a creep if she does.

Emily lets out a heavy sigh and goes back inside, locking her door, and the light switches off moments later. I can now move from my spot and head back to the house. The day has been fun, and I look forward to more with Emily.

After a quick shower, I fall into bed, and it doesn't take long for me to fall asleep. I'm exhausted and not because I've been partying or because I've had way too much tequila, I'm physically exhausted from riding a bike around the countryside.

A GIRL with golden spun hair runs through lavender fields, laughing, looking carefree. I catch her hand, spinning her around before she falls into my arms. Emerald green eyes, rose pink lips, that are ready for me, begging me, calling me to kiss her. I oblige. They taste like sunshine, and the scent of roses tickles my nose.

I WAKE WITH A START, my mind full of color, images, my hand itching to get the images onto canvas. I jump out of bed and rush toward my studio before my inspiration fades.

19

EMILY

"Morning, Gabriel." I make my way into the kitchen with my legs aching. They feel like jelly after yesterday's ride, and believe it or not, my butt actually hurts. I think I need one of those hemorrhoid donuts to help me sit on. I don't think I have ever in my life worked out that much. I should probably start because I'm walking around like an eighty-year-old woman right now, and that tells me more about my physical conditioning than it does about my age.

"Morning." He smiles, handing over a croissant and freshly squeezed juice.

"Is he up?" I ask about our boss.

Gabriel nods. "He's been in the studio all morning." My eyes widen, and Gabriel smiles wider. "I think yesterday has inspired him." *Really?* "He's probably hungry," he tells me, handing me a croissant wrapped in a napkin. "Go... take it to him."

"Um..."

"I have his coffee as well." I shake my head. "I have a lid for it." Gabriel hands over the secure travel mug.

I guess I'm going to have to take it to Louis. Gabriel practically pushes me out of the kitchen.

I wonder what Louis is doing down there?

I hope he's not drinking again. Yesterday was great seeing him so carefree, it suited him, but I'd be naïve to think one day in the sunshine will change him.

Slowly walking down to the studio, I'm enjoying the morning sun. When I arrive, I see a pile of rubbish to one side of the studio filled with destroyed canvases, paint tins, and other random objects.

Everything is quiet, which is unusual. He always has his music playing loudly when he's working or should I say drinking. I lightly rap my knuckles against the wooden door, but there's no answer. Taking a deep breath, I push the door open and walk through.

My eyes trace over the empty studio where the destruction from the other night has vanished, and now it's practically empty. Blank canvases stand to one side, there's neat paint pots sitting on a table. Hanging in the middle of the room is the canvas of the yellow lips I saw the other day. But there's another painting drawing my attention—it's black, but there are silver specks in the middle, which appear like light shooting out from them. Then beside that is another unfinished work—a black sky that hangs over a lavender and yellow backdrop.

They are simply beautiful.

I place the croissant on the side table and move closer to examine the paintings in front of me. I'm lost, far away in thought admiring these new works that I jump when I hear his voice. Turning around, I see a disheveled Louis walk from a back room, his gray pajama pants hanging low against the deep V of his hips, with a trail of caramel hair disappearing under the edge. It's obvious he isn't wearing any underwear judging by the sizable bulge at the front. There are speckles of paint across his bare chest—black, white, purple, and yellow cover his tanned skin.

"You've been painting." My words come out slowly because I'm in awe of this creation.

A smirk crosses his face as he runs his fingers through his blond hair, making the waistband of his pants dip dangerously low. My teeth sink into my bottom lip, and before he can answer, I yell, "Stop!" Alarming him, I pull out my cell and take a snap of him in his finest. The women will go crazy over this image. It's perfect. I mean I'm drooling over it, and I'm seeing him in the flesh.

"What the hell do you think you're doing?" He looks mighty angry, so I bite my lip harder.

"Um... I just..." This is going to sound really bad now that I have to explain it to him. "I thought you looked so good standing there in next to nothing with paint all over..." my hands wave at him, "... your chest. And I thought it would be perfect for posting. Women will go crazy over this image, Louis."

Those blue eyes widen in surprise, then turn from turquoise to an almost sapphire color. "You like what you see?" His voice is deep and low, sending thundering vibrations right through my body.

"I was looking at you aesthetically."

"Like I'm a piece of art?" His brow quirks up, and he smirks.

"I told you... you have an ego the size of Everest," I joke because the air in the studio has thickened.

He moves toward me, and I take a couple of steps away from him. "And like I told you, it's not the only thing that's big." My eyes immediately look down at his crotch. His pants have tented a little, and my cheeks flush because I damn well know the size of his dick. I'm horny, and he's damn well hot, and this is so, so wrong.

"You painted."

Louis' eyes look over my shoulder to the images behind me. "Yes."

"I like them. What is it?" My heart is thundering in my chest as I remind myself he's my boss, and that I need this job. He's looking at me like he's seconds away from ripping my clothes off, and the bad part about that equation is that I want him to. Toby never looked at me that way.

"It's nothing," he says curtly making me frown. Louis' cell starts ringing on the counter, and we both look over at it, the sound echoing around the studio, cutting the tension between us. He picks it up and answers. I turn to leave and to give him some privacy.

"Stay." The word is commanding. "Hold on, Daniel, she's right here," he says, then places the cell onto the counter and presses speaker.

"Morning, Emily," Daniel says happily through the speakerphone.

"Hey," I answer.

"Those photos you took yesterday... are simply amazing. The number of comments on them is huge. A couple of art bloggers have picked up the images and are talking about Louis again. So, thank you. Great job."

Even though Daniel can't see me, his praise makes me happy, and I smile.

"She's already taken some more this morning," Louis adds, his eyes never leaving mine.

"I look forward to seeing them. I hope you two can get out and explore more. I need more images like that," Daniel tells us.

"Don't worry, I have something planned," Louis adds, which surprises me.

"Fantastic. I'm glad to hear you're on board with this, Louis."

"If it means getting me on top, a position I like to be in..."

Louis looks at me hungrily, his meaning coming through loud and clear, "... then I'll do whatever it takes to get me there."

"I don't know what you have done to this man, Emily, but keep it up," Daniel tells me.

Honestly, I'm a little taken aback by Louis' attention. He's hated me since the moment I arrived, and now it feels like he can't wait to take me to bed. Maybe he's bored, and I'm just convenient.

"Anyway, the reason for my call... this weekend you have been invited to a charity gala in Monaco, and I think this will be the perfect place for you, Louis, to get back on the social scene. I have a number of women who will be happy to be seen on your arm. You need someone with a profile, someone who will show you're on your way back. Someone with connections."

"Are you pimping me out, Daniel?" Louis' jaw tightens.

"Of course, I am. Elisabeth and Yves are on every social page in France and Europe. They attend every charity gala, movie premiere, and they rub shoulders with the who's who of European celebrities. They network their asses off, and it's paying off. He's becoming an art juggernaut, and if you don't fight back, then you're going to be left behind."

I can see the anger bubbling under the surface when Daniel mentions Yves, but he's right, all the research I have been doing on Yves shows that he's very well connected. He wasn't well connected four months ago, but once he and Elisabeth got together, he exploded onto the scene.

"Emily, I'll need you to attend the gala as well."

"Wait! What?"

"There's a chance that... *they* might attend." My eyes look at Louis who has stiffened beside me. "I want you there just in case."

I totally understand.

Louis remains completely silent.

"In the top drawer of the desk in the office is a company

credit card. I'm sure Louis won't mind buying you something to wear."

"That's very generous, but I can't accept."

"Yes, you can," Louis comments. "It's fine, Daniel. She'll be dressed appropriately."

"Good. Good. I'm emailing over a list of potential dates."

"No. I don't want one," Louis tells Daniel.

There's silence for a couple of moments.

"Louis... she might be—" Daniel starts to argue.

"No. I don't need a woman on my arm, especially not a fake one."

"You know how these things work," Daniel tries to argue with him.

"I don't care. I will not hide away anymore."

"Fine," Daniel reluctantly agrees. "Probably better to have you pegged as a bachelor. Women will want you more that way, which means all those rich ladies will buy your art to get a piece of you."

"You sound like a pimp again... *not* my agent," Louis says through gritted teeth.

"One and the same at the moment, brother."

Tick goes that vein on Louis' neck, and it's pulsating, but he's remaining calm.

"Anyway, better go. You're not the only person I have to worry about. I'll email all the details through to Emily. Please don't fuck this up. Please don't cause a scene if they are there," Daniel warns, but Louis hangs up on him before he even has a chance to finish, the vein on his neck now throbbing in overdrive. Before I know it, he picks up the colorful painting from this morning and throws it across the room making me jump. He grabs another canvas and places it in its place on his stand, then Louis grabs the dark-colored paint pots and starts angrily painting.

"Louis?" My hand comes out and touches his arm, worried

about his sudden change in demeanor, which only serves to make him flinch.

"What?" he snarls. Those beautiful blue eyes are now more like a swirling furnace of fire. "Did you think one day riding through the fucking countryside would help me?" His paintbrush violently stabs at the canvas, the black strokes only further stroking his black heart. "Did you think you could be my next muse?" he hisses at me.

The hunger that was there earlier has disappeared and has been replaced with darkness again.

His eyes look me over with disdain. "Muse," he huffs, his lip curls in a snarl as he stares at me. "You wish you could inspire someone like me." He points his paintbrush in my face as my throat becomes tight, and I fight back the tears.

I will not let this egomaniac see me cry.

I pick up the pot of paint beside me and hurl its contents at him. The midnight blue paint drips down his chest, while his eyes widen in shock.

"What the fuck?"

Paint runs down onto the wooden floor, and thick blobs drip all around him.

"Go fuck yourself, Louis Marchant."

And with those few words, I turn on my heel and walk away from him.

I don't have to put up with his shit!

20

LOUIS

What the fuck just happened? I grab a spare rag and try to wipe the paint from my skin. What the hell was I thinking to lash out at her like that? Moments earlier, I was propositioning her, seconds from picking her up and fucking her on any surface I could get her onto because, for the first time in a long time, I was inspired to choose another color other than the darkness. A tiny speck of light filtering through the dark has swallowed me whole. Then some stupid asshole switch turns on when people talk about Elisabeth and Yves.

Fuck!

I kick over my easel sending my latest demonic painting flying across the room. The hurt on Emily's face as I said those things to her hits me hard in the chest. She didn't deserve that. I open one of the cupboard doors and find what I'm looking for, my bottle of tequila, my old friend. I screw off the cap and take a couple of gulps to try and erase the images of Emily's disappointed face. I don't blame her for throwing paint at me, I deserved much worse.

Emily doesn't deserve some washed-up has-been. Some

idiot who's messed in the head. A wannabe. A fucking alcoholic. A complete bastard.

I should be so lucky to have her as my muse. Nothing but sunshine flows from that woman, and some of it filtered through to me last night for the briefest of moments before the ingrained darkness took over again.

I slump against the sideboard, my head hanging between my legs, the bottle poised at my lips. I should stop myself falling into that oblivion again, but I don't think I can, or maybe more to the point, I don't want to.

"WAKE UP." A voice filters through my consciousness, my eyes slowly open, but the world is a blur. "Wake up." The voice is louder this time. "God, you're pathetic." The voice pushes me up from where I'm lying, and angrily says, "Drink this." I feel a mug of hot coffee being shoved in my face, the aroma filtering through my nose, waking me a little more.

"Who? What?" I try to work out who's in front of me.

"It's Gabriel," the voice replies.

"Oh." I take a sip of the hot coffee, and it burns my fucking throat.

"You're a fucking dickhead."

My head begins to pound as I try to concentrate on the blurry image in front of me. "What did you say?" My words slur, even I can hear it.

"I said... You. Are. A. Fucking. Dickhead," he annunciates each word, so I comprehend them more clearly.

"That's what I thought you said." My eyes narrow as he comes into focus a little more. His nostrils are flaring, and his eyes are cold and hard as he stares at me. "How dare you. I gave you this job. Sent you to culinary school. I expect loyalty from you." I take another sip of coffee and try to blink away the fog.

"You have my *fucking* loyalty, you idiot. Especially when I turned your wife down numerous times after she asked me to fuck her."

Lunging at him, I drop my cup and push him to the floor.

"Go on, do it. Hit me," he urges me.

My hands are gripping his shirt tightly.

What the hell am I doing? I fall back and slump against the sideboard.

"I'm sorry," I apologize and then hang my head in shame.

When all the shit came out about Elisabeth, he was one of only a few that turned her advances down. He told me he owed me everything. I found him homeless living outside my Paris apartment. Every day I'd chat with him, give him food, blankets and a few bills here and there. It wasn't until I found him bloodied and bruised, almost close to death, that I took him in, got him healthy again, and helped get his life back on track. His parents were drug addicts, and it was safer for him to live on the streets than at home. Gabriel was fifteen at the time, and he's like my little brother. When I found out others I'd employed had betrayed me, I lost it. I don't know if I could have coped finding out that Gabriel was one of the men who had been intimate with Elisabeth. He was one of the only people who, over the years, had told me about the rumors of Elisabeth with other men.

I didn't believe him. Stupid, right?

It was mainly due to Elisabeth telling me Gabriel was jealous because he was in love with me, that he was gay, and that he wanted her out of the picture. I believed her, but I refused to sack Gabriel. In the end, he was the only one who had my back.

"What's happened to you?" Gabriel looks down at me, his eyebrows are drawn together so tightly you swear they joined in the middle.

"I don't know." I scrub my face with my hand, trying to get a grip on reality.

"How have you let *one woman* control so much of you?"

"I thought it was love."

Gabriel shakes his head. "Love isn't supposed to be like this, Louis. Love doesn't take everything someone has worked so hard for. Love doesn't decide to find someone better. Love doesn't fuck around on that person. What you had with *her* wasn't love."

"I know." I sigh. I simply don't have any more fight left in me.

"Honestly, you're acting like a fool." My eyes widen at his candor. "Six months Elisabeth has been gone, but instead of picking yourself up and dusting yourself off, you have been whoring yourself out every damn day. Getting drunk. Painting shit. Yelling at everyone who wants to help you. And why? All because you got your heart broken by some gold-digging bitch."

Gabriel's words shock me, and maybe the reason they do is that I know they're true.

"The Louis Marchant I know is a man who fought until the end of the earth to find the people who attacked me and put them in jail. The man that took a homeless boy into his home and helped me become a man. Louis Marchant doesn't treat people like shit, especially beautiful women." This gets my attention, and I cringe. "The things you've said to Emily..." his eyes narrow at me, "... they aren't words I'd ever expect from the man I look up to." Gabriel's going for the heart on this one, and it's hitting like an arrow. "I like her," he confesses. "But you don't like that, do you?" He smirks, but I stay silent because I'm not sure how to answer that question. "Don't worry, I have my eye on someone else. Otherwise, you would have competition." Gabriel chuckles.

"You have a crush on someone?" This little tidbit of information intrigues me.

Gabriel rolls his eyes. "Yes, but you have been so far up your own ass recently, I haven't been able to talk to you about it." He's right, and I know it, I have been a little self-absorbed over the past couple of months.

"Agreed. But I'm here now, tell me."

His cheeks tinge with pink as he lets out a long breath. "Her father is the butcher in the village." I can immediately see how smitten he is because it's written all over his face. "Her father has been sick, and she's come back from Paris to help look after the shop while he recovers. She's a teacher."

"Have you gone on a date with her?"

Gabriel shakes his head. "I... no. You need me here."

"What? No, I don't. I can fend for myself." Gabriel gives me the side-eye and then raises a brow. "I've looked after myself before you, I'm sure I can again. Take the rest of the week off... wine and dine the girl. Spend as much time as you can before she goes back to Paris."

Gabriel's eyes widen. "Really?"

I nod. "I have to start standing on my own two feet. You're right. I've let my heartbreak consume me. It's taken me over like a flood, and I have been drowning in it. I don't like the person I've turned into. This isn't me. I need to let go of what Elisabeth did to me to move on. I'm sick of living in the past."

Gabriel gives me a big smile. "Good. First stop on this new journey needs to be with Emily."

My stomach sinks remembering this morning and how I treated her. "I know." I wring my hands together thinking how the hell am I going to smooth things over with her.

"She's a good person. You can trust Emily. Don't forget she, too, is going through heartbreak." I'm a self-absorbed bastard, one who doesn't deserve a second chance. "Just... go easy, okay?"

I nod and think *when did Gabriel get so wise?*

"I'm sorry about before."

"I know you are. I've been worried about you, Louis."

I reach out and place my hand on his arm. "I promise you… I'm going to put these dark days behind me starting today."

Gabriel nods in agreement. "Good because there's a beautiful woman living under your roof who can help."

I shake my head. "As much as I might want to, it's probably not a good idea."

Gabriel shrugs. "You're probably right. I think you've fucked up your chances, anyway."

I let out a groan, he's probably right. I need to make amends with Emily, and not because I want to fuck her, but because it's the right thing to do.

Who am I kidding? I want to fuck her too.

21
EMILY

I tried to hold in tears, but when Gabriel saw me coming back into the house, I kind of let it all out. He was so sweet and caring, listening to me go on and on about Louis and the size of his damn ego. I told him about the disaster that was Toby and me. I let it all out, and if I'm honest, I feel pretty good after our chat. It felt so cathartic to let go of everything that's Toby, but it may also have been the dark chocolate mousse that Gabriel made for me—chocolatey goodness soothes the soul.

Now I'm holed up in my room working. I posted the photograph of Louis from this morning, half-naked, covered in paint with the most delicious outline in his gray pants. Ordinarily, I probably would have cropped the picture to disguise his privates, but he's pissed me off, and I don't care.

Daniel emailed the details of the gala he wants me to attend with Louis in Monaco. If my friends heard me moaning about attending a black-tie event in Monaco, they would probably unfriend me.

Louis' words really cut me deep this morning, more than they should have. Maybe I did for a brief moment think that there was a small chance I could be his muse. I mean, one day out in the French countryside, and I was able to get him to use color again.

Geez, I am full of myself. Actually, thinking that little old me could be the catalyst for the genius that is Louis Marchant's comeback.

I fall back onto my bed and stare at the ceiling. Maybe I'm trying too hard, trying to prove that I'm perfect for this job when, in reality, I was probably the only person who applied for the position and definitely the only one who would put up with the boss' shit.

Maybe I need to do my job, let him sort out his messed-up relationship with women, and that's it. Stop trying to be his friend and definitely stop thinking about getting into his pants. This summer is supposed to help me find myself, not end up in another disastrous relationship with a man who cares about only himself.

Yes, that's exactly it. I'm going to concentrate on being the best assistant he has ever had and nothing more. No flirting. No more trying to fix the broken artist. Just doing my job to the best of my ability. The cell beside me starts chirping wildly, so I pick it up.

Oh shit! There are thousands of comments on his page. Everyone is salivating over what's in his pants.

Shit, shit, shit! I think that post has just gone viral.

The phone rings, and I see it's Daniel.

"Hello," I answer cautiously.

"You're brilliant," Daniel praises.

"Thank you."

"Do you have any idea how many magazines have contacted me in the past five minutes wanting to interview Louis? Don't answer that because it doesn't matter. All that matters is that photo you posted has just put Louis Marchant back in the limelight with a bang. You, Emily Chapman, are a superstar. I have to go... my phone's going crazy. Keep up the good work." And with those last few words, he's gone.

A smile falls across my lips, and I mentally high-five myself. See, best assistant *ever*.

"WHAT THE HELL HAVE YOU DONE?" Louis' voice echoes through his empty home.

Apparently, Louis had a lobotomy today and has let all his staff off early, giving everyone an extra-long weekend.

Gabriel was so excited because he's finally going to ask out the butcher's daughter, the one he's been admiring since I arrived. *Ah, young love, it's filled with such enthusiasm.* I hope things work out for him because Gabriel's pretty awesome.

I can hear Louis stomping up the stairs. Here we go! He's obviously seen the photograph. I try and stay calm because he sounds more than a little angry. He pushes open my door without even knocking.

"Excuse you." I jump out of my bed. "How dare you barge into my room."

Louis blinks a couple of times as if he's so upset that it never occurred to him to knock. "This is my house." A flimsy excuse at best!

"And *this* is my room." I wave my hands around and continue, "If you aren't going to respect that, then I'll have to find somewhere else to live."

I've stunned him. He lets out a couple of hard exhales, then runs his fingers through his hair, the frustration radiates from him.

"Everyone is talking about it." Louis starts to pace. "People have made memes and shared the image a couple of million times." I'm trying not to laugh because his over-dramatization is something to watch. "Some sex toy manufacturer wants to make a dildo out of my dick." His eyes are wide in shock, and I simply can't hold my laugh even though I bite my lips together. "You think this is funny?" Once the giggles start, I can't stop them. "Oh my God..." He throws his hands up in the air very theatrically, so much so, it's almost an Academy Award-winning performance.

"Daniel said it's created great interest in you."

"In my dick, not my art."

"At least they are talking about you, and that's a good thing." I try to put a positive spin on the situation.

"Why did you do it?"

"Because it's my job."

"Do you have any idea how embarrassing this is?"

"I'm sorry, Mr. It's-not-the-only-big-thing." Those blue eyes flare at the use of *his* words. "I'm sorry that women and men around the world now know who you are. Did you know your Instagram account followers have gone up by two hundred thousand, and your Facebook account around the same? Did you also know that Daniel has had numerous press agencies calling wanting interviews with you? Oh, and your website has had a surge as well, so much so we have had to purchase more bandwidth. Not to mention five paintings have been sold, and not the ones from when you were at your peak days. No, it's the dark, messed-up ones."

I cross my arms in front of me and continue, "Is this embarrassing? I don't know, I don't have a dick, but it's no different than women being photographed with their nipples showing through their clothing. No one can see anything, it's just an outline. But guess who everyone is talking about? Yes, that's right, it's Louis Marchant, not Yves Blanc. I bet everyone is wondering why your ex left you after seeing that picture..." Oh damn! I didn't mean to bring up the ex and his protégé, but I'm on a roll.

I brace myself for impact, but it doesn't come.

"You're enjoying this, aren't you?" Those blue eyes stay firmly on me, burning into my skin.

"Of course, I am. I did a good job. This is the reason I was hired... to help get you out there on social media. Have I achieved this quicker than anticipated? Yes!"

"That photo has nothing to do with art." He shakes his phone at me rather vigorously.

"I don't know... most comments are saying it's a work of art." I give him a smirk, one I probably shouldn't have. *Don't push the beast, Emily.*

"You... are... *so*... frustrating."

"I know. Aren't you glad I'm not your muse?" I throw his words back at him, and he starts pacing again, then stops.

"I'm sorry about that..."

Um, what? There's sincerity in his voice, and that more than shocks me.

"Gabriel, he gave me a few home truths before he left today." Louis looks a little sheepish. "I haven't been the most pleasant to be around since..." I notice him wince while trying to force himself to say her name. "I guess I've been a little *self-absorbed*, I think that's the word Gabriel used."

"Okay, see... even you agree." I laugh while he rocks on his feet. "I've been a dick. A *big* one." Our eyes meet, and we both burst out laughing at his use of words. "Okay, we're not going to stop with the dick jokes anytime soon, are we?" I shake my head in answer. "Anyway, what I want to say is..." Louis moves closer to me, and the air between us changes the closer he gets. "I'm truly sorry. I've been wallowing in self-pity for far too long and making everyone around me as miserable as I am. I promise no more feeling sorry for myself. I need to concentrate on my art and re-establishing myself. I've given Elisabeth too much already... she doesn't deserve any more."

I give Louis a warm smile. "I'm glad to hear it. Can we start again... for a second time?" Holding out my hand, I greet him,

"Hi, I'm Emily Chapman, your new assistant. I am a big fan of your work, Mr. Marchant, and I look forward to helping you prepare for your next exhibition."

Louis takes my hand and gives it a firm shake but doesn't let go, while his thumb lazily runs circles under my wrist sending white-hot heat through my veins. "It's a pleasure to meet you, Miss Chapman. I'm always delighted to meet someone with impeccable taste in art." I chuckle. "I look forward to spending the summer with you."

22

LOUIS

I'm nervous about tonight, it's the first public art event I've attended since my divorce. There's a chance that Yves and Elisabeth could be there, which has my anxiety at an all-time high. I'm not sure if I'm ready to run into them. But if it happens, I need to suck it up. It's inevitable I'll run into them at some point—the art scene is an incredibly small world.

I'm downstairs anxiously waiting for Emily to head down. I organized hair and makeup for her for tonight because she's been so worried about this event all week. Plus, I've been a pain in my pretty awesome assistant's ass, so it's the least I can do.

"She's ready," Felix, the stylist, tells me as he walks down the stairs and waits patiently at the bottom with me. Emily is a naturally beautiful girl, so I know she'll be gorgeous, but I wasn't prepared to see how stunningly attractive she really is. Standing at the top of the stairs, she looks like an angel dressed all in white. Her hair is cascading around her creamy skin like wavy ribbons of golden silk. She glides down the stairs like she's royalty, utterly elegant and regal.

The couture gown appears as if the white vine embroidery is crawling over her body, the sheer nude panels giving an elegant allure of skin without showing anything. There's a deep V, but you can't tell what's her skin and what is the dress. A full embroidered skirt falls from her tiny waist.

As she slowly makes her way toward me, I watch in awe. When she reaches the bottom of the stairs, she lets out a sigh as if she was holding her breath the whole way down.

"You look..." I'm lost for words, but I can see she's waiting to hear something, anything from me because she's a bundle of nerves. "Stunning." But even then, that word doesn't encompass how truly beautiful she looks. I lean in and place a kiss on her cheek, and she smiles. I watch as those creamy cheeks turn the perfect shade of pink.

Felix and his team are clapping their appreciation of how good she looks, and this embarrasses her more as the tips of her ears have gone a bright red.

"Mademoiselle Chapman, you're a vision," Felix gushes.

"It's all your magic," she compliments him while he shakes his head.

"Tell her, Louis. She's the perfect canvas for me to work my magic."

My eyes don't move from hers. "She's exceptional." Those emerald eyes sparkle at my compliment.

"You pull off a tuxedo well."

I run my hand nervously down my suit wanting to look good for her.

"You two will be the most beautiful and talked about couple at the event."

"We're not a couple," Emily and I say in unison.

Felix looks between us, chuckling, then tells his entourage to move out.

Emily nervously fiddles with her dress.

"You really look stunning." She slowly looks up at me through her lashes. Does she not realize how beautiful she is? Did her ex never tell her how exquisite she looks?

"I'm nervous."

"Me, too," I confess, rubbing my hands together. "How about a selfie?" I ask, then give her a quick wink.

"I'm fairly certain your adoring fans only want to see you, Louis, especially in this tuxedo..." I raise an eyebrow, "... they are going to go crazy."

I don't care about the faceless people online. I want the woman in front of me to go crazy for me instead.

I'm not supposed to be having these thoughts.

We're starting over, remember?

"Where should we take the photo?"

She looks around my home. "Is the limousine here? That will be perfect. You'll look like the James Bond of the art world." Emily gives me a playful wink.

She's just doing her job, Louis. This isn't a date, I remind myself.

She rushes off in search of the limousine.

"Have fun tonight." Felix gives me a wink and walks outside to join his team.

Taking in a deep breath, I join Emily beside the limousine.

"Stand right there..." She points, and I do as I'm told. "Don't pose like that. Give me a natural look. You're not on your way to a school dance. Stop standing like that."

I cross my arms over my chest and sigh. Taking ridiculous photos isn't my scene.

"Relax your arm." Emily directs me, and I try to do as she says. "Give me brooding." Instead, I give her daggers. "Perfect. The women are going to love that smolder."

"Are we finished?" I groan.

"Yes. Yes."

"Let me take a photo of you two," Felix interrupts.

"Oh no, you don't need one of me."

"Come on... if I have to, you do, too." She wrinkles her nose but reluctantly hands over her cell to Felix, then she joins me beside the limousine.

"Now it really looks like a school prom photo," I whisper into her ear as I rest my hand on her hip.

Felix snaps a couple of photos with a huge grin on his face. "Have fun, you two." He hands Emily back her cell and waves us goodbye.

I hold open the limousine door for her. Emily gathers up her dress and attempts to gracefully slide into the car, but there's a lot of dress, so I help push the last bits of fabric into the car, making sure I don't close the door on anything.

I run around the other side and jump in as she gives me a wide smile.

The limousine takes off. It would normally be a two-hour drive from here to Monaco, but sitting in a car with Emily for that amount of time, in a confined space, I didn't think I could be a gentleman for that long, so instead, I have a surprise planned.

"Come on, let's take a car selfie." She rolls her eyes but smiles, then hands over her cell. "Remember, you, too, are showing the world you're fine without him." Emily slides over beside me, letting me place my arm around her shoulders for the smallest of moments. I snap the image and then hand it back to her.

"What hashtag should I use?" she asks, reminding me of our last photograph.

"Think you should use the same #dreamscometrue, #bestartistintheworld maybe even #fangirling." She gives me a light tap on my arm making me laugh. It doesn't take long until we arrive at our first stop.

"Where are we?" She looks up from her cell. "Why are we at a heliport?"

My grin widens. "I wanted to surprise you."

"Well, I'm surprised, but I still don't get why we're here."

"We're taking a helicopter to the event." Emily blinks a few times while her head shakes infinitesimally.

"But why?" she asks when stepping from the car.

"Because who wants to be stuck in a car for two hours."

Emily shrugs as if my answer makes sense and then tells me, "I've never been in one before."

Really? Her ex really was a dickhead.

The pilot greets us and opens the door for Emily to slide in. She looks at the step and then her dress. Okay, I didn't think this through all that well—ballgowns and helicopters probably don't mix all that well. But before she realizes there's a problem, I pick her up in my arms making her squeal, then step onto the step and place her inside. After she's securely in place, I rush around to the other side and jump in.

The pilot hands her the headphones, and she mouths, "Thank you."

"Testing, testing," the pilot talks into his microphone. "Welcome aboard. The flight to Monaco tonight should only take fifteen minutes. The weather is perfect for the flight, and the skyline should be lit up, so take as many pictures as you want."

After his announcement, we're up in the air and zooming along the coastline in minutes. I keep looking over at Emily whose face is planted against the glass, the pilot pointing out landmarks. The bright lights of the Monte Carlo casinos come into view as do the luxury yachts that line the shore.

It's a quick journey, and now we're descending for landing at the heliport where there's another limousine waiting for us. I hold out my arms to her to help her out, and she takes them. I spin her around while holding onto her which makes her giggle. She slowly slides down my body, her warm, soft flesh against mine. We both stay in the moment maybe for a little longer than is professional, but it feels nice. Right. I take her hand and pull her toward the limousine. From here, it's not far to the gala, and there's not enough time for me to do all the things I'd love to be doing to her right now.

"So, are you ready for tonight?" she asks, looking over at me.

"No," I confess.

Emily reaches out and places her hand on my thigh lightly, my body instantly reacting to her touch. "Do we need a safe word just in case?"

"In case of what? Is Christian Gray going to be there?" Now she has me panicking, and she notices, so her fingers dig into my leg.

"Everything is going to be fine. I wish Christian Gray were going to be there," she says with a giggle.

I file that away for later.

"But it might be nice to have a backup plan in case you're put in a situation you aren't comfortable with." She's right—she thinks of everything. "You're a viral sensation now. There might be some rich ladies who might want to… you know? Touch."

My heart begins to beat a little faster at that thought.

They wouldn't, would they?

"How about sunflowers for the safe word?" I tell her.

She smiles. "Sunflowers is perfect."

We arrive not long after. The driver opens my door, I step out, and round the car, then he opens hers. I hold out my hand for Emily to take as she steps out of the limousine. The flashes of the paparazzi go off immediately. They are blinding there's so many of them.

Emily nervously squeezes my hand.

"It's going to be okay," I try and reassure her, but in truth, it's me who needs the reassurance. I don't let go of her hand as we walk the red carpet. Just having Emily close to me is giving me the strength to walk along the red carpet answering mundane questions about my art from the reporters hanging over the red rope waiting for us.

"Louis… Louis," the paparazzi shout. The flashes continue

to go off all around us. I wave and smile for them, but I don't stop, I'm not ready for their inappropriate questions.

"Louis, is this your girlfriend?"

"Miss... miss... who are you?"

They start to hound Emily. She tries to let go of my hand, not wanting to add fuel to the fire, but my hand grips hers tighter. I pull her away from the vultures and finish the red carpet as quickly as possible. Once our names are ticked off the guest list, we walk into the grand ballroom where the charity gala is being held. Tonight, we're raising money for the Monte Carlo Art Society which funds some great art therapy projects.

"Wow! This is..." Emily's jaw is on the floor, and her eyes widen.

"I know, it's spectacular."

"Is that..."

I follow where she's looking. "Yes, that's the Prince. Would you like to meet him?"

Emily shakes her head. "No. No, I can't. Maybe later."

I was nervous too when I first attended one of these events, but when there are so many, you become immune to the opulence of it all, but I have to admit seeing it through fresh eyes is nice. I want to show her everything. Introduce her to everyone. I want to help her become part of this world because she deserves to be here.

23

EMILY

Tonight has been unforgettable. Me, at a casino in Monte Carlo, mingling with royalty, socialites, politicians, and the art society elite is something I never thought would be a reality for me.

At first, Louis was very apprehensive, but as the night wore on and there was no sign of Yves and Elisabeth, he eventually relaxed. Seeing him in his element, charming everyone, dealing with some handsy women who wanted to 'talk' to him was amazing. I took photographs of the event and loaded them online, and I wrote about raising money for art therapy programs. Adding links to the various societies' information, I can hopefully bring some more awareness to the cause from people who can't afford the one-thousand-euro ticket.

"Now, Louis... is this your girlfriend?" an older gentleman asks.

"She's way too smart to date me. Emily is helping me prepare for my next exhibition in New York at the end of the summer."

The older couple nod in my direction.

"Do you paint, my dear?" the older man asks.

"I dare not call myself an artist, but I paint to relax."

The older man chuckles. "Yes. I'm the same. We all can't be made for greatness like this man here." The older man pats Louis on the back in some sort of man-slapping thing that they do.

"Emily tells me I'm her favorite artist, and I guess she should know, she has an art history degree." I raise an eyebrow at Louis as he teases me again over my confession. The older couple laughs at Louis' joke, then utter their well wishes and move on to someone else.

"Would you stop telling everyone I'm your biggest fan. They'll think I'm some art groupie."

"Aw... come on, Emily. I know you have a poster of me up on your wall at home." He gives me a wink.

"Yes, I throw darts at it. Often. I'm a pretty good shot now."

Louis smiles, then his eyes look over my shoulder, and he stills. His face turns pale immediately. I spin to see what's spooked him and notice that Yves and Elisabeth have arrived, and Louis can't take his eyes off of them.

"Sunflowers?" I use the safe word, but he's lost somewhere in his mind—he's not paying any attention to me anymore. There's a soft murmur amongst the crowd as people realize what's happening.

Elisabeth is dressed in a stunning off-the-shoulder red evening dress with a slit that ends at her hip exposing her long, toned, tanned legs. She looks like a goddess. It's no wonder Louis is still so hung up on her.

Yves is a lot younger than her, but he's equally as good-looking dressed in a tuxedo, his face is unshaven, and tattoos are peeking out of the luxury material. A gold earring sits in one ear, his face is hard as he dismisses a waiter who approaches him. You can see why they call him the bad boy of the art world, he's got that look about him.

Then, I see the moment that Elisabeth notices Louis, the

hitch in her body posture gives it away—she's still affected by him. I don't like the way she's looking at him. It's as if he's some tasty treat that she hasn't had in a while.

"Louis, you okay?" I step in front of him breaking his trance. He shakes his head. "Sorry. What did you say?" He seems confused, not with me at all.

"Do you want to go?" He looks over my shoulder one last time then turns back to me. "No, I'm fine. I am heading to the bathroom, though."

I nod and watch as he hastily makes his way out of the room.

Keeping myself occupied, chatting with people from the art community, I realize Louis has been gone for too long, and I'm becoming concerned. I make my way to the bathrooms and wait out there for a couple of moments hoping people don't think I'm being some sort of creeper.

"Excuse me, is Louis Marchant in there?" I ask a man as he leaves the bathroom, that's how desperate I've become. He shakes his head.

Where the hell is he?

I do another loop of the room, but he's not here. Maybe he's out in the garden. I'm going to kill him when I find him. I've texted with no luck. I've called him, and there's no answer. I pace around the garden, but I can't find him.

Now I'm really starting to become concerned. Last time this happened, he was screwing some woman in the bushes.

My stomach sinks.

No. He wouldn't do that to me, would he?

He's single, Emily, he can do whoever he wants. That realization stings, but maybe it's for the best. Just because you have both been joking around the past week and no longer at each other's throats, doesn't mean he fancies you. I'm such an idiot.

"You must be Marchant's new girl." The voice comes from behind me in the darkness, and it surprises me. I turn with my hand over my heart and see Yves standing behind me, and he's smoking a cigarette. His eyes lazily look me over.

"And you are the *other* man." I look around and realize I'm in a darkened part of the garden with no one around but my boss' arch-nemesis.

"I see he's brainwashed you." He lets out a puff of his cigarette, the smoke lingering in the air.

"Oh, no. I formed that opinion all by myself."

Yves raises a brow at me. "You're very beautiful." The change of direction catches me off guard. "Marchant always had good taste in women."

What a creep! My stomach turns with repulsion.

"Well, I hope you have a good evening." I move away from him, but he blocks my exit.

"Why leave so soon? We're just getting to know each other." His finger runs down my arm, and I pull it away quickly.

"I'm okay." I look for another escape route.

"You won't find him." He smirks, but I don't answer. "Last time I saw Marchant he had disappeared with Elisabeth."

My stomach falls.

No. He wouldn't. Would he?

Yves catches my moment of weakness. "I'm surprised you're not running after your girlfriend if that's the case." He moves closer, and I try to shuffle away, but he keeps shifting his position, blocking me in.

"Elisabeth and I have an understanding..." he touches my hair, and I take a couple of steps backward, "... if we see someone we want, then we can have them." He throws his cigarette to the ground and steps on it.

"I'm not interested in your relationship." I move to the side, but a bush blocks my path.

"And you know what I want?" He stalks toward me.

Shit. Shit. Shit.

"I want you tonight." He grabs my arm and pulls me against

him. I bounce off his chest, it's that taut, but his arm is tight across me. I try and push myself away, but his grip on my arm is too tight. So much so I'm sure it will bruise.

"Let go of me," I tell him firmly.

"No." He smiles. "What's Marchant's is mine." Yves tries to kiss me, but I knee him in the balls. "You fucking bitch." He lashes out, ripping the sleeve of my dress as he tries to grab at me.

My heart is racing as I move from his grip. This dress cost a fortune, and now it's ruined. Tears threaten as I run as quickly as I can back toward the party, but in my panic, I trip over the garden's edge, falling harshly against the cement, ripping the sleeves of my dress even further. Blood begins to drip down over my white dress from the cuts on my elbows. I look at the red splatter across the contrast of the stark white material.

"Emily." Louis is racing down the stairs toward me. "Are you okay? I've been looking for you for ages." He notices my torn sleeves and the blood on my dress. His hand reaches out and touches the ripped fabric. His face is torn in confusion. "You're hurt."

"I want to leave, Louis." Tears fall down my cheeks, and he notices my distress. His hand touches me, and I flinch. "Sunflowers, Louis, sunflowers." I use our safe word twice as movement behind me catches his attention.

"You do have great taste in women, Marchant," Yves calls out.

Louis looks down at me. All sorts of emotions flare across his face, but mostly it's devastation followed by anger. "Did he?"

A look must come across my face that tells Louis everything he needs to know, and he tries to lunge at Yves, but I stop Louis putting myself in between them.

Louis doesn't need a public punch up with his ex-wife's lover in the middle of a society gala—that kind of publicity will kill all the good we have done.

"Did. You. Fucking. Touch. Her?" Louis' voice rises as he fumes at Yves.

"Nothing she didn't want," Yves replies, cockily.

Louis looks at me, trying to work out if I'd do something with his nemesis.

"I would never." The words come out in the softest of whispers, along with another tear that rolls down my cheek. "Please... Louis..." I tug on his tuxedo, "Sunflowers. Sunflowers, Louis."

His body is primed for a fight, but I use my safe word again. I need to get him out of here. I tug on his suit one last time, his arm comes out and wraps around my shoulders, pulling me close as he escorts me out.

I attempt to hold it all in, but as soon as the door closes on the limousine and I know I'm safe, the tears fall rapidly.

Louis pulls me into his lap and holds me tight. "I'm so sorry, Emily. I should never have left you. I am so sorry."

I bury my face into his chest and sob.

24

LOUIS

Seeing the ripped sleeve of Emily's dress and the smug look on Yves' face, never in my life have I wanted to kill someone like I do him at that moment.

What the hell was he thinking?

Why would he attack Emily like that?

I'm going to have to talk to Daniel about this situation.

Thankfully, Emily pulled me away from Yves with her safe word because it would have been the best excuse to lay my fists into his smug face. And, to be honest, I'm not sure I could have stopped.

When Emily used her safe word to get away from him, I knew my priority was her well-being.

The moment we stepped into the limousine, Emily broke down, her lithe body shaking, the shock setting in. Her normally creamy skin turned alabaster with all the color draining from her body.

I've pulled her into my lap, hoping it lets her know she's safe, that I promise I won't let anyone hurt her ever again.

Dammit, Louis! I can't believe I've let him hurt her in the first place.

I feel sick that I brought this disgusting human being into her life. Emily buries her face into my chest. My arms automatically wrap around her, protecting her, holding her, while I tell her over and over again that she's safe, and that I promise he'll never ever touch her again.

"I..." she starts to explain, pulling away from me, her mascara-run tears falling over her cheeks.

My palms cup her face. "You don't have to apologize to me." Those bright green eyes widen a fraction. "That man is a predator. Scum. He isn't a real man."

"I was trying to find you, but he found me. You said you needed the bathroom and then... somehow I lost you."

Some socialite pulled me into a conversation about football, and I hadn't realized the time until he was called away. Fuck.

"I would never... not with him."

My thumb wipes away the tears that fall, and I kiss her cheeks ever so softly. "I know." I may not have known her for long, but I believe in her sincerity. She's loyal to a fault, proving it time and time again with my ludicrous behavior toward her.

"He said you were with... Elisabeth."

"What? No. Never."

What is Yves playing at?

"He said they have an arrangement."

I'm taken aback by this statement. Elisabeth was extremely jealous of women who flirted with me—little did I know she was screwing around on me with everyone else. I could have taken up the many offers thrown my way, but I never did. I guess that's more fool me than her, though.

"He told me that if they want someone, they are allowed to..." Her body starts to shiver uncontrollably, the shock of the evening truly setting in.

This isn't the Elisabeth I know.

Am I shocked? No. Because in all honesty, it sounds like I never knew my ex-wife.

"Yves said he wanted me." She looks up at me, those emerald eyes shimmer with more unshed tears. "I told him, no. I made sure he knew I was saying no." Her body is still shaking, her hands are resting on my chest. "I told him I wasn't interested."

I want to kill him. *Where the hell does he get off thinking he can touch a woman when she says no?* Both of my hands cup her face because I need her to listen to me. Really listen to me.

"This isn't your fault, Emily." Those eyes stay wide as I speak, "He is a sick individual, who thinks that because he's famous, he can do whatever the fuck he wants. But he can't." My thumb wipes away more tears that are falling over her lashes and down her cheeks. "No man should ever force himself onto a woman. Ever. There's never any reason where that's okay. And if I had my chance, I'd have fucking killed him. I'll not allow him to touch someone that's not his. Do you hear me?" She gives me the slightest of nods in understanding. "I promise it will never happen again. You're safe with me." Emily nods again.

My hands fall away from her face and wrap around her, pulling her close to me. We stay like that all the way home.

It's a long silent journey home from Monte Carlo, I make my way around the limousine and hold my hand out for Emily, and she takes it giving me a small smile. Thankfully, she's stopped shaking now. It could have been the couple shots of vodka we found in the mini fridge in the limousine that settled her nerves. I don't let go of her hand as we move through the dark corridors of my home.

We stop outside her door, and I finally let go of her hand.

"I can run you a bath if you like."

Emily smiles at me but shakes her head. "Thank you, but I think I might grab a quick shower and head straight to bed."

Neither of us moves for a couple of moments.

"Okay. I'm just down the hall if you need me," I tell her.

She nods sucking her lip between her teeth. Emily pushes open her bedroom door and disappears.

Letting out a heavy sigh, I make my way to my room where I close my door. My back hits the door, and I take a moment, the tuxedo starting to suffocate me. So, I desperately pull it off, throwing on a white T-shirt and gray track pants. I find my cell and call Daniel, starting to aggressively pace my room until he picks up.

"Hey, I hear the night was a success," Daniel answers happily.

"That fucker touched Emily." My nostrils flare with hate, I want revenge.

There's a couple of silent moments before Daniel speaks again, "What are you talking about?"

"He ripped Emily's dress." The words come out stilted and angry. "I wanted to kill him." I rake my hand through my hair followed by a loud groaning sound.

"Louis, calm down. I don't know what you're trying to say."

My chest is heaving, and I'm sure there's steam coming out of my ears. "Yves. He fucking touched Emily."

"What the fuck?" Daniel fumes on the other end of the phone. "What happened?"

"I'd gone to the bathroom, but on the way out, someone pulled me into a conversation, and Emily had come looking for me. She was in the garden searching. But... fuck... I left her alone, Daniel. I thought she'd be safe. I didn't think..." My words become louder as I pace the room.

"What the hell is he playing at?"

"He's fucking with me." Now I sound paranoid. *Why would he screw me over like he did?*

"You might be right," Daniel comments sadly. "Remember a while ago before everything happened when I told you that Yves seemed jealous of you, of your success, of your life." It was an interview Yves gave just before I found him with Elisabeth where he told the magazine that his dream was to be me. I shrugged Daniel's comments about the article away at the time because I was flattered he thought so highly of me. But now? Now I see he was telling the world that he wanted to be me and not a copy of me but actually me.

"But he has it all now."

"Maybe having it all hasn't fulfilled him the way he thought it would," Daniel adds. "Maybe he wants more."

"How much more does he want? He has my wife, my career, my home."

"Maybe it's not about having the physical things, maybe he enjoys the chase even more."

"And now he wants Emily?" I sink onto my bed and look at the floor.

"Judging by what you're saying happened in the garden, he must."

"Fuck," I yell.

"She was so scared, Daniel. It took me ages to get Emily to stop shaking. I can't put her through this. She's innocent."

"You want me to fire her over this?" he asks angrily.

"What? No!"

"Good. Because one, it would be an HR nightmare, and two, a PR nightmare and three, she's great at her job. Plus, I've heard that you experimented with color recently."

Of course, he did. Damn Gabriel.

"What has that got to do with anything?" Daniel chuckles at my defensiveness.

"Just saying it's interesting."

I frown at him even though he can't see me, and I don't comment.

"Anyway, look... I think Emily is perfect for the job. I'll make sure we beef up security, that you don't attend any events where Yves will be, and if we have to, I will give Emily a bodyguard. The best way to mess with this little prick is to show him you're the *real* man and to bury him in your art. Your exhibition needs to be your best work yet." A small groan falls from my lips at the stress he's putting on me. "I'm not trying to put any more pressure on you, Louis, but..." He lets the words hang.

"But you want me to fuck his shit up as much as I want to fuck his shit up!"

This makes Daniel chuckle. "Yeah, pretty much."

A smile forms on my face for the first time all evening.

"Nothing like revenge to fuel creativity," I joke.

25

EMILY

The music is pumping, the lights in the club are strobing, and I have started to sway. Is there a smoke machine? Why can't I feel my lips? I don't think I've drunk that much, have I? I stumble amongst the crowd. Where did my friends go?

"Stupid drunk bitch," someone hurls in my direction.

"I'm not drunk," I slur back. Oh shit, maybe I am.

"Are you okay?" a male voice asks.

"Um, no. I... I don't feel so well."

"Let's get you some fresh air." I feel arms wrap around me, the kind voice is helping me, and it makes me feel safe. My body sags against his hard body. My legs begin to wobble, but I'm able to make it with his help.

I hear a door creak open, and then the cool night air is against my face, which feels divine. My blood feels like it's on fire, bubbling underneath my numb skin. We keep moving even though we are outside.

"Where are we going?"

"I'm just taking you somewhere more comfortable." I nod my head, which is pounding. I could use a nap.

Everything's dark. I'm being tugged. I feel a hard body against mine. My hands try and push them away, but they just laugh.

"I've wanted you for so long, Emily. I knew one day you would notice me." The voice filters through the darkness, a breeze blows across my skin, my vision starts to return, but my head hurts while I begin to struggle as I start to come to.

"Get off me," I scream, but it sounds like I'm in a tunnel. "Get off me! What are you doing?" I feel more tugging at my clothing.

"You're mine, Emily. Mine."

I WAKE UP WITH A START, my body is laced in sweat, and my heart is pounding. I haven't had a nightmare about my attack in years. Obviously, tonight has brought it all back up. I jump out of bed and make my way into the bathroom to splash some cold water on my face. I look like shit. My eyes are red raw from crying, and my face is splotchy.

I need a drink or two to get back to sleep.

Making my way downstairs in the darkness, the house is quiet, there's no staff around because Louis gave them all the weekend off. My feet pad on the cool tiles, the only light coming in is via the moon. I make it into the kitchen and scream.

"Emily!" The male voice echoes through the darkness.

I scream loudly and fall to the floor, pulling my knees up to my chest.

"Shit, Emily." Louis is in front of me, but I can't look at him. My whole body is shaking, and I'm trying to stave off a panic attack. "You're safe. You're safe." Louis wraps himself around me, pulling me into his lap. "I'm so sorry I scared you, I didn't think you'd be up."

It feels good being in his arms, the hard plains of his body are pressed against me, and this all helps to bring my heartbeat slowly down, so I can come back to normal.

"I couldn't sleep."

Silence fills the void between us for a couple of moments.

"Me either," Louis confesses as he pulls me tighter against him.

We stay like that for a little while until Louis tells me his legs have gone dead, which makes me smile. I jump up out of his lap, and he shakes his legs out.

"Sorry about that."

"Do you want something to drink? Eat?" Louis makes his way over to the refrigerator again, opening the door, and the light fills the darkness. "I've got cheese, chocolate, maybe some ice cream in the freezer. Fruit—"

"Actually, I could go for a toasted cheese sandwich."

"Consider it done. Take a seat."

I watch as he moves his way around the kitchen, the muscles across his back tensing and moving as he prepares my sandwich. I take in the sight in front of me. He looks magnificent. The women would be swooning if they saw him cooking in next to nothing—an idea springs in my mind.

"Hold on," I tell him. I rush back to my bedroom and bring down my cell.

He's still working by the stove when he looks up at me and frowns upon my return.

"I just want to get a photo." His frown deepens. "The women on your Instagram are going to wet themselves when they see this." He just shakes his head and ignores my craziness. I snap a couple of pictures which I'll upload in the morning.

"Are you pimping me out?" Louis asks, placing the sandwich in front of me.

"Yep, totally." I smile, waiting for my sandwich to cool slightly. "Look at you, the women go crazy for it."

Louis' blue eyes hold mine. "You like what you see?" His question surprises me.

"Do you need your ego stroked again?" I sass back, then quickly take a bite of my sandwich, the burning hot cheese hits my mouth and scolds it. His eyes never leave me, and his stare is utterly intense. I feel totally awkward.

"No. I was simply curious, that's all."

Is he flirting with me?

"I think that you're a very beautiful woman." My cheeks turn an instant shade of red, and I can't look at him. "Hey…" he steps closer, his hand comes out and lifts my chin, "… do you not like compliments?"

"I'm not used to getting them," I confess.

Louis' hand drops away, and he steps back to his sandwich, then takes a bite.

"Did your partner never tell you how beautiful you are?" I shake my head. "How your smile lights up the darkest days." Nope. Toby never did that. "That your laugh is the best sound in the world." No, he hated my laugh. "Did he have a big dick?"

I choke on my sandwich at Louis' question.

"Um, no…"

Louis frowns, and his blue eyes stare at me. "Then why the hell were you with him?"

I shrug. I've been asking myself the same question. "I don't know, honestly. I think we just started dating, got into a routine, and continued until…" I don't need to say it, we all know what happened next.

"Was there any passion?"

Thinking back, I don't remember a time when I looked at Toby and wanted to rip his clothes off, so I shake my head.

"I think you're lucky he cheated. You deserve more." I look up at him, and he gives me a smile that lights up his face. Damn him, he's so gorgeous.

"I'm starting to see that now."

Silence falls between us as we eat our sandwiches.

"Can I ask you a personal question?"

"You can ask. Whether or not I answer, that's another thing."

"How did you meet Elisabeth?" I'm guessing my question wasn't what he was expecting from the stillness that falls over him.

"I think I'm going to need a drink to tell this story." We place our plates in the sink, and he takes me through to his bar area. "Tequila okay?"

"Wait." I stop him, my hand touching his. "What if this starts you on another bender? I don't want to know, okay?" I've just gotten this good version of Louis going, and I want to keep it that way.

"I promise. No bender from me." He gives me a reassuring smile.

"Okay, then I'll take a tequila."

26

LOUIS

I hand her the tequila shot and take a seat at the opposite end of the sofa. I grab the throw blanket and give it to Emily, which she pulls up high and snuggles into it. We both throw back the shot, and I pour another. If she wants to talk about Elisabeth, and it takes her mind off of what she's been through, then I'll take one for the team.

"I met Elisabeth six or seven years ago. She was the mistress of my mentor." Emily's eyes widen, and her eyebrows rise significantly. "I know. Karma, right?"

She frowns at my lame joke.

"Anyway... we started off being friends. She was my mentor's partner, one of five he had at that time."

"Five?"

I smile at her shock. "Yes. He has his wife, Ellie, and five mistresses, who he changes whenever their time has run out."

"Men!" She rolls her eyes.

"He's an artist. We are lovers." A small smirk forms across her face as she takes a sip of her tequila. "Anyway... we started spending more and more time together as we were closer in age than she was to him."

"Of course." She gives me a cheesy grin.

"Stop being judgmental." I waggle my finger at her.

Emily zips her lips and pretends to throw away the key.

"So, we would spent all our time together like we were in our own little bubble. I know Victor noticed."

"Victor Kazalausks?" she questions.

"Yes. He was my mentor."

"Wow! I love his work."

Of course, she does.

"I thought I was your favorite?" I tease her.

She kicks me lightly, but I grab her foot in my hands and hold it. She tenses for a moment, but then I let my fingers sink into her foot finding the right pressure points.

"Oh, wow." Her head falls back, and she closes her eyes. "That feels so good." Her voice is relaxed. I want to tell her I can make her feel better, but that's for another time.

"Yes, Victor Kazalausks was my mentor, and Elisabeth was one of his many mistresses over the years." She nods, now enjoying my foot massage. "One weekend Victor was gone, and he took everyone except Elisabeth with him. He gave her some bullshit excuse and left."

"He was pushing you together."

"Yeah. The old man saw what was happening between us, and I guess he wanted to see if something was really there. Nothing happened for a while until we got drunk at dinner. That's when the obvious sexual tension between us snapped, and we fell into bed with each other." My heart aches a little bit remembering those times, so I pour myself another shot of tequila while Emily is still sipping hers.

"What happened?"

"Once we slept together, my art took off. It was like I finally saw life in technicolor. The world seemed so bright... I was excited and inspired." She nods. "When Victor came home, we continued to see each other. Elisabeth and I sneaking away whenever we could, but my art couldn't hide the fact that Elisabeth was my muse.

"Maybe three months of us hiding behind Victor's back was when he pulled me aside. He told me he could see that I was inspired, that my muse had come to me, and that I was painting some of my best works. He then told me that sometimes we don't pick our muses, but once we find them, we shouldn't let them go."

"He gave you his blessing."

"Yeah, he did. Weeks later, Elisabeth and I moved out, got our own place, and then my paintings really took off. I made my first big sale after that. With the money, we bought a house, and we made a life. My star grew brighter, and I thought I had everything I could ever want in my life." I laugh sadly.

"She threw how we met in my face when I caught her with Yves." Emily tilts her head and screws up her forehead. "She told me it wasn't sex... she was just his muse. Didn't help that I caught him using her as a human paintbrush, fucking her all over his canvases."

Emily's eyes widen.

"That's what his paintings are?"

I nod and watch as the information sinks in.

"Don't you get paint everywhere, like you know..."

God, she's cute, and it makes me laugh. Something I haven't done about this situation before.

"Wasn't my first thought when I caught them fucking." I pour us both another tequila as she's finally finished her shot.

"Do you still love her?"

"No."

Both of us are quiet for a moment, my answer falling more easily from my lips than I thought it would.

"Wow! Wasn't expecting that answer."

"Neither was I." I grab the shot and throw it back.

Both of us are now sitting in silent contemplation.

"How did you meet Yves?"

I pour myself another shot before speaking, "I found him selling his paintings in Montmartre. I could see the diamond in the rough." Emily smiles at me as she knocks back her shot. I pour her another. "Yves had a hard life. His family was refugees from Algeria, he grew up in camps, moving around a lot until finally settling in Paris. When I saw him practically begging on the streets, selling these incredible paintings for next to nothing, I wanted to help. Elisabeth and I had set up our mentor program by this time, so we offered him a scholarship, free room and board, and a mentorship for his art. He'd never had a loving and stable home life before."

Emily moves forward, taken in by the story.

"Come here." I motion to her. She gives me a strange look. "Just, please," I say. She moves and settles between my legs, her back to my front, and I pull the blanket around us as the cool night air wafts over us. I wrap my arms around Emily, absorbing her warmth while she rests her head on my shoulder. "That's better."

She gives me a lazy murmur, "Yes."

"Now, where was I. Right... Yves. As the years passed by, we become one big happy artistic family. I didn't think I could be happier. I thought of him as my brother."

She turns in my lap and looks at me. "Sorry... side note. Is Daniel your brother? You both have different surnames, but he calls you his brother."

I smile. "Yeah, he is my half-brother, but that's another story we might save for another night." She nods and settles back down against me. "My workload increased over the years, and I was away a lot more than I normally had been. Each time I came back, I heard whispers that some of my staff had concerns about Elisabeth."

"Like Gabriel." I still, how on earth did she know? "He told me," she answers my unasked question. I knew they were close, but I didn't realize they were that close.

"Yeah, like Gabriel. And, of course, I didn't listen to them, not after Elisabeth got into my ear, told me they were jealous of my success, even convinced me that Gabriel was gay and in love with me, and that was why he was making up these rumors about her."

"Oh my God, Louis, that's..." She doesn't finish, instead she trails off.

"I know. And I fell for it."

"She was your wife, of course, you would have. How would you have known what she was really like?"

Emily and I look at each other—I like that she gets it.

"Elisabeth was always a flirt, but I thought she was just being the life of the party. I never once realized until recently what her flirting consisted of." *I was such a fool.* "I started to notice how close Elisabeth and Yves had gotten after my trips away, but he was like family, so I never suspected a thing. However, I did notice things like how he slowly became competitive with me, with each painting sold, especially the more expensive ones, and the more he sold, the more his confidence soared. He'd joke that he was going to take my place one day, that everyone would be talking about him in the same way they talk about me."

"That's some *Single White Female* stuff there."

"Yeah. I think you're right, especially after tonight." A shiver runs down Emily's skin at the mention of Yves' attack tonight.

"You think he hates you that much he would..." She doesn't finish the sentence, and I turn her face to me.

"I won't let anything happen to you, Emily." She purses her lips, and I see the concern in her eyes. "I mean it. Daniel and I are organizing extra security for you. Even a bodyguard for events."

Emily turns and looks up at me, those green eyes widening. "That's a little overkill, don't you think?"

"I don't trust Yves. Not because he has run off with my wife... sorry ex-wife. But because I think there's something more going on with him. He has a lot of issues left over from his youth. We've sent him to counseling, and I thought it worked, but now... I just don't know. Maybe his ego has gotten so big thinking he has taken everything from me, that he can take anything he wants from me."

I let my hand reach out and brush her face. "I won't let him this time."

Emily closes her eyes and presses her face against my palm. I lean forward and kiss her cheek. She sucks in a startled breath, but I move away from her. I won't touch her, not after tonight. Those green eyes open, and there's intensity behind them.

"He may have all the materialistic things, Louis, but he doesn't have your talent when it comes to his art. And that's what truly matters. He may have learned from the master, but he'll always be the apprentice, and I think he knows that, and it's what's fueling his fire."

"Good to know I'm still your favorite artist," I tell her, breaking the serious moment.

"I get paid to say that. You do remember you're my boss." She gives me a cheeky smile, but at this moment, the thought of her being anything other than a beautiful woman between my legs has left me.

"I know I'm your boss," I say through gritted teeth. "Every moment I see you prancing around the house in those sheer singlets you wear to bed, I have to remind myself *I'm your boss* because the impure thoughts I have about you are something I shouldn't have." Emily just looks at me, her cheeks turning a beautiful shade of pink. "I replay our kiss over and over in my mind. The..." I can't believe I'm going to tell her this, "... the sunshine lips... I painted them after kissing you. I couldn't sleep. I just—"

"Louis," she says my name breathlessly.

"I know." I scrub my face with my hand. "I wasn't cold before, I just... I simply wanted you in my arms, and I don't know why. I like having you around me."

Wow. Okay.

All that shit just came out of my mouth without my permission.

Being sober-ish sucks.

"You like me?" She points to herself, and I sigh which makes her laugh. "I'm your favorite assistant, aren't I? I know I am. I just need to hear you say it."

This girl.

"Of course, you are, but you're more than just my assistant." My eyes flick down to her pink lips and back up again. Emily's tongue comes out and licks them subconsciously.

God, I want to lean forward and kiss her.

Maybe I should.

No.

You can't take advantage of her like that.

"You're also my pimp." Her eyes widen, and a slow smile forms on her face. "I mean you showed my dick to the world."

"It's a nice dick." She quickly covers her mouth realizing what she's said—sometimes she has no filter.

"Oh, I know how nice you thought it was. You couldn't stop looking at it." She huffs at me, but I know the truth.

"I was just appreciating God's art."

"You can appreciate it anytime you want."

Why am I flirting?

"Is that so?" She bites her bottom lip as I nod while teasing her. The last thing I expect is for her hand to slide between us and over my dick.

Oh God! I suck in a harsh breath.

"Emily…"

She shakes her head, her hand moving over me again, the thin fabric of my sleep pants not hiding anything.

My hand comes out and stops her, a tiny frown mars her face. "After tonight… I want to, I really do. I just…"

She shakes her head. "I want you to touch me. Take away the feeling of his fingers and the cigarette breath on my body."

"Are you sure, Emily?" I don't want to make matters worse for her.

She moves in my lap, her legs straddling me on the sofa. "I trust you, Louis."

Fuck. Her words hit me like an arrow to the heart. After everything I have put her through with my asshole behavior, she can still say that she trusts me. I internally promise never to break that trust, not when she's freely giving it over to me.

My hand comes up around the base of her neck, I slowly pull her face to mine. "Thank you," I tell her before our lips meet. When they do meet, it's like a spark between us that sets us both on fire. Hands start pulling off clothing and throwing them in all directions. My lips are all over her skin, my teeth nipping at her—it's like an elastic band has snapped between us, and we have both lost control.

I want to be gentle and slow with Emily, but she's equally as frenzied as I am. The sexual tension between us over the past couple of months has taken over.

My hands find her exposed breasts, my fingers twisting those pink buds. Her teeth sink into my shoulder, and it makes me shudder. I pick her up, her legs wrapping around my waist, and I lay her down on the sofa. My hands pull down her shorts and underwear in one fell swoop. I throw everything to the floor. I move back between her legs, pulling them open, exposing her to me.

"Stop."

My body freezes.

Shit.

I've pushed her too far.

Emily sits up and looks at me, her hand covering her pussy.

"Um. You don't have to... you know?" She bites her lip.

"Excuse me?" Confusion rocks me.

"You know... go downtown." Her skin is flushing pink as she says the words.

"You don't want me to eat your pussy?"

"I just mean... you know... like don't feel obliged to because... you know..." She's squirming with embarrassment.

"You think I only want to taste you because I feel obliged to?"

She nods, pulling the blanket around her tighter. Her shield has come up again.

"Did he tell you that he was going to eat you out because he was obliged to?" My blood begins to boil.

"Um... yeah."

Her ex—he's a fucking loser.

"Did he never willingly go down on you?"

Emily shakes her head. "He said he didn't like doing it."

Calm yourself, Louis.

"But you sucked his dick?" She nods slowly. "Did you like doing that?"

She shrugs.

"But he didn't think he needed to return the favor?"

Emily shakes her head.

This girl deserves more than a quick fuck on a sofa, she deserves for me to pray at her altar, she deserves for me to spend all night worshipping her like the goddess she is. How dare this dickhead think of only himself when making love to this woman. How could he not want to wring out every possible orgasm from her body?

"Get up." My command is a little harsher than I wanted it to be.

She scrambles up, wrapping herself in the blanket.

"Jump on my back."

"What?"

"Jump on, Miss Chapman."

She hesitates, so I turn around and look at her. "I want you in my bed, so I can worship your essence with my tongue, all... night... long." Her teeth sink into her lip again. "Do you want me to do that?" She quickly nods. "Good. Now jump on and let me show you how a real man does it."

27

EMILY

My body aches. Every muscle got some kind of workout last night, I mean even muscles I never knew I had are sore. Now, I totally get the saying *thoroughly fucked*. Lordy, Lordy, Louis knows how to fuck.

I stretch my body as the sun streams in through the windows, wincing a little because my vagina took such a pounding. I got to appreciate Louis' dick too, in every single position known, and some I had no idea about.

I'm sorry, but Elisabeth is an idiot. The man is a sex god and a giving one at that.

Toby never liked oral sex, and I thought there was something wrong with me downstairs because of his abhorrence with the idea. But that was totally blown away by the hours—I swear it was hours—that Louis spent between my thighs.

"*Open wide for me, Emily,*" he commanded. "*Let me taste your sweetness.*" He runs his nose along my seam. "*Do you have any idea how long I have wanted to taste you?*"

I shake my head, not sure if he really wants me to answer the question.

"*Ever since you stepped out of the pool that first night. I watched* in utter fascination as the droplets of water traveled down your skin." Louis runs his finger over my body retracing the droplets. "I watched in fascination as they dipped down over your underwear." His finger slides over me. "I could see this right here." He runs his finger through the strip on my pussy. "My tongue ached for you."

Louis' tongue traces the strip, and I almost buckle off the bed. "Hmm," he murmurs. "Open wider for me." His fingers move my legs apart while I suck in a deep breath feeling exposed, but the appreciative noises coming from Louis spurs me on.

"That's it. Fuck, you're perfect," he growls as he moves between my legs. I almost launch myself off the bed at the first lick against my slit. A quick suck of my bud, and I'm hyperventilating.

This is embarrassing, mere seconds of Louis between my thighs, and I'm almost ready to come.

God, his tongue is magic.

He continues torturing me, over and over again, soft and hard licks, quick and slow. Louis doesn't move away from me, instead he devours me while he tells me all the filthy things he wants to do, and I'm gone. My hips almost fly off the bed as he takes me to places I never dreamed I could go.

My body is primed and ready to go again reliving last night's thoughts. I turn over hoping for round four, I think. I've lost count as I was in ecstasy for most of the night.

The bed is empty.

The place where Louis was is cool to my touch, meaning Louis has been gone for a while.

Panic fills me.

Where is he?

Does he regret it?

Was it just a one-night thing?

I pull the blanket around me tighter and close my eyes tight. Damn! I'm such an idiot. Tears begin to well in my eyes.

No.

There will be no tears.

I jump up and grab my clothes and quickly get dressed. I want this humiliation over with. While getting dressed, I notice a note on the bedside table.

Emily,

You inspired me. I'm in the studio.

Louis.

Oh. I sit back down on the bed rereading the note over and over again.

I inspired him?

He's in the studio.

I need to see this.

I rush downstairs and into the kitchen, grabbing us both a coffee, and then I head quickly out to his studio. I'm careful not to spill the coffee as I rush along the grass. I don't even bother knocking and walk straight in and come to a complete stop.

I can't believe what I'm seeing.

He's painted so many canvases, and he's concentrating on another one.

He's dressed in his paint-splattered jeans and nothing else. Every muscle in his back is moving as his paintbrush glides over the canvas. The floor creaks under my foot, and he swings around. He looks different. A huge smile falls across his face when he sees me.

"I made you coffee." I'm not really sure what else to say. "Here."

Louis takes it from me and puts it down without taking a sip. "What do you think?"

"You're painting with color." He nods in agreement. "They are different from your normal work, but the colors, they are there again."

"Someone new has inspired me." He takes my coffee from my hand and places it beside his. Louis walks me backward until my back hits the wall. Large palms caress each side of my face, soft lips touch mine as he kisses me slowly, seductively. His hands pull off my T-shirt, and he discards it onto the floor. He gets on his knees and pulls my sleep shorts down.

Louis stands again, his lips meet mine as he kisses me then pulls back. "I need you, Emily."

Oh my goodness, I can hear his need by the tone of his voice.

"I'm all yours." My fingers fumble as I unbutton his jeans, they fall open at his hips, and I realize he's not wearing underwear. My hand reaches inside and pulls him out.

Louis lifts me, my legs wrapping around his waist as he walks me across his studio then places me on the paint-splattered velvet couch. My legs widen for him as I feel his hard body pressed against mine. Then, without warning, he's inside me, stretching me. I'm still sore from last night, but I don't care, he feels so good, and this feels so right with him being inside of me.

"You've inspired me." I gulp down my feelings as he continues to move against me. "You... I never expected... I've been waiting for you." He looks down at me in awe. The shield that has been wrapped around my heart begins to break, it starts crumbling with each forceful thrust inside of me. "You're my muse, Emily. You." He kisses me forcefully.

I've never been anyone's muse before, let alone a freaking genius like Louis Marchant.

"I need you, Emily. I need you to help me stay in the sunshine with you. I don't want to sink back into the darkness."

"I've got you," I tell him as he pushes himself deeper inside of me.

Moments later, we're both falling over the edge.

Louis moves the hair from my face. "I'm so thankful you came into my life."

Damn him. He needs to stop saying these things. They are giving me hope, and I don't know if I want hope because we only have the summer together. Plus, he's Louis Marchant, I could never keep a man like him for long.

"I'm glad I can help."

Louis frowns at me, we're still joined together. "Emily." His thumb rubs over my cheek.

No. This is all a little much.

"I better go clean up." I push him away from me. "And let you finish your work while you're feeling inspired."

He moves away from me, and I quickly jump up and grab my clothes.

"Talk to me, Emily." I turn and see he's dressing while I slip my T-shirt on over my head.

"About what?" I try to play it cool, but I see Louis' assessing eyes.

"Was this too soon for you?"

I laugh his question off pretending everything is fine. "I've got some emails I have to attend to." With that, I turn on my heel and rush out of his studio.

"Emily, wait!" Louis comes after me, his arm reaches out and spins me around. "What did I do? Tell me, please? You have always been honest with me."

I have but, right now, I have no idea why I'm freaking out.

"Is it the muse thing?"

I look up into his blue eyes. "I don't want to be blamed for ruining Louis Marchant's comeback."

"What?"

"I'm only here for the summer. What happens when I go back to London? Who will be your muse then? What happens if you can't find someone? I can't... that's too much pressure to put on me. I can't ruin you." He looks at me and smiles, which kind of freaks me out.

"You're pulling away because you're worried about *me*?"

"You've just started to come back to the art world, I don't want to be responsible for you going back to the way you were."

"Then I guess you're going to have to stay."

I shake my head slightly because I'm not following him.

Louis pulls me to him. "Whatever is happening between us, Emily, I'd like to see where it goes."

What? I'm stunned.

"I like you."

"Only because I'm your muse?"

"No. Even if you hadn't inspired these paintings, I'd still want you."

"You want me as what? An assistant?"

Louis shakes his head. "I want you, Emily. In my bed, in my home, going on bike rides, taking selfies in front of sunflowers. I want to spend time with *you*. You make me want to be a better man."

Boom. The last crash of armor around my heart fails and falls directly onto the floor.

"So, would this be like… an exclusive kind of thing?" I won't share him.

He smiles. "Damn straight it is. I'm not sharing you with anyone. So what do you say? Wanna give a washed-up artist a chance?"

"Yes. I guess I do."

Louis pulls me into a kiss, and it feels right. I'm going to give Louis Marchant a chance. This might be the stupidest decision I've ever made, or it could be the best. Who knows?

"Good. Then come away with me. Just the two of us. Away from being my assistant. Away from all this."

"But you've only just started to get it all back."

"I can paint anywhere." He grins. "I have a house in Ibiza. Let's go. Let's get to know each other as Louis and Emily."

"But what about the show in New York. You need to prepare for that."

"I have a studio at my home, I can work there." Seems he has it all worked out.

"I can't just go on vacation with you."

"You can work from there if you need to." Louis pulls me into his arms again, his face nuzzling into my neck.

Butterflies flutter in my stomach. I did just say I'd give us a go. Plus, hello, Ibiza.

"Okay."

His face lights up. "You mean it." I nod. "Just the two of us." I nod again. "Thank you." He kisses me. "You won't regret taking a chance on me, Emily."

His words, they make me smile.

28

LOUIS

"How's Emily?" Daniel asks.

"She's doing well. Really well."

There's a long pause.

"Oh, for fuck's sake, you've slept with *her*," Daniel yells.

"It's not like that. I like her."

"What like a boss does a good employee."

I let out a sigh. "No. As a man who has found a woman who's special."

"Oh." Daniel goes silent.

"She's my muse, Daniel."

Silence again.

"You only see her as your muse?" I hear the accusation in his voice, and I don't appreciate it.

"No, I see her as someone I want to spend my time with. To get to know. To maybe, I don't know... maybe one day be my partner."

Silence again.

"You have that strong a feeling for her?"

"It kind of just happened. I wasn't expecting the feelings nor was I looking for them, but here we are."

"Wow."

"Don't sound so shocked."

"But I am."

"Are you upset because you wanted her?" I ask through clenched teeth.

He laughs loudly. "I only said that to get you riled up, and I see it's worked."

"You're a fucking asshole."

"What are you going to do?"

"I want to take her to Ibiza."

"Seriously?" He knows that's my special place, my sanctuary.

"I want to see what life is like... just the two of us. Spend some quality time really getting to know her outside of work."

"And you think she's going to agree?"

"She already has."

"So, you're going to do the boyfriend thing?"

"Early days, but I want time to get to know her properly while I'm sober and not an asshole."

"That would be a good start." He chuckles.

"I see colors again, Daniel."

"That's good."

"But I want more."

"More?" Daniel asks.

"I love art, but after everything I've been through, I realize I want more in my life."

"But art is your life," Daniel adds.

"I know it is, but I'm not getting any younger, Daniel. Sometime in the future I'd like to think about having a family, having something more than art because I won't always be the best. There will *always* be a new up-and-coming artist hungry for my title."

"Who the hell are you, and what have you done with my brother?"

I chuckle. "I don't know. Losing everything kind of makes you work out what's important to you, and what you thought was the most important thing in your life may not be what you thought it was."

"Have you... fallen in love, Louis?" Daniel asks tentatively.

"No, not yet, but Emily is special. And maybe I should take the time to find out if we could be more."

"As long as you get me enough paintings for New York, which is in five weeks, then I don't care what you do. Just try not to break her heart, Louis."

"I don't plan on it."

"Most people don't plan on it, but somehow they do."

And with that, he hangs up, giving me some food for thought.

"I'M SO EXCITED." Emily grins as we make our way from the private airport to my villa in Ibiza. Jumping into my old convertible, I throw our bags into the trunk, then give Emily a kiss as I close her door. The smile that forms on her face quickens my heartbeat. I jump in beside her, taking her hand in mine and kissing it before speeding off into the Mediterranean sunshine.

"It's so beautiful," Emily marvels as we drive along the windy, rocky coastline of the island.

"It's been too long since I have been here."

We soak in the warmth of the Ibiza sun as it pours over us. Emily's strawberry blonde hair is blowing around her like golden spun silk, her eyes are closed, her creamy skin turning a light shade of pink, and there's a smile curved against her rose-colored lips. I try and commit that image to my memory—Emily looking so carefree and relaxed.

A little while later, we're pulling into my whitewashed villa's driveway. It's been way too long since I've been back here. Thankfully, I got the manager to air it out before we arrived, and I also asked them to fill up the cupboards with food and, of course, wine. I want Emily to relax and enjoy her time here.

Emily's emerald eyes take in the villa in front of her. It isn't as grand as my home in the South of France, but it's simple and has everything you need. The view of the ocean is the reason I bought this little home on the coast. Once you step through those front doors, the turquoise blue of the Mediterranean calls you to her like a siren to a sailor.

"Louis," Emily whispers my name in awe. That's the exact reaction I had when I first saw what was hidden behind the front door.

"I know. It's beautiful, isn't it?"

Emily rushes to the edge of the balcony, the land below falls away as the home hugs the rocky cliffs. The pool is on the next level which juts out over the cliff like a white springboard to the ocean below it. You can't tell where the ocean and the sky begin because they are the same colors.

"This is paradise, Louis." Emily squints staring into infinity. I move in behind, wrapping myself around her, and she leans back into me.

"I'm glad you like it here."

"I love it." She turns to me. "How could anyone not?" I can see by the look on her face, she means every word.

"Elisabeth didn't."

Emily freezes.

Dammit! I didn't mean to bring my ex up—it just came out. "I... sorry..."

Emily shakes her head. "Don't ever feel bad for mentioning her, Louis. I'm a big girl, I can handle it. She was a huge part of your life."

Fuck! How did I get so lucky with this woman?

I kiss her cheek. "She said this house was too simple for people like us."

Emily is silent for a couple of moments before she speaks, "Simple can be good."

I stare out into the horizon, my stomach somersaulting as she agrees with me. My arms tighten around her—I don't think I want to let this woman go.

"I want a simple life," I tell her. "I've had the other, and honestly, I don't want that life anymore." I'm hoping that maybe she too wants that type of life. I hope she's not interested in the glitz and glamor of the international art world.

Emily absently nods in agreement.

"What do you want?" I ask.

Please say the simple life.

Please, I try and telepathically tell her.

Emily is quiet as she thinks over my question. "I want someone to love me for me." Her confession is a direct arrow to the chest. "To accept me for who I am."

I turn her in my arms and look down at her. "I accept you for you." I hope she understands that I have feelings for her.

Emily's eyes glisten. I didn't mean this to get so deep so quickly. I thought maybe we would discuss things when we were drunk, not stone-cold sober.

"I'm glad I am sharing all this with you."

"Me, too. I don't know if I'll want to leave. This place is paradise. You might be stuck with me," Emily jokes.

"Here's hoping," I tell her.

She sucks in a breath. "Well, you're saying all the right things." Her arms wrap around my waist.

"They're not just words, Emily."

"I know, Louis, and that's what scares me."

I frown. Maybe I'm coming on too strong, but it's the artist in me. I'm a passionate kind of guy, and I know I can be a little intense. "Come on. That pool looks inviting." I change the subject.

Relief washes over Emily's face at the sudden change of conversation.

"Let's see if we can recreate the first night we met. But this time with a very different outcome." I grab and swing her over my shoulder making her squeal. My long legs eat up the distance from the balcony to the pool.

"Louis, no!" Emily screams as I launch us into the water fully clothed.

Emily comes up spluttering. She's wearing a thin sundress, and it instantly becomes see-through showing her white bra underneath, and that too is giving everything away with those perfect rose nipples now on show.

I pull her to me and kiss her hungrily. Her protests die quickly as she pulls me to her. I start to pull off my soaked T-shirt and throw it to the side. It lands with a thud, her dress joins it as do my shorts, then our underwear.

Emily wraps her legs around my waist as I move her through the water. I place her bottom on the hot tiles, and she hisses at the sudden heat, but then her lips are on mine again, her legs opening for me as I slide between them, the perfect angle to slip right inside of her. We groan at the connection. We need it, moving in unison as I make love to her on the side of my pool with the sunshine all around us in one of my favorite places in the world, the place that makes me feel the freest I've ever been. My sanctuary. And now I have found someone I want to share it with, to appreciate and enjoy it with.

"I'm falling for you, Emily," I tell her as I push inside her deeper, needing that connection, needing to show her what she means to me.

"I know." She smiles up at me before I push her over the edge in ecstasy.

WE MOVED our lovemaking from the pool to inside. Emily's skin isn't used to the bright Mediterranean sun, and the longer we stayed outside, the brighter shade of pink her skin glowed.

I carried her limp form to my bedroom where I tried to revive her with my dick. It worked for a while until she passed out after another round of orgasms.

Being back here, in a place I never tainted, has inspired me. So, I reluctantly leave my strawberry blonde goddess asleep in my bed and make my way to my studio. Opening the door, a wave of nostalgia, inspiration, and freedom hits me. I see old pieces and products from at least a decade ago. Some of these pieces are my first paintings. My fingers run along the thick paint, hoping they'll inject me with new life, new inspiration, and help me find the *new* Louis Marchant.

The next thing I know, I'm grabbing a canvas, opening the windows to the studio which look out over the ocean, and my hands start moving on their own, muscle memory taking over as I grab my brushes and pour out the paint that I need.

For the next couple of hours, I lose myself in my work.

"THERE YOU ARE." Emily's voice makes me jump.

I turn and see her standing like a disheveled angel at my doorway. Her hair is pulled up in a messy ponytail, she's wearing one of my T-shirts, and her feet are bare.

"You're painting." Those green eyes widen as she takes in the canvases I've been working on. She steps into my space and looks over my work. I suck in a breath wondering what she's thinking as they're a little different from what I have been doing.

"You're using the colors of Ibiza."

How did she see that?

"The whites of the villas, the greens of the gardens, the browns of the stones, the blue of the ocean..." I nod. "These are perfect, Louis. The perfect balance between your angrier, demonic phase..." she gives me a smirk, "... to your older brighter colors. You should be so proud."

She understands.

I rush to her and kiss her passionately.

"You get it." I hold her face. "You get me."

"I try." She gives me a shy smile.

"Then, paint with me." I step off to grab another blank canvas.

"No. I can't." She shakes her head.

"Why not? You told me you used to paint."

"Yes. That was a long time ago. I can't anymore. I'm not very good."

"So what? You're not painting for the Louvre... you're painting for me." She shakes her head again, this time more forcibly. "Please?"

"No." Her answer is definite. Those emerald eyes sparkle with tears, she turns on her heel and rushes away from my studio.

"Emily. Emily, wait," I call after her.

"Don't, Louis. Please... just don't." She waves me away.

My steps slow, and I let her go. I don't want to push her any more than I have.

I've triggered something, I have no idea what, and I didn't mean to.

29
EMILY

"I'm so embarrassed," I cry into the phone to Ava.

"You have nothing to be embarrassed about. Talk to him, Emmy. Tell him. It sounds like he wants to help."

"But he's Louis Marchant. He's a genius," I moan.

"Um... he is also your boyfriend," she tells me.

"Well, he hasn't asked me to be his girlfriend, so I don't know." I sniffle.

"He's asked you to be exclusive. He's told you he's falling for you. He's whisked you away to Ibiza. Yeah, I'm totally calling boyfriend material."

"Anyway..." I try to change the subject.

"Anyway," she repeats. "Don't forget you helped him find his way back to whatever genius art he used to do, and it sounds like he just wants to help you find your art again."

"But I'm crap."

"No, you're not. What was crap was Toby and his negativity about your painting. He killed your creativity. He took so much from you, Ems. He dulled your spirit. Your fire. We never said anything because we thought you were happy, but Toby changed you, and I hope it's not too late for you to find yourself again. Ever since you have been in France, we can see the old Emily coming back. The fun-loving, carefree girl you once were."

Tears fall down my cheeks. "Did I really change that much?"

"It was gradual, but he dulled your sparkle and now... now we can see your sparkle has come back. So, why not make yourself shine again." Ava's words ring true. "Toby wanted the limelight to be solely on him. He liked having power over you. He liked that you needed him, that you relied on him, and that he called the shots. He was like your damn dad."

Well, that just hit far too close to home for my liking.

"Shit. You're right." I've known Ava, Rosie, and Georgia all my life. We grew up in a little coastal town down in the South of England where everyone knew everyone, and that was generation after generation. Not many people left the village. They became farmers, fishermen, or housewives.

That's not what any of us girls wanted. So as soon as we could, we all left the village. I thought I hit the jackpot when I met Toby. He was this rich, well-traveled guy. The guy all the girls wanted because he was a catch. We were opposites from our backgrounds to our interests.

Was I that desperate not to be alone that I let myself fall for someone who was exactly what I was escaping? Someone like my father who hated art and who despised anything that he didn't understand that wasn't in his norm.

"You don't have to be the best, Emily. You just need to try. You need to find your passion again."

"You're right, Ava. You're so right. I let Toby's irritation ruin my love of art. I let my passion die. Maybe that's why I couldn't ever get an art position because I was no longer passionate about it."

"I think you might be onto something," she agrees.

"I miss you guys so much."

"We miss you, too, but you're hardly alone. Hello, hot French artist. 'Jack, I want you to draw me like one of your French girls,'" Ava quotes *Titanic,* and it makes me laugh. "Just have fun, Emmy. You deserve it. You deserve him. The photos you've posted of the two of you on Insta, you can see the spark between you two. You look good together."

"He's so far out of my league, Ava." She huffs at me. "Have you seen his ex? She's a damn supermodel."

"Do you even see yourself, Emily? Stand in front of the mirror because you're beautiful, too."

"But I'm not sexy." I pout.

"Pull yourself together. A hot, French artist, with a giant dick..." *How does she know that?* "I saw your post. The world saw it," she answers my unasked question. "And holy hell, that's a big paintbrush he has there." Ava giggles. "He's whisked you away to his special place in Ibiza. He's painting again. He wants you to join him in making art together, and that's not a metaphor for sex, which I know you have been having heaps of. *Bitch!* He wants to make art... art with you. Forget about everything else."

Wow! I'd expect a pep talk like this from Rosie or Georgia but not from Ava. I like it. Maybe I do need to start having a little more confidence in myself.

"I love you, Avie."

"I love you, too, Ems. Now go jump that hot man and take one for the team."

I hang up, smiling.

Louis pops his head into the bedroom. "I wasn't eavesdropping..." I bet he was because there's guilt written all over his face. He totally was.

"How much did you hear?"

"Um... okay, well, all of it." He gives me a shameful smile.

"Come here." I call him over and pull him into my arms, surprising him as I cuddle into him. "I'm sorry about before."

"You don't have to apologize."

"I haven't had much support when it comes to my art, and I guess I didn't know how to cope when I finally got some."

He kisses my forehead. "I'd support you in anything if it makes you happy."

Oh my God, this man!

"That's new for me. So, sorry for the freak-out."

Louis shakes his head. "Whenever you're ready, the studio is yours. Any time of the day or night. If you need it, help yourself."

"Thank you." I nuzzle into him, my heart bursting with this unfamiliar feeling.

"I have to agree with one thing your friend said…"

"Yeah, what's that?"

"I do have a big dick." I burst out laughing. "And I think you should take one for the team and ride it, right now."

We're both smiling at each other.

"I think that sounds like a great idea."

THE LAST COUPLE of nights I've woken up to my hands itching with the need to paint, but I've forced myself back to sleep. I am too nervous to try.

This morning, however, is different. I'm forcing myself out of my comfort zone determined to do at least one painting. I tiptoe out of bed trying not to wake Louis as he lightly snores. The sun is about to rise—the first beams start to hit the horizon—as I follow the rocky path down to the studio.

I tentatively open the wooden door and step into Louis' inner sanctum. Taking in a deep breath, the smell of the paint, the thinners, the canvases, it all tickles my nose. Oh, how I have missed this.

There's a blank canvas on the easel waiting for me. *Did*

Louis do this for me? Hoping that one day I might fill the white canvas with my artwork, the chasm in my heart just shrunk a little more. My fingers lightly touch the different size brushes laid out before me. I hold the different sizes, feeling their weight in my fingers, the familiar feeling permeates through my entire being.

I scan the various colors of paint from the brightly colored to the dark tones. There's pretty much any color I could desire laid out before me.

Nerves tickle my veins. My breathing quickens as I walk around the studio. I decide to open the windows that surround it and let in some light. I used to enjoy painting in natural light. Then it hits me—the images that have been playing over and over again in my mind. So, I don't think, I pick up a paintbrush, scan the paint tins again until I find the colors I'm looking for and start.

30

EMILY

"Hey. There you are." Louis' voice makes me jump, pulling me from the canvas I'm working on. "You've..." His words fall away as he rushes over to the couple of paintings that I have completed in secret over the past week. He picks one up, and my stomach sinks. I turn to tell him not to look at it, but he's already shaking his head as if anticipating my reaction.

He whips around quickly and stares at me.

"What?"

My stomach sinks further.

He hates them.

He thinks I'm no good.

Oh my God, I'm the biggest loser.

To think I could be an artist.

The paintbrush falls from my fingers and thumps on the floor. Louis must see my face because he places the canvas down on the table carefully beside him and rushes to me.

"No. Don't you dare retreat again, Emily." He grabs my shoulders, stopping me. "Did you do all those paintings?" He motions with his head behind me.

"Yes," I squeak out.

Louis lets go of me and rakes his hand through his hair.

"Emily. Fuck. Emily... they are amazing."

Huh. Did I just hear him right?

"Never, ever, ever, believe anyone who tells you that you shouldn't paint. These are..." he rushes back to my canvases and points to them, "... these are magnificent. They are just as good as any known modern artist out there at the moment. They should be in a gallery. Why are they *not* in a gallery?" He is so excited that he's flicking between English and French.

"You need to paint more. I need more." He throws his hands up, then comes rushing back over to me. Louis picks me up and swings me around the room making me squeal. "You're brilliant, Emily. Brilliant." He kisses my face, my cheeks, and then my lips.

I'm so caught up in his enthusiasm. "Really?" I squeak out with a tiny bit of self-doubt creeping in.

"Chérie, yes." He nods. "In fact, I want these two." He points to my first two canvases. "I want to hang them." He picks them up. "Come... come now." He stomps off while I jog to try and catch up. We go back along the rocky path and enter the house. He's on a mission to somewhere, and I'm just following behind, utterly confused. He stops in his long white hallway where some of his paintings hang. He takes them off the wall and hangs mine instead.

He stands back and admires them. "Look... look at your work."

I take a step back and try to see what he's seeing. I push all the negative thoughts from my mind and look at what I've achieved, then finally a smile forms on my face. "See? Now you see what I see." He smiles at me. "You're amazing, Emily Chapman."

Tears begin to threaten as he pulls me into his arms, and I let them fall. "Thank you."

"It's what any partner would do." I look up at him. "You're mine, Emily." He looks down at me. "I'm not letting you go. Not now. Not ever. Okay?"

I simply nod, the tears falling down my cheeks. They are happy tears for once.

"Okay."

And with those few words, I'm all his, and I don't want him to let go of me either.

31

LOUIS

"How's it all going with Emily at the house?" Daniel asks.

"Amazing," I tell him. My brother bursts out laughing. "What's so funny?"

"Are you pussy-whipped." He chuckles. "You sound like you're on cloud nine."

"One, fuck you, and two, I am. I am so fucking happy."

"I'm happy for you," Daniel's tone turns serious as he speaks. "I think Emily is the right fit for you."

"She is. I've never felt like this before. I thought what Elisabeth and I had was love. But this... this is something different. It's easy, effortless, it's just natural."

"I'm glad to have my brother back."

"You're just happy I'm painting again. Let's be serious."

"Of course, I need to pay off my new Maserati somehow." He chuckles.

Dick!

"Anyway, I want to ask you something, and just hear me out before you say no."

"That isn't a great way to start a conversation." I ignore Daniel's pessimistic tone.

"Check your text messages." I've just sent Daniel some pictures of Emily's work. I listen as I hear him messing around with his cell.

"Where did you find these?"

"What do you think of them?"

"Is this a local Ibiza artist?" he questions.

"I'm not telling you until you tell me what you think of them?"

"I instantly want to represent them."

Yes. I fist-pump the air.

"The artist's name is Emily Chapman."

Silence.

"Did you hear me?"

"Yes."

"And?"

"Are you serious? Emily did these?"

"Yes. I wouldn't mess you around like that. I also don't want you to blow smoke up her ass because she's with me either."

"These are incredible. I was ready to sign them on, no matter who they are. But—"

"But what?"

"You're dating her. Don't you think people will assume she slept her way to the top."

I frown. I want to say 'fuck them,' but Daniel has a point.

"She's got talent, Daniel," I reiterate.

"I can see. Just ask her if this is something she wants first before organizing her life." I hate it so much when Daniel makes sense. "Can you ask if the New York Gallery is interested in her work? If they would be willing to add her to my exhibition."

"Louis," Daniel says my name sternly.

"Please, Daniel. Just ask."

My brother lets out a heavy sigh. "Fine. I will, but if they aren't interested, don't push it, okay?" I agree, but I know that once they see her work, they'll want her. It's my superpower, finding artists in the rough and turning them into diamonds.

"Also, I have another favor."

Daniel groans and says, "Fire away."

"Emily really misses her friends, and I'd love for them to come out and see her. Maybe a girls' weekend in Paris. They can stay at my apartment."

"Who the hell are you?" Daniel asks.

"I just want to make the girl I love happy."

"*Love?*" Daniel's voice rises.

"Yeah. *Love.* I know it's too soon. Hence, I'm not ready to tell her yet. But yeah, she gives me all these feelings."

"Yes, I can help my lovesick brother. Are her friends cute?"

"They are off-limits," I warn, but he just laughs.

"Fine! Leave it with me." He hangs up on that note.

Now I need to find my woman and make love to her.

WE'VE BEEN BACK from Ibiza for a week. Emily and I walked hand in hand back into the home to the shocked faces of my staff.

"I knew it!" Gabriel grinned when he welcomed us back with open arms.

I told Emily that I wanted her in my bed now that we're back home, and it took her all of two seconds to agree. Mainly because my fingers were kind of distracting at the time, even though I think they were incentivizing.

But tonight, we're debuting as a couple at an art society gala in Geneva, Switzerland.

"I'm so nervous." Emily looks over at me, holding my hand

as the helicopter lands. I can feel her visibly shaking underneath my palm.

"It's going to be okay. You look beautiful... like a princess." I look over at Emily who's wearing some couture frock that Felix found for her. A black, off-the- shoulder tulle evening dress with a front split. Gold floral embroidery across the front makes it look like she's stepped out of the pages of a fairy tale. I pick her up again and help her from the helicopter, and we quickly make our way to our limousine, which will be taking us to a mansion that sits along the banks of Lake Geneva. "You and me," I tell her, making sure she understands exactly what I'm saying.

"You and me," she repeats.

I kiss her forehead as the limousine slows down to the entrance of the event. The driver opens our door, and I slide out first then help Emily out of the car. The bright flashes of the paparazzi give her pause as she gathers herself. We step onto the red carpet for the first time as a couple. The paparazzi scream their questions at us, many remembering Emily from the Monte Carlo event. There are a couple of reputable reporters lining the red carpet, and when they see me holding Emily's hand, they try and vie for my attention by shouting their questions. Eventually, I stop at one.

"Monsieur Marchant, it's so good to see you in public again," the reporter starts. "Can we expect any new works from you soon?"

"I am socializing again, but I'm also busy working in the studio. I've been recently inspired." I pull Emily into my side. The reporter picks up on my not-so- subtle cue.

"Ah... so this young woman with you tonight is the reason for your new inspiration." I lean over and kiss Emily's cheek, her fingers squeezing mine tightly. I know she's uncomfortable about this.

"Yes. Without her, I'd probably be dead in a ditch somewhere." Emily looks up at me, those cheeks flush pink with embarrassment. "She inspires me to be a better man. Every. Single. Day." I take her hand and kiss her knuckles, the paparazzi lapping it up. The reporter is eating up the exclusive I'm giving him.

"Everyone is so happy for you. It really has been a trying year for you both professionally and personally."

Okay, I guess the reporter is going there, I should have expected it

"Yes. It has been, but I'm happy to be on the other side in a better, healthier mindset. Sometimes you have to hit rock bottom before you can rise again." Emily squeezes my hand, giving me her strength.

"And will Louis Marchant rise again?"

"Of course. But I'm more focused on my art, not popularity contests or how many celebrity friends I have." Yes, that was a direct dig at Elisabeth and Yves and their fake online life.

"Sounds like you have changed." The reporter gives me a warm smile. "Do you think it will be awkward tonight seeing your ex-wife and protégé?"

Emily stills.

What the hell? I didn't think they were coming to this event, that's why I said yes. I turn and look at Emily, her face has paled a little, and I know we need to get out of here. My body is on high alert.

"It will not be awkward for us," Emily answers for me. "Louis and I wish them nothing but good fortune. They are having a very successful year, and we wish them all the success for their future."

Fuck! I love this woman.

"Thank you." I cut the interview short and pull Emily away from the spotlight. I walk quickly along the red carpet, ignoring the rest of the reporters.

"Louis, hold up," Emily calls from behind me. She's practically running as I push through the gilded doors and out of the glare of the spotlight.

My hands cup her face. "We can go. We can turn around and walk straight out the backdoor. No one will know. I don't want to put you in a dangerous situation again."

"Louis." Her voice is soft. "It wasn't your fault last time. I'll be fine. I'm sure he's not stupid enough to try something again."

I wish I had the same optimism as Emily, so I say, "I can have a bodyguard with us within the hour."

"Louis, please. It will be okay." She reaches up on her tiptoes and kisses me softly. "I love that you're so worried about me, but I promise everything is going to be okay," she tries to reassure me.

"If you feel uncomfortable at any moment... sunflowers, okay?"

She nods. "I promise. Sunflowers." She gives me a wink, which relaxes me the tiniest of bits.

Thankfully, the room is so large that we're seated nowhere near *them*. They are all the way over on the other side of the room with maybe a thousand people between us. I still want to punch Yves in his smug face, but luckily, they have stayed on their side.

"Louis, I need a bathroom break." Emily pulls on my sleeve as I'm chatting with the gentleman beside me. I try to excuse myself from the conversation, but Emily stops me. "I'll be fine. He's still seated at his table. If he moves, you can come and get me." I look over to where Yves is sitting, and she's right, he's sitting in his seat.

While Emily is gone, I keep a close eye on Yves' table, and when a body slides in beside me, I relax. I turn around to welcome Emily back safely, but instead, I see Elisabeth. *What the hell?*

"You're looking good. Much better than the latest gossip reports on you. You've cleaned up well." Her bright red lip curls up into a smile. "I hear it's because you have a new *muse*." She says the word muse as if it's acid on her tongue.

"Yes, you were replaceable, after all."

Elisabeth doesn't react to my dig. "I'm sure she won't last. No one is as talented as I am as your muse." Her hand slides up my thigh trying to find its target. I jump at her touch, my entrée wanting to make a second appearance.

"Actually, she's better." I take her hand and remove it from my leg forcefully. "I've never felt this way before. I now know what real love is." Each barb finds its target, and I see the barest of flinches.

"You and me both, Louis," she throws back. "Yves doesn't put me on a pedestal. He understands that sometimes a lady likes it a little rough." My fists ball, bile creeping up my throat. "I hope your new love can handle the pressure of being the perfect partner to you." *What does she mean?* "You treat your women like glass dolls, Louis. But guess what? We won't break if you manhandle us a little. Keep that in mind next time you're fucking your muse."

"Fuck you." I take a swig of my wine, and my hand starts shaking with rage.

"You wish you could. Come find me when you get bored with Miss Strawberry Shortcake." Elisabeth stands and walks away, while my heart is beating a million miles a minute.

Emily. I look up and see that Yves is still sitting at his table, but Emily isn't back yet. My phone vibrates in my pocket, I pull it out and see the word 'sunflowers' flash across it. *Shit!* I jump up out of my chair and rush toward the bathrooms. I don't even think just run straight into the ladies' bathroom, and a couple of women scream with surprise.

"Emily. Emily," I call out frantically.

She's not in here.

I run back out and see her step out of an alcove. She's shaking, holding a white envelope in her hand, and her face is white.

"Emily." I pull her into my arms. "Chérie, what's the matter? What's happened?"

"This." She hands me the note, she has screwed up into a ball. I pull it open and start to read.

I haven't been able to stop thinking about you since Monaco.
When the time is right, you will be mine.
Yves
xoxo

My hands shake with rage.

How fucking dare he?

I'm settling this once and for all.

"No." Emily grabs my arm before I stride off. "Please, let's go home."

"He needs to be taught a lesson."

Emily shakes her head. "No. I want to go home. I want to go back to our bubble." Emily is shaken, and she's pleading with me to get her away from here. As much as I want to punch his face in, Emily's welfare is more important. I take her hand and escort her outside and along the red carpet. Moments later, the limousine arrives.

Emily slides in first and hits the privacy screen. As soon as I close the door to the car, she's on me, her legs straddling my lap, nimble hands are fumbling with the zipper of my tuxedo pants. In seconds, she has them open and down, and her hand is pulling out my hardening dick. "I need you, Louis." She's almost breathless when she talks.

"You have me," I tell her.

Seeing that she needs this, needs me in this moment, I push

aside her panties and then her pussy in engulfing my dick. I let her control the pace. This is all Emily, all about her needs and wants. She bucks against me wildly, riding me like the good girl she is. My God, she feels so fucking good. Harder and harder she rides me, taking me deeper, making me fill her up.

"Yes. Yes. Yes." Emily bucks and moans as her orgasm takes over, and only moments later, I follow behind her.

We're a sweaty, messy heap.

Emily gives me a satisfied smile, then her face pales. "Oh, Louis. Shit." She tries to move off me, but I hold her there."

"Chérie, what is it?" She looks down between us, but a mountain of tulle covers where we're joined.

"I... we forgot protection."

I stop, now feeling her bare, and fuck me if my dick doesn't get hard again just at the thought.

"I'm clean. I promise you. I was checked before we slept with each other. I was kind of optimistic."

She gives me a weak smile. "I'm on the pill," she whispers. "I just..."

I move the hair away from her face. "You needed me. I don't regret it, and if by some chance something happens because of it..." I let the words hang in the thick air between us as a tiny frown creases her brow. "I would be happy."

"Happy?"

"It may not have been in our plan, and I do hope we're together a lot longer before babies came along, but sometimes life throws you curveballs, and well, I for one, would embrace it."

Emily's face softens. "I would, too."

My eyebrows shoot up. "You would?"

She giggles. "Let's not go planning anything just yet, but I'm happy with the practice we're having."

"Yeah, me, too." I grin at her, my dick twitching inside of her, making her giggle. "I love you, Emily Chapman." She freezes. "I just need you to know that because if anything happens, you know I mean it, not because of an accident." Her long lashes slowly blink as she stares at me. "I know it's way too soon, but I've been feeling this for a while now."

"You have?"

"Yes. But I didn't want to scare you off."

"You think your love would scare me off?" She smiles.

I shrug. "Kind of... it's too soon, I know this."

"I love you, too, Louis."

"You do?"

"Yeah, I do. I've been fighting my feelings for you because I thought it was too soon as well, or maybe one-sided, but now I see you feel this as well."

"I do."

"Good. Well, let's go home so you can make love to me, Mr. Marchant."

I groan as she says my name. "Say it again."

"Mr. Marchant." This time she says it so seductively, my dick springs to attention.

"Thank fuck for the helicopter because I can't wait to get you home."

32

LOUIS

"Where are we going?" Emily laughs as the wind blows her golden hair across her face. We've taken my vintage sports car out for a spin today, and I'm taking her on a date. A proper one because I realize I haven't done that yet.

We stayed in bed making love over the past two days after returning from Geneva, exploring each other with new loved-up eyes.

"Just somewhere." I don't want to give anything away. She eyes me suspiciously but doesn't push it, just enjoying the sunshine and the amazing views that are passing us by. We don't have to travel far, but I have driven her around in circles to confuse her.

"Louis, this is spectacular."

I knew she'd be blown away. The lavender fields of Provence are divine, add in an old castle and some vineyards to the mix, and you have a winner. I open the car door for Emily and hold out my hand, she loops her fingers with mine.

"Monsieur Marchant, it's an honor to have you at our winery today. Please follow me. Everything is set up for you."

Emily looks at me and smiles. I'm waiting for her to say something, but she keeps her mouth shut and just takes in her surroundings. Little does she know I have hired the estate just for the two us, so we won't be disturbed. The manager walks us through the grounds giving us a detailed history of the castle. Emily, of course, takes it all in. I assumed that since she has an art history degree, she'd also like normal history.

Once we finished the tour, the manager leads us into the garden where the staff has set up two easels for us with two fresh canvases and paints. Emily looks at me, bewildered, and rushes toward the blank canvases.

"I thought we could paint together." I look down at her. "Let me be your muse." I kiss her neck as I wrap my arms around her. "Just paint what you see. What you feel."

"I can't guarantee it's not going to be X-rated," she teases.

"Then, the painting will be for my eyes only." I kiss her nose.

WE SPEND all day painting and have now finished. We laughed, talked, and took in the beautiful scenery together.

Now it's time for the big reveal. I made sure I didn't peek at her painting because I know she's self-conscious about her work.

"Okay, are you ready to see my masterpiece?" Emily smiles.

"Hit me."

She turns her canvas around, and I'm blown away by just how extraordinary she can paint.

"You're incredible." Leaning in, I kiss her forehead. I stare at the couple making love in the lavender fields. I'm used to Emily drawing modern, abstract kind of paintings, definitely not something like this which is so lifelike.

"You're giving me so many ideas." She wiggles her eyebrows

playfully at me. "Don't tempt me," I growl as I pull her into my arms and swing her around. "You make me so happy, Emily."

"You make me happy, too." She wraps her arms around my neck and kisses me. There's an awkward throat-clearing moment, and we pull apart to see the waiter has arrived with our food. I forgot I'd organized that. He sets down a new bottle of wine, another cheese board, some fries, and a selection of appetizers. Emily takes a seat and pops a few fries into her mouth while I thank the waiter and send him away.

"It's so beautiful here. I've had such a great day. Thank you."

"That's what happens when you start dating your favorite artist."

She throws a French fry at me, giggling.

We fall into a comfortable silence, indulging in the great food, and maybe one too many glasses of wine.

"Does anyone else in your family paint?"

Emily stills, and that's when I realize she hasn't spoken much about her family.

"Well, um... that's a bit of a long story."

"Lucky we have all the time in the world. Plus, lots of wine." I hold up the bottle, and she rolls her eyes at me.

"Fine," she groans. "My mother's French." This surprises me, but it does explain why she speaks impeccable French. "She was an artist. From what I remember, although the years have strained that view, she was this bohemian woman who didn't fit in. I come from a small town in Devon. You know the kind where everyone knows everyone else and their business. The people are simple and live lives simply... either fishing or farming, and they love having a few pints down the pub. They aren't interested in culture and the arts."

I nod. I've never been anywhere like that, but I know of these places and that type of culture.

"My mother met my father when he was on holiday in Paris... it was supposed to be a holiday romance. It was exactly that until my dad came home, and he found out Mum was pregnant. She had written, telling him about her pregnancy."

That's something that could happen between Emily and me since we have stopped using protection.

"He sent her money to catch the next ferry to England, so he could marry her, and they could be a family. Of course, my mother not having much and wanting a better life for herself, did just that. She loved it at first... the quaint little fishing village with the most idyllic views, but the locals didn't understand her, and they were not open to newcomers like she thought they would be.

"My father was a fisherman. He'd be away a lot, so my mother had to fend for herself. She had her art and would paint to keep herself occupied. Things went downhill when she had my brother, and from what I hear, I think she suffered from postpartum depression.

"After that, things quickly turned sour between my parents, but she became pregnant with my sister six months after the birth of my brother. She knew she was stuck. Of course, my father went away fishing, and she was left at home with a baby and a stomach that was growing bigger every day. Her art helped her again, but when she'd lose herself in her art, she would forget about Ryan, my brother. Neighbors complained to my father that they could hear him crying all day and that he appeared dirty while she was busy with her artwork."

I reach out and hold her hand. I can see this story is upsetting for her to relive, and she gives me a weak smile.

"He banned her from painting. He took all her art and threw it away. She must have been devastated. I can only imagine the feelings of betrayal she must have felt. But Dad was a simple man... he didn't understand her world, nor did he care to. Of course, after the birth of my sister, Sara, Mum took a turn for the worst. At the time, the doctors didn't know what the problem was, but eventually she was diagnosed as bipolar. Her moods became erratic, so much so that my father had to find another job because he was too scared to leave her alone with their children. But that didn't stop them bringing me into the world."

I squeeze her hand letting her know I'm listening.

"I came at the worst time in their relationship, and my birth added more fuel to the fire. Mum's moods and behavior became more and more erratic. Once the doctors had found and prescribed the right medication for her, everything seemed a little better, but the damage was done, and even though I got what I thought was a normal mum, in reality I got nothing but a shell.

"My father decided, in a last-ditch effort to save his family, to encourage her to get back into art. Once she held those brushes in her hand, everything changed. She was so happy... or so we thought. But in reality, it wasn't the art that she was happy about, she was happy because she was having an affair with a local French artist. A couple of weeks after my fifth birthday, she left, and I've never seen her again.

"When she left, my father demanded we stop speaking French, he outlawed art and anything to do with her, but I couldn't give it up. Speaking French and art were the only links I had to my mother, and I held onto them tight and in secret.

"My father passed away just after my graduation from high school, and as sad as I was, I was also relieved because I was able to accept my scholarship for art history, something he'd have never have let me do if he were alive."

Wow! What a story.

"And where's your mum now?"

"Here." I frown. "Apparently, she lives in the South of France somewhere, married to the artist she left my father for."

"And you haven't tried to seek her out since arriving."

"Well, I've been kind of busy." She gives me a look that suggests the amount of trouble I have given her is the cause.

"Oh, that's right, you have an asshole boss."

She giggles. "He's growing on me," she says flirtatiously.

"I'll do more than that on you." I bite her neck which makes her squeal. "Do you want to find her?"

"What would I say?"

"Maybe 'hello' would be a great start, followed by 'how have you been.'"

"You make it sound so easy."

"It can be. I'll be by your side."

"I like this Louis." She waves her finger in the air and smiles. "He's much nicer than that other one."

"That's because he's crazy about some English woman." I pull her chair toward me, so she's almost sitting on my lap.

"Is that so? You're crazy about her?"

I nod with a smile on my face. "Yep, and I have a feeling she might be crazy about me, too."

"That's a little presumptuous, don't you think?"

"Well, she did tell me I have a big ego as well as a big…" She kisses me silencing my words before I can finish.

"Yes, this woman is crazy about you."

"Good. Now let me help."

"Fine."

"Perfect. Now can I take you home and fuck you?" A huge smile falls across her face.

"I'm all yours."

33

EMILY

There's a knock at the front door. The staff is still on extended vacation while Louis and I explore each other, and I'm really glad we have had this time together with no interference because I feel closer to him. Not because we hate leaving the bed, but because we laze around and talk and paint. I don't think my life can get any better than what I have at the moment.

"Daniel, hi." I'm surprised to see him at the front door. Louis told me he had spoken to Daniel and told him we're a thing, but actually seeing him here makes it real, I guess. We've been living in our own little bubble, just the two of us for a while now.

"You look happy." Daniel smiles, kissing both cheeks.

"Um..."

He chuckles. "I'm not upset, Emily. I'm happy that the two of you are together. I think you're good for him."

"He's come a long way by himself without my help, though."

"I know my brother. He wouldn't be making a comeback if it weren't for you." Tears begin to well in my eyes as I think about just how far Louis has come since when I first met him. "Anyway, I actually came here as I have a surprise for you. Well, no, Louis has a surprise for you. I can't take all the credit."

What's going on?

"Come." Daniel takes my hand and pulls me out the front door, and that's when I notice a limousine parked out the front. The door swings open, and I scream because my three best friends jump out of the car and rush straight into my arms. We're all crying tears of happiness at seeing each other once again.

"We missed you," Georgia tells me.

"I missed you girls, too." I hug them all.

"Wow, that's loud." Louis comes out resting his shoulder against the door.

I'm a mess. There are tears rolling down my face. I untangle myself from my friends' arms, run to Louis, jump into his arms, and kiss him multiple times.

"Thank you, thank you, thank you." I kiss him again but more passionately this time, much to the hollers of my girlfriends behind me.

"You're welcome. I thought you might be missing them."

"I was. I just..." The smile on Louis' face says it all. "Tomorrow we'll take you to my Paris apartment, and you can have a girls' weekend there. I'll stay with Daniel and get some overdue business stuff done."

This man. I adore him.

I untangle myself from him and go back to my girls.

"THIS IS THE LIFE." Georgia lays back on the sun chair as we laze by the pool.

"Seriously, Emmy, that man is fucking hot," Rosie whispers beside me.

We have had one too many bottles of champagne catching up with each other, but who's counting, anyway?

"His brother is hot, too." Ava lifts her sunglasses as she ogles Daniel, who's walking back with Louis from his studio.

"You look happy, though," Rosie adds. "France suits you."

"I'm painting again." The girls are all shocked into silence. "I know. I know… I started in Ibiza, and then Louis took me on a date to this castle in the countryside which was surrounded by lavender fields, and he set up private painting sessions. We talked and painted for hours. It was great."

"I can't believe he's gotten you painting again. This is phenomenal news," Ava adds.

I've known these girls all my life. We all moved to London from our tiny little town seeking adventure and fun, and we found it with each other's experiences.

"I know. It took me a little while to warm up, but once I lost myself in the stunning views, plus the great conversation and maybe a couple of wines, it felt good to be painting again."

"He's your muse." Georgia winks.

"Maybe he is."

The girls all ooh and aah and then burst out laughing, which sends us into fits of giggles.

Maybe we have had way too much champagne.

I'M surprised to see Gabriel back. Louis has had the staff on leave since we have been together, wanting us to have some alone time together, which is code for screwing me on every surface of his home. I walk over and give Gabriel a big hug and a kiss on the cheek. I've missed him.

"Long time, no see."

"Bossman has been keeping you busy." Gabriel looks over my shoulder. I can just imagine the looks he's giving him. "And he looks mighty jealous, too." He chuckles, flipping Louis off behind me.

"Ignore him." I giggle. "How are things with the girl?"

Gabriel's cheeks flush. "Good. She's good, but I have to finish getting dinner ready. We'll catch up when you get back from Paris."

"Okay, but I want *all* the details." Gabriel gives me a salute and heads back to the kitchen. I make my way to where everyone's seated and take one beside Louis.

"Everything okay?" he whispers in my ear.

"Are you jealous, Mr. Marchant?" My hand moves across his thigh, grazing his lap. He lets out a frustrated huff, those blue eyes glaring at me. "We're just friends." Louis holds my stare as my fingers wrap around his, giving his hand a tight squeeze. "How could anyone compete with this." I squeeze harder, and he leans into me.

"Keep teasing me like that, Miss Chapman, and I'll bend you over this table and fuck you in front of everyone to make sure they all know you are *mine*."

I swallow hard. *Damn, that is hot.*

"Would you two cut it out? Us single people don't want to lose their appetite before dinner," Georgia groans but gives me a quick wink.

Oops, she totally heard Louis' dirty threats.

Louis ignores my friend and pulls me closer, then kisses me, making my friends and Daniel gag.

Not long later, dinner is served and, of course, it's spectacular. Gabriel made a traditional Provençal. We all ate way too much and drank too many bottles of wine, but the conversation around the dinner table never faded.

"Daniel, did you know Emily's mother is French and also an artist," Louis tells his brother. He's tipsy, we all are. I notice the girls look over at me a little shocked that Louis knows about my family's past.

"Really? I guess it must be in her genes." Daniel takes a sip of his wine. He's lost his suit jacket, rolled up the sleeves of his dress shirt, and Ava hasn't stopped flirting with him all night. *Where did this confident woman come from?* Ava rarely makes the first move on guys.

"She lives here, too, somewhere." Louis waves his arm around the room.

The girls look over at me again, questions lacing their faces going by their raised eyebrows and widening eyes.

"Have you seen her since you've been here?" Gabriel asks.

I shake my head. "I haven't seen her since I was five."

The table goes to quiet contemplating my confession.

"Would you like to meet her?" Daniel asks.

I shrug because I'm not really sure.

"The reason I ask is that I know people, who can, you know..." his voice lowers, "... find anything."

My eyes widen as do Ava's.

"They could find her?" I look over at Georgia and Rosie who are staring at me with their mouths open.

"Yeah." Daniel waves his hand. "I could have her address by tomorrow if you want."

Holy heck, that's quick.

Is this what I want?

My pulse quickens—it doesn't give me much time to process it all.

"You wouldn't have to meet her, but you could write her a letter if you had her address," Louis adds.

He's right. Maybe I could write her a letter to start off slowly. That way, if she rejects me, it's not face-to-face, and she ends up devastating me.

"Okay," I whisper.

A hush falls across the table.

"Are you sure, Emily?" Rosie asks.

"I think I need to know why she didn't keep in touch, especially after Dad died. She's had so many chances, and I guess I just want to know. Maybe then I can have some closure on that part of my life."

My friends all nod in agreement. They've been through all of this with me throughout my entire life. They know what my family was like growing up.

Louis kisses my forehead. With him by my side, I feel like I can conquer this last hurdle in my life.

34

LOUIS

We have dropped the girls off at my apartment. Thankfully, Daniel organized cleaners to tidy the space since I haven't been there in months. The last time I was there was during one of my many benders, so I can only imagine what the place looked like.

"We need to talk." Daniel looks serious as I take a seat in his office. "It's about Emily's mother."

"Is she dead?" I ask.

"No. But..." Daniel is fidgeting, he never fidgets. "You have a connection to her mother."

I look at Daniel. *Is he high?* Then panic fills me. Fuck! Did I sleep with her mother? During those four months of darkness there were some rich older ladies that I slept with and, oh fuck! How could we move on from that?

"I didn't sleep with her, did I?" Daniel bursts out laughing at my question, which can only mean I didn't. Thank God!

"Seriously, Louis?"

"Look, I was in a bad place."

"Not sure if it's worse than that, to be honest. But anyway, Emily's mother is Ellie, or also known as Eloise."

Oh shit.

"Victor's wife?"

Daniel nods.

I stand and begin to pace. I've spent more time with Emily's mother than she has. *Shit.* I still catch up with Eloise and Victor, not that much since my hiatus. I rake my hands through my hair.

Shit. Shit. Shit.

"Should we tell her?"

"I don't know, Louis."

"Eloise never said anything about having kids. She and Victor would always say they're devoted to their art, and that the artists they mentor are like their children. Shit, Daniel! How can I keep this from her?"

"Give her this weekend with her girlfriends, then maybe slowly broach the subject afterward."

"If Emily doesn't want to know… then how can I keep this from Eloise and Victor?"

"This isn't your secret to tell."

"Yeah, and if that were true, then we would never have met."

Daniel and I share the same father but different mothers. I grew up as an only child to a single mother who struggled to make ends meet. Apparently, the apartment we lived in was paid for by my father, but that was as far as his generosity went. Just before Daniel's mother passed away, she confessed to Daniel that he had a brother a year younger than him, his father having had an affair with his secretary. She was sworn to secrecy by his father, not wanting to destabilize his company with the bad press an affair would cause.

He threatened Tina, Daniel's mother, that if she ever told anyone he'd divorce her and leave her penniless. So, she told his secret on her death bed, when he couldn't blackmail her anymore.

Daniel looked for and found me, ignoring my father's request which meant giving up his family legacy by choosing me. He has no relationship with our father, and I've never met him, but at least I got my brother out of the whole messed-up situation, and he has my mom, who adores him.

"I know, but this is tricky."

I rake my fingers through my hair. "Of all the women you could have hired as my assistant."

"Sounds like fate had some plans for you both."

Maybe's he's right.

If Emily had one day come and found her mother, we would have eventually met. *Would we have fallen for each other then?* I probably would have been in a better place and not been as mean as I was to her when we first met. But I think I'd have pursued her if we were introduced because she has that effect on me, and it was immediate when I met Emily.

DANIEL and I stayed in for the night while the girls went out. I wanted to be sober just in case Emily needed me, so I could be there for her. We watched some football and caught up on some business.

"Ava couldn't keep her eyes off you," I press, taking a sip of my beer.

Daniel doesn't say anything. I take a glance over, and he's refusing to look at me.

"You didn't?"

"Of course not. That's Emily's friend."

I eye my brother suspiciously. "And if she wasn't?"

"It doesn't matter, she is, and that's the end of it." My brother is interested but isn't pursuing her because of Emily.

"She's beautiful."

"That she is," Daniel agrees.

"She seems smitten with you."

"That she does." He gives me another curt answer.

"And you got on well last night."

"That we did."

Ugh, he's getting on my nerves.

"Yet?"

"Yet, nothing, Louis."

I hold up my hand at my brother's terse words. He's being very defensive over her. I'm going to ask Emily about it. I bet she knows what's going on. Girls talk about this kind of stuff, don't they?

"Don't fuck her around," is all I say.

Daniel lets out a frustrated sigh beside me, and we go back to watching some action movie that I have no real interest in.

MY CELL RINGS. It rings and rings continuously then stops. It starts again, and I pick it up rubbing the sleep from my eyes.

"Louis. It's Emily."

Those few words get my immediate attention.

35

EMILY

"I can't believe we're here." Ava looks around the luxurious nightclub where Louis has organized for us to be seated in a VIP suite.

"I can't believe this is your life." Rosie elbows me.

"Um... it's not my life, it's Louis'," I remind them all, but they don't believe me.

I understand Louis is famous—like you know, in the art world—but I didn't realize just how famous he was in celebrity circles. His name opens doors. Not that I'd ever use his name because I'm not like that. Louis set up this weekend for my girlfriends and me.

Earlier today, we went shopping, we took selfies in front of the Eiffel Tower, we walked along the Champs Elysées, then Louis organized a private dinner cruise along the Seine for us.

The man is going for *boyfriend of the year*.

I'd marry the hell out of that man.

No. I'm not supposed to think those kinds of things.

There's still a tiny little niggle in my mind that what we have has an expiration date, and it's in a month in New York.

No. Don't think like that, Emily.

The man is crazy about you. You both love each other. Whatever happens after New York, you will sort it out. Paris is only a train ride from London. I push my doubts from my mind and concentrate on the here and now, not some distant future that may or may not happen because why ruin a perfect evening.

I'm having the best time, dancing with my girlfriends, enjoying the VIP treatment. There's a group of guys hanging around near our booth in the VIP area. I assume they're okay as they are in the VIP section and should be okay to mingle with. The girls don't seem to mind the men's attention, and I can't deny my girlfriends the chance to hook up with some hot French guys. *I'm a good friend like that.* But as the night wears on, I realize I've had one too many drinks because my words are becoming slurry.

Maybe I should go home.

Yeah, I should totally go home.

I have a hot French man waiting in bed for me. I pull out my phone and try and text Louis.

Emily: Mess you

I hit send then giggle to myself.

Umm, that doesn't feel right. *Why are my legs wobbly?* Stupid French champagne. I sit. *Ugh, why am I so sweaty?* Ewww, that's not cute.

I look around at the flashing lights of the VIP area. There are a fair few people up here now, they should really turn up the air conditioning.

"I'm just going to head to the bathroom," I tell Rosie who's sitting beside me, talking to some hot guy.

"Want me to come?" she asks.

"No. Stay and lock lips with a hottie." I wiggle my brows at her.

Rosie hugs me and turns her attention back to the hot guy. I stumble a little bit. Dammit! I'm not used to these ridiculous heels. *Who makes heels this high?*

I'm thirsty, and my tongue is dry. So, I grab a bottle of water off the bar and start to drink. *Why am I still sweating profusely?* Actually, I feel clammy, and now my head hurts. I grab my cell and check the time. It's 1:43 a.m. It's been a long time since I have partied this hard. *Am I getting old?*

I notice that Louis has sent me a message.

Louis: Hope you're having fun tonight. My bed isn't the same without you.

My heart swoons. *God, I love that man.* The screen becomes a little fuzzy, so I purposely blink a few times, then force myself to concentrate on writing out a message to him.

Emily: I msk u 2 and yore deck.

There, that was totally a super flirty sexy text message. I put my cell back into my pocket and make my way to the bathroom. Thankfully, they're empty in the VIP section and clean. Being important is kind of awesome. I trip over my feet and land hard against the cubicle door.

Ouch. That's going to hurt. Probably going to bruise too.

I eventually get into the cubicle somehow. It takes me a couple of tries to fix myself up.

On the way out, I catch a glimpse of myself in the mirror. Oh wow! What the hell happened? I look like shit. My makeup has completely run, my eyes appear bloodshot, my skin has a gray tone. I don't look cute at all.

Maybe it's time for bed.

I'm feeling really tired.

I wish Louis were here to carry me. My legs feel heavy.

I make my way to the exit. The swirling colors of the lights are blurring, and the music is becoming muffled in my ears. *What's going on?* I'm not feeling well at all.

"Enjoying your girls' night?"

That voice. It's the one that gives me nightmares.

"What are you doing here, Yves?" He just chuckles, moving closer to me as I stumble against the wall. Stupid heels.

"Just having fun with my boys, who seem to have taken a shining to your girls." I try to look over his shoulder, hoping to catch someone's attention, but everything behind him is a blur. I don't feel good at all.

"Please leave me alone." I take a step but stumble right into his arms.

"See. I knew you would come around. Louis' women always do."

I try to push him off me, but I don't have the strength, he's too strong. I stay slumped against him.

"Someone has had a little too much fun, I think. Lucky, I'm here to look after you. So many dangerous people out there." His laugh sounds maniacal bordering on evil.

"No." I try and scream, but my voice comes out more like a whisper.

I can't fight him off.

I now know what I'm feeling.

My heart constricts in my chest as a panic attack starts, but I'm becoming immobilized. I can't feel anything except for living a nightmare that I can't stop from happening.

We move through the crowd with Yves' arms wrapped around me. I try and gain people's attention by screaming and shouting, but it's all internal because nothing comes out of my mouth.

My eyes are becoming heavy.

No. Fight it, Emily.

I can't fall asleep.

I won't fall asleep.

But I know I can't fight the drugs that are having this effect on me.

The world is becoming darker and darker until blackness consumes me.

Please, Louis, help me.

36

LOUIS

"I'm going to fucking kill him." I'm pulling my hair out. Rosie called to tell me that Emily didn't return from the bathroom. When they started looking for her, one of the staff said she had left with a man. Thankfully, the girls have location finders on their cell phones because they were able to find her moving on the GPS locator. The girls are currently in a taxi following the blinking dot just like we are.

Our driver rushes through the Paris streets, following the directions the girls are giving us. The girls let me know the blinking has stopped and give us the last known coordinates.

My stomach sinks.

I know that address.

Daniel looks at me, his face a little paler than normal. "He wouldn't?" His question is faint, but I hear it.

"If he touches a hair on her head, I'm going to fucking kill him."

"Louis," Daniel warns me.

"No, brother, the bastard has my woman. Emily hasn't done anything to him. She doesn't deserve this. Not after everything she has been through in her past. Did you know she was raped when she was a teen?"

Daniel looks at me, horrified.

"Exactly. She told me about it after Monaco. The incident still gives her nightmares."

"I have a friend in the Gendarmerie. I'll call and get him to meet us there. We have to do this by the book. He needs to be put away if he's touched her."

"I don't know if I can wait." Daniel gives me a pleading look but also a profoundly serious one as well. "He has her, and God only knows what he's doing to her."

Daniel's phone beeps.

"My friend is five minutes out. He lives around the corner."

My heart is racing. How are we ever going to get back from this? Just when things between us were moving forward, this happens. Fuck!

The driver pulls up out the front of Yves' Paris apartment as Daniel's friend arrives. They shake hands and talk about a plan.

"Louis, this is Marcus." We shake hands and both do a chin lift.

"I'm not waiting," I warn them both.

"Depending on what we find…" my stomach sinks at Marcus' words, "… I'll give you your moment with him." Marcus looks at me seriously. "I promise you that."

I nod.

We make our way to the apartment with my fingers crossed that Yves isn't smart enough to have changed his code. I enter it in, and the door unlocks. *Fuck! Someone up there is looking out for me.* All three of us rush in across the courtyard, then through the doors that lead to the stairs. We make our way up four floors to where his apartment is located. We take them two at a time, every minute she's with him is killing me.

We make it to his level.

"Let me pick this lock. I need to catch him with my own

eyes to prosecute. Okay?" Marcus tells me to which I reply, "Hurry the fuck up."

He picks the lock in under a minute, then he stands and pulls his gun from his holster and holds it out in front of him. We rush through the hallway behind him, and we all stop. In front of us is an unconscious Emily on the couch, and Yves is ripping her dress clean off her body.

"Stop. Police."

Yves freezes. His face pales when he sees a gun aimed at him.

Then they widen when he sees me charging at him.

"You motherfucking piece of shit." My fist slams into his face as we roll to the floor.

Yves fights me—I get a punch to the stomach which winds me, but I don't care and just shake it off launching myself at him again. My fist hits him in the stomach, the ribs, the face. "I'm going to kill you."

"Fuck you," he spits, blood pouring from his face.

"Louis," Daniel calls out. "*Louis*," he calls to me again. "Get. Emily. Now." This stops me. My chest is heaving as I hold Yves by his ripped shirt, turning my head.

Quickly, I get to my feet and rush over to Emily, who's out cold.

"We need an ambulance... a doctor."

"I've organized for one to meet us back at your place," Daniel tells me. "Pick her up and take her away from here. We'll clean up this mess."

"She wanted it, Louis. She wanted me," Yves yells at me.

My blood boils, and I turn to go for him again, but Daniel punches Yves instead, flooring him.

"Shut the fuck up, you piece of shit. You're about to be fucked," Daniel states.

"The boys in lock-up are going to love a pretty boy like you," Marcus tells him. "I'm going to make sure I put you in with the best." The sneer, followed by a bark of laughter, makes me take a second look. Marcus follows that by rubbing his hands together, where I see he's taking pleasure in his actions. It makes me feel better knowing Marcus is going to take care of Yves once and for all.

I take off my shirt and place it over Emily. She doesn't need the world to see her in her underwear—this gorgeous woman has suffered enough. I pick her up, cradling her, then slowly walk back the way I came and out into the darkness. Headlights light up the courtyard, and I can hear her friends frantically talking. They notice me coming and gasp seeing Emily's limp form in my arms. I push open the door, and they crowd around us.

"Fuck! Emmy... we're so sorry." Rosie is crying.

All of them have tears running down their cheeks—they know what she has been through.

"He didn't?" Ava asks.

I shake my head.

"You made him pay, didn't you?" Georgia asks.

"Fuck, yeah."

The girls all nod, but shock is setting in. I watch each of them needing something to support themselves in an upright position. They all lean against the car as their breathing becomes rapid, and they all start sobbing.

"There's a doctor coming to my place to check her over. I think she's going to want to see your faces when she wakes."

They all give me teary looks but nod.

The driver opens the door for me to slide in while cradling Emily to my chest.

I won't ever let her go again.

"Do you think she's going to be okay?" I ask her friends once the doctor leaves.

It appears like we got there in time. Yves hadn't had time to assault her.

"I don't know, Louis," Ava tells me. "We've been here before. It took her a *long* time to get over what happened last time. Not sure she ever did."

"I can't lose her," I tell her friends.

They all give me sad smiles as if they know it's inevitable.

"The guy who did this to her last time... he was her best friend." My stomach sinks at Rosie's words. "She trusted him. We all did."

"We didn't realize how his crush had turned into an obsession," Georgia adds. "He stalked her, and he was right there under our noses."

"I brought this man into her life." I scrub my hand across my face.

"How would you have known he'd do this?" Rosie questions.

"He tried it on at the gala. But I thought... I tried to make her safe."

"How could you have known?" Ava tries to reassure me.

"That's the thing... I did know. I thought he was dangerous, but I had no idea..." I run my hands through my hair. "Not only has he destroyed my past, but he's also now destroyed my future."

"Not going to lie. Prepare yourself, she's probably going to want to run," Georgia warns me.

I look up at her friends, my heart aching at this thought, but how can I blame her. I wouldn't want to stay here either.

"Just give her time. She'll come back to you."

"And if she doesn't?" I look at them.

"Then you fight for her... if she's what you want," Ava tells me.

"She *is* what I want. More than anything," I confess. "She brought light back into my life when all I could see was darkness."

"Then don't give up on her, Louis," Rosie pleads. "She was happy with you, even when you were an asshole." Her words make me smile even if it's fleeting. "Just remember what you had together before everything got fucked up, especially when she pushes you away."

Please come back to me, Emily. Please.

37

EMILY

How much did I drink last night? I haven't stopped throwing up this morning. Thank goodness I have a bucket beside my bed. My head hurts so, so much. My mouth is dry. I turn and see Louis asleep on the chair in the corner of my room.

What's he doing here? It looks like he slept here.

Why does my body hurt so much? I look down and see a multitude of bruises, ranging from light to dark in color.

My brain feels foggy just like...

Oh God! Then it hits me, and I jolt up in bed and scream.

"No. No. No. No." My body begins to shake uncontrollably.

"Emily." Louis rushes to me, but I flinch away from his touch.

He swallows hard, the color draining from his face as hurt flames in his eyes.

"Emmy," Ava says.

I watch my girlfriends flood into the room, and I break. Tears stream down my cheeks and drop off onto the bed as a panic attack begins, and I struggle to breathe.

"Emmy, you're safe," Ava tells me.

"Breathe, babe, just breathe," Rosie instructs. "You're having a panic attack."

"Look at me, Emmy. Focus on me and only me." Georgia holds my face making our eyes connect. "You. Are. Safe. No one is going to hurt you." Hands begin to rub my back, and somehow, I start to calm. "We're here."

I nod, focussing on my friend, slowly getting my breathing under control.

"That's better." Georgia smiles at me.

My friends hold onto my shaking body, giving me their strength and courage.

"I'll go get you some water." Louis leaves the bedroom.

"He saved you, Emmy," Ava tells me.

I don't want to hear it.

"I want to go home," I tell them.

I watch as they all look at each other.

"What about Louis?" Rosie asks.

I shake my head. "I don't want to be here anymore. I need to get away from him."

Louis walks in at that moment, hurt is written across his face. He hands the glass to me, but I can't look at him.

"If you want to go home, Emily, Daniel will organize a private plane to take you back to London." I lift my head and nod. "I'll message him now." Then he walks out of the room.

"He loves you, Emmy," Ava tells me.

"I don't care. It's his fault that man touched me."

"Emmy." Georgia's tone is angry. "Did you not see the cuts and bruises on his face... on his knuckles? He attacked Yves, he defended you. He saved you."

I shake my head. "He'd never have touched me if it wasn't for him."

"No, Emmy," Georgia argues, which surprises me. "I'll not let you place blame on Louis. The person you should be upset with is Yves. He is the fucking cunt who spiked your drink and took you home. He's the one who deserves your anger, not that man in there. Not that man who thought his world was crashing down around him because he'd lost you. Not that man who would have killed Yves if the police weren't there."

I just keep shaking my head.

"Not now," Rosie tells Georgia.

"Rosie, he's a good man. He loves her."

Rosie shakes her head at Georgia as if asking her to stop.

"I just want to go home. Coming to France was the biggest mistake of my life."

My friends pull me in tighter as I breakdown further inside my mind.

HOURS LATER, Louis has organized a private plane for us to fly back to London. Daniel joined us. The girls said goodbye to Louis, but I couldn't. I just wanted to get away from this nightmare of a place.

"If you need anything, anything at all, let Daniel know."

Not sure who Louis said that to, but I know I won't be needing anything from him ever again. I curl up against the butter-soft leather seats and stare out the window.

"You need to eat something." Ava sits down beside me, handing me a sandwich.

"No, thanks." I push it away.

"Take one bite, please?" She pushes the plate in front of me again, and I give her a dismissive hand gesture, take a bite to please her, then push it back. "Thank you."

Ava moves away leaving me alone.

There's a black town car waiting for us at the airport.

"The driver will take you wherever you need to go. Emily's things will be packed up and shipped back to London as soon as it can be arranged." Daniel's talking to someone—I have no idea who. I'm so lost inside my head. "Here's my business card, if any of you need anything, please don't hesitate to call."

I let out a frustrated sigh.

"Thank you so much, Daniel. We'll be in touch," Ava tells him.

I roll my eyes. Of course, she will be, she wants to fuck him. It's not like I didn't witness the fuck-me eyes she's been throwing him all weekend.

Whatever. I don't care.

I jump into the back of the town car and curl into the door. I wait patiently until the others join me, and the car starts moving.

"You don't mind sharing an apartment with me again?" Rosie asks, attempting to cheer me up.

I just ignore her and stare out the window watching the city go by.

One by one, we drop off all the girls, and then it's our turn. Rosie helps me out of the car and up to her apartment.

"I'm going to go to bed," I tell her.

"Okay. Well, I'm here if you need me." She gives me a tight hug, a little longer than is necessary, but I don't pull away. "I mean it, Em. I'm here for you. We all are."

I nod and make my way to the spare room where a bed is made up for me. I pull back the duvet and sink into the soft bed —a bed that makes me feel safe. I take the pill the doctor prescribed and fall asleep not long after.

HANDS TOUCH ME. *I feel hands all over my body. Lips against my skin, and I can't free myself. I scream and shout trying to get free, but I can't. I call out for help, but no one is there. Hands try to pull my legs apart. I attempt to kick and scream, but nothing comes out.*

. . .

"Emmy. Emmy… wake up. It's a dream."

I jolt up in my bed, my body is bathed in sweat, and Rosie is sitting beside me on the bed with a look of concern on her face.

"He tried to…" I burst out crying.

Rosie pulls me into her arms and holds me as I sob. Hours later, I eventually fall back to sleep with Rosie right next to me.

When I wake in the morning and realize it's her who's sharing my bed, I feel relieved.

38

EMILY

"He's been charged with sexual assault." I hear Georgia say as I enter Rosie's kitchen.

It's been a couple of days since that fateful night. They stop talking when they see me.

"I heard you." I grab a juice from the refrigerator.

"Good. So, you now know you're safe, and we don't have to repeat it," Georgia tells me.

Rosie and I have been sharing a bed these last couple of nights. I'm too scared to go to sleep because the images of Yves keep playing in my mind on repeat, and I'm too frightened to close my eyes when I'm on my own.

"He's not convicted yet," I state, then take a sip of my juice.

"This is true, but…"

I shake my head at Georgia. "The man is a national treasure. He's rich and powerful. Do you seriously think he's going to be convicted?"

Are these girls stupid?

"He will if you testify," Georgia adds.

My eyes bug out. "Are you fucking serious? You think I'm going to testify against him?"

"You're not?" she asks.

"Of course, I'm not. The media is going to get a hold of this and twist it. They are going to make me out to be a whore, or even worse, a serial reporter. I can't do that. I can't handle it." Tears well in my eyes. "It's going to be a national scandal."

"We're here for you. We'll support you. We will protect you," Ava reassures me.

"Like you did that night?" The room falls silent. "Like you all did with... with... Connor?" Tears fall from my friends' eyes, and I'm not sorry. "Both times something has happened to me, you have all been there right beside me. You were supposed to protect me. But you *didn't*," I scream at my friends. "You let them take me. Touch me. Destroy me." They're all sobbing now at my words. "How can I ever trust you all?"

"That's not fair, Emmy," Georgia argues.

"Not fair! *Not fair!* What's not fair is having someone forcibly take your virginity. Someone who was your best friend. The person you thought you could trust. That's *not* fucking fair."

"We're sorry, Emmy." Rosie is sobbing.

"*You're sorry*. That's good, yeah, that makes everything all okay then, doesn't it. Because *you* are sorry."

I'm angry, so fucking angry.

Why me?

Why is this happening to me again?

"THERE'S ANOTHER BOUQUET OF FLOWERS." Rosie places the vases of sunflowers in the kitchen and adds it alongside the others. Every single day for the past two weeks Louis has sent me a vase of sunflowers. No note, just the flowers. Every single time they arrive, I want to throw them into the bin, but Rosie stops me and tells me she loves sunflowers, and she'd rather look at them than waste them.

What I have been doing to occupy my time is painting.

Rosie has let me set up an art space in the spare room, and I spend most of my days locked away in the room. There's a gorgeous view of the private residents' gardens from there. I'm not painting happy, light paintings. They are more angry, aggressive, dark, and haunting, which is all the emotions that are inside of me at the moment and are flowing out through to my artwork.

Every day when Rosie comes home from work and sees my latest creations, her smile fades just a little more. She thinks it's fantastic that I'm painting again after all these years, but I can see the concern on her face when she sees the images I've painted that aren't so *nice*.

She's worried about me, I know she is, all my friends are. They think I should go to therapy, and maybe I should, but I want to process this myself. Art is my therapy. If I can get rid of the demons that haunt me overnight when I close my eyes through painting, then I'd rather that than some doctor prescribing me drugs like they did last time. Those drugs simply added to my misery and sent me into a deep depression. I never want to be like that ever again.

The girls finally explained to me what happened that night. I needed to know—I needed to know how far Yves got. Apparently, the friends that had surrounded our table in the VIP section were his crew. Yves had used them as a distraction. One of his friends placed something in my drink while we were talking. I hadn't noticed, but the cameras from the VIP section caught it all. Unfortunately, security had missed it happening as there was a fight on the lower level which conveniently happened at the same time.

Yves waited for his moment, and when I went to the bathroom, that's when he took it. Louis told the girls that they busted through the door just as he was taking my clothes off. The doctor's report showed no physical or sexual assault had taken place, only a few bruises. I'm so thankful. I don't know if I could have coped with being defiled for a second time.

Georgia made sure I knew that Louis attacked Yves, pummeled him to within an inch of his life for touching me. There's a small section deep inside of me that's happy he did, that he cared enough to fight for me.

But I should never have been put in that situation—I should never have been around someone so evil as Yves.

There's a knock at Rosie's door which I find rather strange as it's the middle of the day. I've been holed up in my studio for hours lost in myself.

Maybe Rosie forgot her keys?

I make my way to the door and peek through the hole. *It's Daniel.*

What the hell is he doing here?

How did he get in?

This is a secure building.

My heart begins to race, my hands shake, and my skin becomes clammy. I suck in a deep breath calming myself, then I open the door. He seems surprised that I'm even opening the door as a friendly smile eventually lands on his face.

"Hey," he says awkwardly as if he doesn't know what to say to me.

"Hey." Well, that's the start of a great conversation.

"You're painting." He points to my paint-splattered clothes.

"Yeah, I am." My curt answer makes him shift from one foot to another nervously before me.

"Can I come in? I want to talk to you about something."

Every part of my body is screaming 'no you can't come in,' but for some reason, I go against my inner thoughts and reply, "Yes." Opening the door for Daniel, I allow him to pass. He walks into the living room and stands awkwardly.

"Would you like a drink?"

He nods. "Water, please."

I busy myself in the kitchen getting us both a glass of water, then hand it to him, and we both take a seat on the sofa in silence for a couple of moments.

"How are you doing?" Daniel looks over at me, and I shrug because, to be honest, it's a daily struggle. "I see you've received Louis' flowers." He points to all the sunflowers filling up the apartment.

"Rosie seems to like them." He frowns a little but doesn't say anything, then takes an uneasy sip of his water. "Why are you here?" My question is filled with accusation.

Daniel places the glass on the coffee table. "I have an offer for you."

Well, that's not what I thought he was going to say.

"No amount of money can make me go back there, Daniel," I tell him.

"That's not what I'm here about," he tells me. "Before everything happened, Louis asked if I'd contact the New York gallery to see if they would be interested in sharing the space they have for him with another artist." Okay, not sure what that has to do with me, so we just stare at each other. "The gallery said yes."

"That's all good, but this has nothing to do with me. I don't work for Louis anymore."

"I know, but the artist they want is you."

My heart stops in my chest.

What the hell did he say?

Me?

How? Why?

Am I actually dreaming?

Because this seems like a dream. Something like this wouldn't happen in real life, would it?

"Louis sent photos of the paintings you did while in Ibiza. He asked if he could share the showing with you." That was weeks ago. Why would he do this for me? I don't understand.

"Louis thinks you're talented. No, extremely talented."

I shake my head. No. I don't want to hear this.

"I'm no artist, Daniel."

"I want to represent you."

My heart is beating loudly in my chest.

What the hell is going on? Am I being punked?

"You're only saying this because of what happened. Is this some sort of hush money?" I stand up abruptly and begin to pace the living room. "You're both trying to absolve yourselves."

My chest feels tight. My head hurts. I don't feel great. Goddammit! I stumble, feeling dizzy.

Daniel rushes over and holds me steady, but I pull away from him feeling so vulnerable.

"Emily, you have no idea how sorry I am about what happened to you." I can't look at him, but the sincerity in his voice is killing me. "Louis blames himself. He's..." I hear him sigh heavily. "He's not doing so well."

I don't react, I can't. Knowing Louis is hurting, there's a tiny part of me that feels bad, but I stuff it away deep down inside of me.

"He wants to help."

"That's why he's offering this?" My eyes well with tears, and I try to blink them away, but one rolls down my cheek.

"God, Emily, no. He knows you're talented. He's had this planned for ages. He was going to tell you after you got back from Paris." I wrap my arms around myself, a flutter of hope beginning to take flight inside of me. "I think you're talented, too." I look up at Daniel. "I'd love to see what you've been working on."

Really?

"You don't have to say yes to New York but think about it. We can make sure that you and Louis are never near each other if that's what you want. Whatever makes you feel comfortable. But please, please, just think about it?"

This is all sounding way too good to be true. I close my eyes and try to calm myself. I take a couple of steps and make my way toward my makeshift studio. It takes me until I'm halfway across the room before Daniel follows me. I push open the door to my inner sanctum exposing myself to him.

He passes me giving me a reassuring smile, then he stops. He stands there taking in every inner thought I have had these past two weeks. He steps forward and touches the work, the bright red paint catching his attention, the long strokes across the canvas. I guess this is where Louis and I differ in our melancholy. His art was dark, and you could tell he wasn't in the right headspace compared to his normal colorful artwork. But mine, it's the opposite containing bright vibrant colors swirling across the canvas, but it's the images that show what's really going on, the pushing and pulling of hands, the snarl of an ugly face, the tears falling from a fragile girl huddled in a corner.

"Emily, these are..." Daniel stands in awe, his head moving from side to side taking it all in. He pulls out his cell. "May I?" he asks.

I nod my head, and he starts taking pictures, documenting every single canvas.

"These are spectacular." His fingers run over one canvas, the only one that I allowed myself to paint that wasn't dark or disturbed. It's an image of a couple embracing, making love with every twist and turn of the couple in their lovemaking on show. He stares at this one the longest, and I wonder what he's thinking.

"He'd love this." Daniel taps the image.

The words stumble out of my mouth before my brain has time to compute what they are saying, "Take it."

Daniel turns and looks at me, surprised. "You're giving me

this?" he asks for clarity. I move forward and pick it up, handing the artwork to him.

"Give it to him. If it helps him move on." I don't want Louis to fall back into the hole that he has only just climbed out. If this painting can help him move on, start afresh, then he needs it more than I do.

"He'll love it," Daniel tells me taking the canvas from my hands.

I shrug.

"You'll think about my request?"

"I don't know."

"The event is in a month's time." My chest tightens, that's not long. I don't know if I can produce enough before then. "You know where I live, I'm not far. If you want to do this, I can help you. Anything you need, I can help."

I give him a small smile. "I'll think about it."

This makes Daniel smile, popping that dimple of his. He leans in and kisses my cheek. "Don't be a stranger. No matter what your answer is, no matter your relationship with Louis, know we're friends. Okay?"

I'm a little taken aback by his sentiment. "Thank you." I reach out and hug him. Strong arms envelop me, his hard chest presses against mine, and something inside of me breaks, but I have to try to push it back in.

The tears, the fears, the shock.

"Hey." Daniel looks down at me, shaking in his arms. "Emily, are you okay?"

I shake my head, the tears fall further down my cheeks, soaking my T-shirt.

Daniel pulls me in closer. "Let it out. You're safe now. Just let it out."

He holds me until there's nothing left inside of me.

39

LOUIS

I've let myself sink back into that dark place again with my trusty bottle of tequila by my side. The demonic colors are back against the white canvas. I haven't heard from *her* in weeks. I've checked her social media, and the last images are of her running through the lavender fields. An image that I now have as my screen saver. I'm such a fucking stalker.

Daniel's seeing Emily today, and my nerves are a jumbled mess. I've told the staff that they can have holidays as I won't be requiring any help. Honestly, I want to be left alone. I want to wallow in my misery, and as much as misery loves company, I do not.

"Wow! I love the new direction."

That voice.

A voice that months ago, I'd have longed to hear again, but now, now it's like fingernails running down a damn chalkboard. The sound makes my stomach turn, the tequila curdling and wanting to make a comeback.

"What the fuck do you want?" I seethe. Her motherfucking boy-toy tried to rape my girl, and I detest Elisabeth for it. I hate her for ruining my life and for creating the monster that is Yves.

"Wow! That's not how you should greet your wife," she purrs.

Elisabeth is dressed in skin-tight jeans making her legs look miles long, her generous chest on display with the deep V of her cream top showing off her cleavage. Ordinarily, my dick would twitch at the sight of her, but now, there's nothing.

"Ex-wife," I remind her, but she just waves her hands in the air as if it means nothing.

"I like this new direction you've taken, Louis. It's so dramatic." Elisabeth smiles.

"I am going to count to three, and if you're not gone from my property, I'm going to have security escort you the fuck out." She lets out a heavy sigh, but she doesn't move, which enrages me even more.

"Calm down, Louis." She gives me her 'fuck me' eyes, and no shit, I want to hurl. "I hear Yves has been a naughty boy," Elisabeth purrs.

"He tried to rape my girlfriend." She bristles at the word *girlfriend*, and I think that's what she has a problem with, not the fact that her boy-toy is a potential rapist.

"Girlfriend? That woman was your girlfriend?" Her lip snarls.

My eyes narrow on her. Never in my life have I ever wanted to harm a woman more than I do at this moment.

"I'd even go as far as to say she's the one." That comment hits its mark because she recoils.

"Is your so-called girlfriend going to be pressing charges?"

Ah, so that's what she's worried about. Her golden goose may be losing his shine.

"Yes," I say confidently, even though I know she isn't.

Elisabeth straightens herself. "It's her word against his," she tells me.

"There were witnesses. Plus, there's a video of him putting something in her drink." Usually, Elisabeth is hard to read, but

I can tell by the small gasp that leaves her mouth that the comment has surprised her.

"Is this true?"

I nod my head. "Your little boy-toy is going to be going away for a very long time, especially if I have anything to do with it."

Elisabeth's nostrils flair at my comment. "Don't you think people are going to wonder if this little story is about you seeking revenge on the man who stole your wife?"

"I don't care, and there's proof. I wasn't the only one who saw it. He won't get away with it. He attacked her in Monaco as well." I've surprised her again with that little tidbit of information, but somehow she stays composed, and I give her credit for that.

"We're on the verge of a multimillion-dollar contract, Louis. It's something I have been curating for months. I'm not going to let some whore take it away from me."

I rise to my full height, my face is red with anger, and my body rigid with rage.

"He tried to rape her, Elisabeth. Rape. Her. Do you understand what that means, or have you lost all of your moral compasses?"

Elisabeth doesn't back down. "How much will it cost to make this all go away, Louis? Name your price? Ten million? Fifty million? One hundred million?"

"What? You think you can buy me?"

"Maybe not you, but I bet I could buy Emily." Just hearing Emily's name from her lips makes me splinter inside. I take a couple of steps toward her, and I watch as fear quickly wipes that smug smile from her face.

"You fucking go near Emily, and I'll make your life a pure living hell. Do you hear me?" She doesn't flinch, I don't think I'm getting through. "I mean it! It will become my life's mission to make sure that Yves is behind bars, and your career is in ruins. Furthermore, I will make sure you're shunned from the art community, and I'll ensure everyone knows how much of a piece of shit you and your boy-toy asshole boyfriend are."

Elisabeth huffs. "You don't scare me, Louis Marchant. You are a washed-up has-been artist. Maybe in your tiny little mind you think you're still someone, but in reality, no one could give a shit about you, especially when you're up against Yves. I made him. He has become even bigger than you ever could be. You never had the drive to be the richest, biggest, art superstar in the world. No. You wanted to have a family, the white picket fence, the mediocrity of suburban life. I wasn't made for that, Louis. You were not made for that. You could have been a master, but you didn't have the balls. Unlike Yves, he's hungry. Hungry for it all."

"Get the fuck out of my house, Elisabeth, before I do something I know I'm going to regret."

She grins widely, knowing she's getting to me. "You have twenty-four hours to accept, Louis. Otherwise, I'll take matters into my own hands." And with those parting words, she walks out of my studio.

Fuck! I want to scream. I want to trash everything. I want to hurt someone.

I grab the bottle of tequila and bring it to my lips, but stop.

What the hell am I doing? I'm not going to let that bitch destroy my life again. Elisabeth has just proved to me that she's nothing but a gold digger. The fact she's okay that her boyfriend nearly raping someone confirms it all.

There's only one person who can help me take down Elisabeth, and I just pray that he will.

"LOUIS," Victor greets me warmly.

"It's so good to see you, old man." I pat him on the back, making him chuckle.

"I'm not that old." He waves his arms around. "Come in, come in... it's been ages seen we've seen you."

"Is Eloise here?"

"I heard my name." Eloise enters the foyer, and my chest tightens because I know this is Emily's mother. I see the resemblance, they could almost be twins they look so similar. She pulls me into her arms and kisses my cheeks. "To what do we owe the pleasure of your company?"

"I need your help." They glance at each other. "I'm going to need you to listen to me first, then I'll answer your questions when I'm finished. Do you trust me?"

They both nod their heads.

"Come, we'll sit in the garden, maybe a bottle of wine is needed for this chat," Eloise states.

We all take a seat outside on the terrace, Victor pours the glasses of wine, then he sits back in his chair. "Please start."

Taking a large sip of the wine, I'm hoping it will give me the courage to tell them the whole story. I begin with Elisabeth and Yves, about the darkness I had lived in, how my art had taken on a more somber feel, and about the New York show. Then I begin to tell them about Emily, about how she took me from the darkness and brought me back into the light, that she showed me how to appreciate color again.

Eloise pats my hand, giving me a warm smile as I talk about Emily—if only she knew. I tell them about the party in Monaco, and Victor's face blanches, then I hear his breathing increase. I continue to talk about what happened in Paris. I see he's now fuming beside me, and that he too wants to stand up and destroy something.

"Oh my," Eloise gasps.

I tell her that Emily was assaulted previously. That this attack has brought on flashbacks, and she ran away back to London the minute she knew what had happened to her. Emily blames me, but I don't blame her for leaving me and the country because I brought Yves into her life.

Eloise squeezes my hand. "This isn't your fault," she tells me.

I give her a weak smile, then continue to tell them that Elisabeth came to see me, offering to buy me off, so Emily won't press charges.

These words set Victor off as he jumps off his chair and starts pacing around the garden.

"There was always something about Elisabeth that I couldn't put my finger on," Eloise adds.

"Then why did you let her..." My eyes look up at Eloise as I trail off. I don't understand how she's okay with Victor having girlfriends, sharing the man she loves with others.

"Not everyone is made for a monogamous life, Louis." She pats my hand. "I don't expect you to understand, but Victor and I have an agreement. We're both artists, we both follow where the creativeness takes us, sometimes different people bring out different things in each of us. Doesn't mean I don't love him any less." She looks up adoringly at Victor. "He just can't always give me what I want and vice versa."

I guess if that's what makes them happy, then who am I to judge their lifestyle.

"I wish I'd never introduced the two of you," Victor adds, the strain of the conversation weighing heavily on his shoulders. "Elisabeth pretended with me. There were glimpses of something, but I thought it was the age difference. Because when I saw her with you, she was different, not as guarded, freer, and I thought maybe you were the better fit. And you were for many years but..."

Yeah, he doesn't need to say any more.

"I never knew her. Not really. I think you're right... she masks the real person behind whatever you want her to be.

She's cunning, conniving, and manipulative. The blinders are off now, and I see the true person behind the mask she wears."

"I'm sorry you had to learn it the hard way, sweetheart." Eloise smiles at me.

"Whatever you need from me, whatever contacts you require to put a stop to these two, I'll help you," Victor tells me.

"Thank you." He has said exactly the words I was hoping for.

"Can I see a photo of her?" Eloise asks.

My stomach sinks. *Should I?* It will be strange if I don't show them. It's been over twenty years since she saw her daughter. Would she even recognize her?

I hand over my cell to Eloise, she pulls out her glasses and stares at the image for quite a while. It's the picture of the two of us in the sunflower field after our bike ride where she's carefree and happy.

"Oh my God." Eloise clutches her chest. She looks up at me, but her eyes are wide as saucers.

She knows I have no choice but to say something.

"Yes, Eloise. She's your daughter."

40

EMILY

It's Saturday night, and the girls have come over for girls' night and to check up on me.

"So, I heard Daniel came over." Ava fishes for information as she pours herself a wine.

My eyes narrow. "How would you know that?" I question her.

"Daniel told me," she says quickly, not making any eye contact.

"And why would he tell you that? It's not like you're friends or anything. Are you?"

Ava's cheeks turn a little pink. "We've spoken a couple of times since we got back. Basically, he's been worried about you. He just wanted to check in while giving you some space."

"I never got a message from him?" Georgia smirks.

"Me either," Rosie adds.

Ava becomes flustered and gulps down her glass of wine quickly then pours herself another.

"Is something happening between the two of you?"

"What? No," Ava answers way too quickly.

"Do you want something to happen?"

Ava doesn't look at us, and we all smirk.

"He's pretty hot," Georgia adds.

"His accent is delicious," Rosie chimes in.

"Ugh, you guys." Ava rolls her eyes, which makes us burst out laughing.

I've needed this. I think this is the first time in weeks that I have truly laughed and meant it.

"So, I have a crush on him, okay?" she confesses. Ava never pursues a guy, especially one she has a crush on, so her pursuing Daniel is out of character for her.

"Ava has a cru-ush," Rosie sing-songs as she teases Ava, which makes us all fall into fits of laughter again.

"I know. What the hell is wrong with me?" Ava complains.

"He's a sweetheart. And that dimple…" I add, then sigh.

The girls are a little shocked at first at my comment then burst out laughing again.

"I'm glad me having a crush is so amusing to you all." Ava pours herself another glass of wine.

"You were flirting with him in France. Did anything happen?" Georgia asks.

"I wish. He rebuffed all my advances." Ava pouts.

"You made advances on the guy?"

Ava pokes out her tongue.

"Is he the first guy that's ever said no to you?" Rosie teases.

"Fuck you, guys." She laughs. "But yes, he is." She folds her arms in front of her, pretending to scowl at us all like we have highly offended her.

"Aw… there, there, Ava. Welcome to the real world." Rosie pats her on the head.

"So, what did Daniel want?" Georgia asks, changing the subject.

"Oh. Um… yeah, about that…" They all look at me with

expectant eyes. "He wants me to join Louis in New York to showcase my art."

The girls are all a little shocked, but once that information settles, they all jump up to congratulate me by jumping on me. It takes me a while to get them off, but the smile on my face is wide.

"Apparently, Louis asked Daniel about it before..." I don't need to finish that sentence.

"And what do you think?" Georgia asks.

"I don't know." I shrug. "I showed Daniel the art I have been working on in the studio, and he loved it. He actually took a painting I did of Louis and me to give to him."

"Aw, that's nice of you," Rosie adds.

I shrug again not wanting to discuss that part of my life.

"I think you should do it," Ava adds.

"That's because it gives you an excuse to stay in touch with Daniel," Georgia teases.

"Well, of course, but also because I think you deserve this, Emmy. You're so ridiculously talented, and you haven't had many, if any, breaks over the years. And if anyone deserves this, you do," Ava tells me.

"But I'm only getting it because I slept with Louis."

"What? No, you're not. Do you seriously think Louis or Daniel would do you this sort of favor simply because they know you?" Rosie asks.

I don't know. *Maybe.* Probably not.

"Why not take a chance?" Ava adds.

"We love you, babe, and we know what happened over the past couple of weeks has been hard on you, but in all this bad, maybe something good can come from it." Georgia raises her eyebrows at me.

Tears well in my eyes, which brings my girls closer to me, and we all hug.

"I want to take a chance, but I'm scared, guys."

"You have us," Rosie reassures.

"We'll help you get to where you need to be. If that means we have to get you coffee so you can work all night, or buy you paints, we'll do it," Ava tells me, and her words make me cry.

Far out! I am so lucky to have these girls right beside me.

"I'm sorry, guys. So sorry that I said those horrible things to you all. That wasn't me, it was the situation, but it's still no excuse. So, again, I am sorry."

"Hey. No. Don't think like that. What happened was disgusting, and you were in shock." Rosie lifts my chin to look at her.

"But it wasn't your fault, and I took it out on you all." Tears stream down my face as they do on my friends' faces.

"You needed to blame someone to make sense of it all. We understand, and we're happy to take your angry outbursts as long as it helps you. We all love you, and we knew you were hurting. We're all just so worried about you," Georgia tells me.

"I'm sorry. I didn't mean to scare you all," I tell them.

"You were processing, we understand that. You take all the time you need. We'll always be here for you." Ava squeezes my hand.

"I love you guys."

"We love you, too."

"One day at a time... that's the only way for me to move forward," I tell them.

"Then we'll be there every step of the way. One day at a time if that's what it takes, right beside you." Rosie hugs me.

Fuck, I'm lucky.

"But I do have a question?" Ava asks. "What about Louis?"

My stomach sinks.

"Yeah, every day he sends you sunflowers," Rosie reminds me.

I let out a heavy sigh. "I am going to work on myself, and I'm going to focus on my art."

"But he's going to be in New York?" Georgia adds.

"Fingers crossed I have my shit together by then, and that he still wants me."

My girlfriends all give me sympathetic smiles.

I need to become a stronger, better version of myself because if there's one thing I'm sure of, Louis deserves a woman that has her shit together.

41

LOUIS
BREAKING NEWS

Yves Blanc and Elisabeth Bernard are embroiled in a multimillion-dollar art charity scandal. Their non-profit charity has been embezzling millions of dollars to support their lavish lifestyle. This information came to light as Yves is embroiled in a sexual assault case. Video footage has been obtained of him putting a date rape drug into a non-identified woman's drink, then he's seen walking the unconscious woman from the club to his car, and then through the front gate of his apartment complex.

Now that this information has come to light, more women have come forward recounting their tales of sexual assault via Blanc.

With the mounting evidence against Blanc and Bernard, many people in the art industry have distanced themselves from the two of them, and they have lost many of their multimillion-dollar endorsements.

It also appears that Blanc and Bernard have parted ways, with Bernard putting out a press release exclaiming her shock over the accusations about her partner. That she no longer feels safe around him, which is evident in the video footage that was shown of Blanc screaming at a cowering Bernard outside their Paris apartment a few nights ago.

. . .

"Revenge is a dish served cold." Daniel laughs as he reads out the latest report about Yves and Elisabeth.

"They got what they deserved." Not that I like seeing the demise of people, but they deserved it, so I smile.

"Everything she has is gone. All her assets have been seized. Everything. She's going to have to declare bankruptcy and start again," Daniel informs me. "Apparently, she's in Moscow. Currently, she's the guest of some film producer. A woman like her will always find a way..." Daniel trails off.

"It's good news that all these women are coming forward to tell their stories of his abuse." My blood boils reading about what he's done, including ex-employees who he's terrorized. I hated the fact that I was so blind to it and had no idea about any of his escapades.

"Have you heard from Emily?" I ask Daniel.

"Actually... hold on." My heart begins to thump. What does he have planned?

Daniel walks back in with a canvas in his hand. "Emily gave this to me weeks ago, but I wanted to wait." He turns it around, and I'm blown away. Instantly, I realize it's us making love. "She thought you should have it. This was painted when she wasn't in a great place. Before she said yes to New York."

I have shipped all of my paintings to New York, and I fly out in the coming days. I haven't spoken to Emily since that fateful night months ago because I know she needs time. If she hadn't said yes to New York, I'd have gone to find her, made her see me, have her tell me face to face that she doesn't want anything to do with me anymore. I would respect her wishes, of course, no matter what she wants, but if she rejected me, then my heart would be broken, and I'd understand. After everything Emily's been through, I have no choice but to understand.

I stare at the painting, the colors, the imagery. What was she thinking when she painted this? Did she remember the good times we shared? Does she remember my feelings for her?

"Her other stuff is good," Daniel tells me. "The gallery is so excited to have you both. The buzz surrounding your comeback and this debut artist's work is intensifying."

I want to be excited about making my comeback, but in all honesty, I just want to see Emily again.

"Is she... I mean how is she doing?" I hate the fact my brother has seen Emily multiple times. I hate that she's okay with him and not me, but I have to accept her reasons and decisions.

"She's turned a corner, especially now Yves is in custody, and that the world knows what he's done. A great weight has been lifted off her back."

I nod because I'm happy for her. I just wish the same weight I have could disappear so easily.

"She needed the time, Louis. She had to rebuild herself again."

I nod while staring at the painting. I wish Emily would have let me help her rebuild. I'd have been there for her, seen her through those excruciatingly tough times I know she would have been experiencing.

"She's excited about New York."

Hope. His words give me hope that there's a portion of excitement there at seeing me again. Maybe?

"The girls are all coming, too. They have been planning... I don't know... some kind of *Sex and the City* meets *Gossip Girl* tour. They lost me somewhere between the mention of the two television shows."

I'm glad she'll have her friends there with her to share in this experience.

"I'm glad for her," I tell Daniel. "I just hope she's ready to see me."

"It will all work out, brother. I promise you." He slaps me on the back and leaves me to stare at the painting in front of me.

I can't help but smile at the image and the memories it brings back to me.

42

EMILY
NEW YORK

My friends and I flew in a couple of days before the event to have girl time in the Big Apple. We've explored everywhere. We've done a photoshoot in Times Square, and we sailed along the Hudson past the Statue of Liberty. We checked out the sex museum and giggled like teenagers at all the penises. We re-enacted *Sex and the City* by sipping cosmopolitans at some hipster bar. We ate lunch on the stairs at the Metropolitan Museum of Art as if we were some cool kids on the set of *Gossip Girl*, all while wearing our headbands like Blair. We took a carriage ride around Central Park, which reminded me of dickface and his American Barbie. I made sure I used the hashtags #soulsisters #betterthanbarbie #britsdoitbetter. It might have been juvenile, but I totally felt so much better.

I left the girls shopping on Fifth Avenue because I don't have any money to spend, not until I sell some of my paintings. I made my way back to the Met to lose myself in the art. Walking past the great masters is humbling because I can't believe that my art is hanging in a gallery just like this. Okay, maybe not like this specifically, but it's in a very hipster part of

Brooklyn. The space is nice, not as grand as this stone and marble in front of me, but anyway, it's still awesome, and it's a dream I never thought would happen for me.

I'm thankful my girls could come with me on this trip. They all lead such busy, hectic lifestyles. Rosie works as a producer for a reality television show. Ava works in communications for a high-end boutique, and Georgia works in PR for a top football team. So, the fact they took time out of their busy lives to be with me during this time speaks volumes of what kind of friends they are.

And for that, I'll always be grateful to them.

I'VE LEFT the girls at a bar in Brooklyn near the gallery as I have to do my first walk through to see if the art is hung the way I expect to show it off to its full potential. I knock on the glass door, but no one answers, so I push on it, and it opens.

I walk into the white space—one wall is a giant window overlooking the street. There are floor-to-ceiling white walls that I can see are showcasing Louis Marchant originals. The first couple of paintings are some of his older work before his split with Elisabeth. The colors and vibrancy are all there and depicting that phase of his work. I walk past another wall, and you can see the art change significantly. These pieces were done during his darker period. The blacks, the grays, the angry reds that slash across the canvas represent his feelings well during that period of time. What surprises me is he has even left the slashes in the ones he had ripped in a drunken rage.

Then, I see the sunshine lips and that make me smile. These lips, he told me he painted for me after our first kiss, and they are the same ones that moved him back into using colors.

I stare at them, my hand touching my lips, remembering

what it felt like to have his lips against mine. My heart aches. I miss him.

Not going to lie, I've stalked his social media pages. Granted his images have changed since I was there—there are no gratuitous shirtless pictures, which is good to see. He has even deleted the ones I took of him and posted. He's taken more images of his art, his studio, the surrounding villages for inspirational ideas. I'm really proud of him doing something I know he hates. Louis looks happy and healthy. Obviously, there has been no falling down a tequila-induced hole again.

For some reason, it feels a little like a punch to the gut because he appears as if he's gotten his life in order. Maybe he doesn't want me anymore? Maybe he just wasn't that into me? Maybe too much time apart has extinguished the burning flame between us?

Melancholy seeps into my veins as I continue along looking at every one of his paintings. I see the color start to come back gradually, the moody colors making way for more muted colorful tones.

Then as I look over at the next wall, they are dark again. I frown looking at the images in front of me now. There are a lot of bright red hearts with slices cut deep into them. Goosebumps race over my skin as I realize these are the work he did after I left.

Tears well in my eyes.

I've ripped his heart out.

I broke it in two.

The more I move along, the more heartbreak I see, and I can't hold back a sob as I realize how much I've hurt Louis by pushing him away. That while I was breaking, so was he. I clutch my shirt against my heart and let the tears slowly slide down my cheeks as I stare at the heart-breaking art—so many pieces of him falling apart.

"I didn't mean to make you cry." His voice startles me, so I turn around and see him for the first time in months. His blond hair has been cut. The five o'clock shadow has been shaved away. He's dressed in old-look designer jeans and a white dress shirt, and his sleeves are rolled up his tanned arms. He smells like a combination of the earth and sea. He takes a couple of steps toward me, his large palm reaches out as he wipes away the tears falling down my cheeks with his thumb.

"I never meant to hurt you, Louis."

He gives me a sad smile. "I never meant to hurt you either." Louis' palm cups my cheek, his warmth seeping through my skin. We stare at each other for what feels like an eternity until his hands fall away from my face, and the loss is felt down to my very core.

"Your paintings are incredible." I'm not sure what else to say right at this moment.

"Thank you," he answers.

Silence falls between us again, but then he holds out his hand. "Let me show you the rest." My heart is thumping uncontrollably in my chest, but I reach out and link my fingers with his, anchoring him to me. "As you can see... I went a little dark here." He gives me a timid smile but continues, "However things seemed to turn around." I notice the colors have come back only not as bright as they once were, but they're most definitely back. "These are where I got closure."

Oh no. Does he mean this is the end of us?

That he got closure from being a couple?

"And the rest... well, that's to be determined," he says as we reach the end of his section.

"You must feel so proud finishing your exhibition and having so many wonderful pieces on display."

"I am. I never thought I'd be here again, not after everything I've done this year." He has come such a long way since I first met him. "But I couldn't have done it without a no-nonsense calls-me-out-on-my-bullshit, assistant."

My head turns up to look at him. There's a wide smile across his face as he looks down at me. It makes my heart skip a beat and my stomach flutter with so many butterflies.

Maybe I'm not too late?

Maybe there's a chance for us?

"Come... I want to be the first person to see your reaction at your first exhibition." Louis pulls me further into the gallery, and I pause when I see my paintings, pulling Louis back to me. Tears form in my eyes again as my hand rises to my mouth in awe.

There, in all their glory, are my innermost thoughts and feelings, my own vulnerabilities staring right back at me.

"They are amazing, Emily." Louis walks forward, and I follow. "Even though they are about a horrific time, they are still brilliant." The painting of hands ripping at the invisible girl catches his attention.

"I had to paint it out of me," I whisper.

"I know. I understand. That's what I did." Louis turns to look back at me. "But I don't ever want to go back to the darkness, Emily."

"I don't either," I confess.

Silence hangs between us again.

"I also don't want to be alone."

I look up at him, but he's staring at my paintings. I reach out and touch his arm pulling his attention back to me. "I'm sorry, Louis."

He nods. "I understand. I wouldn't want to be with me either after everything that has happened to you."

"You don't think I want to be with you?" My stomach somersaults, twists, then does a cartwheel. "You think I haven't missed you?" His confused look is all I need to continue, "It killed me to leave you." I thump my chest, hard. "It killed me that a monster could take me back to a place I never thought I'd return to. I hate that he fucked us up. But what I hate more is..."

I suck in a deep breath, "... that I let you go. That I pushed you away."

Louis' eyes search my face as if he doesn't quite believe what I'm saying.

"I thought..." He takes a step toward me. "I thought you despised me?"

I shake my head. "Oh, God, no, but I did hate myself. I retreated inside, it was all I knew how to do. My guard came up. I shut you out trying to protect myself."

Louis steps closer, his hands coming out and grabbing my face. "You were in shock. I understand."

Tears flow freely down my cheeks when I say, "I needed you, Louis, but in the same breath, I couldn't be near you. I was broken. I needed to repair myself. I wanted to make sure I was whole again before..." I let the unfinished words hang between us.

"Before?" He moves closer, our bodies almost touching, hope touching his eyes.

"Before..." Those blue eyes intensify as they train in on me. "Before I gave myself to someone."

"And would that someone be... I don't know... someone like a sexy, French artist? Perhaps?"

Breaking the tension between us, I laugh at his words. "Maybe." Heat races over my body when his hands grip my face.

"Someone who has a big dick and knows how to use it."

My eyes widen, and a smile crosses my face. "It's been a while, I'm not sure if I remember the size exactly."

"I can easily remind you. Just say the word." He winks.

"Maybe you could just kiss me first and see how that goes."

"Sounds like a plan." Louis bends down taking my lips against his in a soft, slow kiss. The instant our lips touch, my body relaxes, and I know I'm home. This is where I'm supposed to be with this man who's right in front of me. My hands move and wrap around his waist pulling him against me intensifying our kiss.

"I've missed you so fucking much, Emily," Louis says against my lips.

"Me, too," I add.

Eventually, the kiss ends, and we reluctantly pull apart.

Louis' forehead rests against mine. "I love you, Emily Chapman."

"I love you, too, Louis."

"Never push me away again," he tells me. "I want a future with you, Emily. You and me creating art together. Maybe creating more later down the road."

"I want that, Louis. I want it all with you." I throw my arms around his neck and kiss him again.

"Can we go back to my hotel room now? I need to show you just how big my dick is."

"Lead the way."

43

EMILY

I'm so sore from last night. I texted the girls to let them know I was going home with Louis, much to their delight. Of course, as soon as we made it into the hotel room, Louis had me out of my clothes and in his bed. As frantic as we both were at the beginning, as soon as we were naked, he slowed down and made love to me all night and then again in the morning.

Waking up to Louis beside me makes the world feel right again. All the shit I went through to get to this moment made me appreciate what's right in front of me.

We spent the night talking about our future together. He asked me to move in with him, and he suggested that could either be in London or France or both, wherever I wanted us to be as long as we were together. He wants us to have our own studio spaces, spending our days painting, making love and drinking wine, in that order. If I don't want to spend my days painting, he told me he'd introduce me to people I could speak to about art curation at museums. I guess my future all revolves around what happens tonight if the exhibition is a success or not. Hopefully, the critics like it, but I'm a nervous wreck.

"You're going to be fine." Louis pulls me toward him. He's just stepped out of the shower, his warm body wraps around me perfectly, his towel slung lowly against his trim hips.

"Easy for you to say, Mr. International Bad Boy Artist."

He laughs. "Look, everyone is going to have an opinion. Art is subjective. Some people get it, some people don't. If they don't like it, then it wasn't for them, and if they do, then great you've found your people."

I look up at him and smile. "Seriously, how did I get so lucky?" I wrap my arms around his neck.

"You hooked me coming out of my pool nearly naked in your innocently white underwear."

A laugh bubbles up and out of my lips. "I was *not* trying to seduce you."

"I beg to differ. It worked. I was seduced."

"Um... if I remember correctly, you yelled at me. You were *so not* seduced," I tell him.

"My dick was hard as a rock, and I was trying very hard not to think about fucking you right then and there." God, he's an asshole, but he's all mine. "Come... you need to get ready. You don't want to be late for your debut." He gives me a heated kiss then pushes me toward my clothes.

I guess I have an art exhibition to open.

"Breathe, Emily. It's going to be okay," Louis instructs.

"But look at all the paparazzi out there." The entrance is swamped with cameras, people all yelling, and I'm a nervous wreck.

"Just hold my hand and follow me."

I don't think I'm ready.

Surely, we can just head back to the hotel room and fuck again.

I like that, that's fun.

This is not!

As if reading my mind, Louis nuzzles my neck. "You look sensational." His lips leave tiny trails of warmth against my goose-pimpled skin.

The girls chose my dress from the many styles submitted to me at Louis' request. We drank champagne, and I tried on every single designer dress that was sent for me to wear this evening. It was like a competition between the designers as to what I'd wear and with what shoes and accessories.

In the end, I settled on a beautiful Versace emerald green cocktail dress. My strawberry blonde hair was pulled up in a messy bun, and the makeup artist did an all-natural look with bright red lipstick, and of course, sky-high Louboutin shoes.

"You ready?" Louis bites my shoulder. "You look stunning... and those shoes... they're staying on later when I fuck you into the middle of next week."

"Y-Yes." How to get a girl all sorts of turned-on right before she steps out into a paparazzi nightmare, Louis knows all the tricks.

He grins widely then opens the door. The flashes go off, and everyone is screaming for Louis, asking him questions about Elisabeth and Yves.

Louis expertly navigates us through the paparazzi, totally ignoring them, then he twirls me around and kisses me. It's not a Sunday-at-church kind of kiss, it's a turn- the-thermostat-up-to-one-hundred kind of kiss. The flashes go crazy getting their image of us. I'm a little shell-shocked, but Louis calmly walks us inside the gallery.

"What was that?" I tug on his arm.

"What?"

"Um, that kiss... in front of those vultures."

Louis smirks and raises his brows up and down. "I'd rather

them write about our love than dwelling on Yves and Elisabeth's drama."

"I hate it when you're right."

"Better start getting used to it because forever is a damn long time." He smirks again, kisses me once more for good measure, then starts introducing me to all the people standing around wanting to talk to us. Whoops, I mean *him*.

"Congratulations," my girlfriends all say in unison while pulling me into a huge embrace.

"You look happy," Rosie teases.

"I am." I smile.

"So, Louis and you... are back on again?" Ava asks.

"Yeah. He just declared 'together forever.'"

The girls all squeal with delight.

"He's asked me to move in with him after all this is finished."

"So, you're moving to France?" Georgia asks.

I shrug. "He said he'd move wherever I choose."

"Don't leave us," Ava pleads.

"Stay in London." Rosie flutters her eyelids.

"France isn't really that far," Georgia adds.

"Let's worry about that later. Tonight, we need to celebrate all my paintings selling out," I joke.

The girls squeal again which makes me laugh.

I'm on the biggest high I think I have ever been on.

Nothing could ruin this night.

I take it back.

Something can most definitely can ruin my night.

Toby is here with a big bouquet of red roses, and he's dressed in a suit. When he sees me, he smiles and waves. I excuse myself from the guests I'm talking to and make my way over to him.

"What are you doing here?" I place my hand on my hip and push it out to the side.

"I've come to celebrate your night." Toby goes to lean in and kisses me, but I take a step back. He frowns as he hands over the bouquet of flowers.

"Where's your American *friend*?" I can't help but enunciate the word, it's not that I care, but I'm curious.

"We broke up. She was sleeping with someone else at work, one of the executive bosses." I raise my eyebrow in surprise, but deep down I'm screaming 'loser.'

"So, you thought you would try your luck with me again?"

"I was a fool, Emmy. You were right. You were the best thing to ever happen to me. And now... now you're this huge artist. Everyone loves you."

"So, I'm desirable? Dateable? Maybe even marriage material now that I'm a somebody?"

"Emmy, don't be like that." Toby takes a step toward me, but as he does, I feel arms wrap around me and warmth against my neck.

Toby's eyes widen at whoever is behind me. *Who am I kidding? I know exactly who's there. Louis.*

"Bonsoir, I'm Louis Marchant, Emily's partner. And you are?" He holds out his hand to Toby.

"I'm Toby, an old friend from London wanting to say congratulations." Louis knows exactly who he is, and I know it. They shake hands briskly.

"That's nice. Can you believe she sold out of all her paintings? That's over a million dollars in sales in only a few hours."

What did Louis just say? No! Really?

I'll ask if he's serious once he's finished marking his territory, which I'm more than happy to allow.

"That's truly incredible, Emily. I always knew you would do something with your art," Toby adds.

"That's strange because she said she hadn't painted anything in the last five years because her last partner hated it. How bad is that? To stifle such a creative genius!" Louis stares at him.

Toby stays quiet.

"I guess it just takes the right man, mon coeur." Louis nuzzles into me again, and I love the feeling.

"Yeah, I guess it does."

I try to hide my laughter but just smile.

"Well, I should let you get back to your party. I just wanted to say hi and congratulations. You look good, Emmy."

I give Toby a smile, but that's it. Plus, Louis has a tight hold on me, and I know he's not going to let go anytime soon. So, even though I wouldn't want to hug Toby goodbye, I can't even if I wanted to.

"Stay in touch," Toby adds.

"She won't. She'll be really busy… with me," Louis replies.

Toby frowns and rushes away. I turn in Louis' arms and look up at him. He has the biggest smirk on his face, raises an eyebrow, and asks, "Too much?"

"Never."

"Good because what I really wanted to do was punch him in the face, but I didn't think that would be appropriate tonight."

"I love you, Louis Marchant."

"I love you, too, Emily Chapman."

44

LOUIS

TWO MONTHS LATER

Emily and I have been living in London for the past couple of months since coming back from New York. Daniel has let us stay with him while we settled on a new townhouse. Emily has turned into the new 'it' artist. Actually, we're the 'it' couple of the art scene.

The demands for more shows around the world has been overwhelming, plus the media attention surrounding us and our love story is kind of intense. Daniel's received a ridiculous amount of branding deals for us, for companies that have nothing to do with art but who want us because we look good together.

We haven't been so keen, but the money they are offering is becoming irresistible. So far, we have stayed strong to our ideals but not sure how long it's going to last.

Emily thinks if we take all these deals, we could donate the money to good causes, and I like that idea. We're making more than we need from our art, so we might as well try to make a difference in the world. That's the huge difference between Elisabeth and Emily. Emily wants to do good with the money while Elisabeth just wanted it all for herself.

Speaking of Elisabeth, apparently, she's disappeared off the radar, and no one knows where she is. Her last post on social media was about her staying in Russia with friends, and that's the last we've heard from her. I don't wish her harm, so I hope wherever she is, she's okay.

Yves, well, he's skipped town. He left France and is on the run. To say I wasn't surprised was an understatement. I knew when they let him out on bail he'd bolt, and that's exactly what he did. I just hope wherever he is, he's rotting in some cesspit of hell. I'm not going to dwell on that scumbag because Emily and I are going strong.

I just hope today goes well.

Daniel and I told Emily that we had found her mother while we had everyone over for dinner one night. I thought if we told her in front of her friends that they could help her work through her feelings on the issue.

Emily surprised me yet again when she said she wanted to meet her and that she didn't care if she never wanted to see her mother again after her first visit. Emily told me she'd had enough time over the years not to focus on her mother, and that she needed to move on with her future, our future, and it didn't matter if that included her mother or not.

But I know Eloise wants a future with Emily. I've also told her that I already know her mother, and that fact really surprised her. I filled her in on how she's the wife of Victor, my mentor, which, of course, she remembered that Elisabeth was one of his mistresses. She got angry over that fact for a while that her mother was being cheated on, but then I explained the situation to her just like Eloise had to me. She didn't understand or like it, but as she said, it's her mother's life, and she can live it any way she wants.

"Do you think they're going to like me?" Emily asks me nervously as her hand is wrapped in mine while we drive to their home.

"I know they will."

She stares out the car window at the passing farms. "What happens if I get angry at her?"

"Then, you get angry. You're allowed to. She hasn't been in your life for years, well, most of it. You're allowed to ask questions. You're allowed to be mad and angry for all those lost years, but I know Eloise, and she's wonderful. Honestly, I think you're going to love her."

Emily nods and goes quiet again. "It's weird that you know them."

"Yeah, it is." I chuckle.

"I think fate had some kind of weird plan for us. That it may have been inevitable we would meet."

"I think you're right. That you would have found your mother, met her, fallen in love with her. They would probably have thrown a party and invited me, and I know as soon as I'd have stepped into that party and seen you for the first time, that would have been it for me."

Emily looks up and smiles at me. "You're very confident, Mr. International Artist."

"Sorry to break it to you, Miss International Artist, but have you seen me?"

She bursts out laughing, and it's great to watch her.

"You would be up on all this." I wave my hands over my body. "Plus, once you saw my dick... well, that would have been game over. You would have been begging me for another turn. Lucky for you my dick is always ready for beautiful women." Her eyes narrow at me. "I mean *a*... as in singular... beautiful woman. One named Emily, *my Emily*." She nods, giving me a playful smile. "What I'm saying is... I'd have fallen in love with you the moment I saw you."

She rests her hand against my arm. "Yeah, I would probably have fallen for you as well."

"That's because I'm your favorite artist."

Emily bursts out laughing.

Not long after, we arrive at Victor's home. I can feel the nervous tension emanating from Emily, and her hand is shaking in mine.

Victor and Eloise are already waiting for us at the front door. They both look equally as nervous until Eloise breaks away and runs toward Emily along the driveway with tears running down her face.

Eloise pulls Emily into her arms. "My baby girl." Emily is tentative for a couple of moments as Eloise hugs her so tight, but then Emily wraps her arms around her body and hugs Eloise back.

Eloise steps back and looks at Emily. "You're so beautiful." Emily smiles. "Come... we have much to talk about." She grabs Emily's hand and makes her way inside, quickly stopping to introduce her to Victor, then they disappear.

"I think that went well," Victor says.

"Yeah, surprisingly."

"Eloise has been a bundle of nerves all day."

"Same with Emily."

"Come on in, son."

THE DAY HAS GONE SO well. Eloise and Emily catch up on everything that has been going on in their lives. The similarities between them are crazy, and the wine seems to relax Emily.

"I have to ask... why did you never keep in touch?" Emily questions.

"Sweetie, is that what you think? I tried. I sent letters. I attempted to see you, but your father would never let me. Once I left, he cut me out of your lives, cut you all out of my life. I would secretly see you, though. I did all sorts of things to make sure you were doing okay. You looked so happy, I thought it was best not to interfere anymore, especially when your brother and sister told me they never wanted to see me again."

"Wait! What? They never told me that." Emily looks confused.

"I'm not really surprised... they were very close with your father. It was one afternoon... I think you were at a friend's house when I decided I'd take a chance and ignore your father's wishes and see you all. Your sister answered the door, but she wasn't happy at all to see me. She told me to go away, that you were all better off without me, and that you were happy. The words... they broke me, especially when I could see the anger and hate in her eyes. I knew the damage was done, and it was best for me to leave." Tears form in Eloise's eyes, and she blinks a few times to keep them under control. "But I attended your high school graduations. All of you, and then your university graduations."

"You did?"

"Yeah. Just from afar. We also went to New York to see your debut, too."

"You did what?" Emily's eyes widen.

"When Louis showed me the photo of the woman he loved, I knew straight away this was a picture of my baby. I knew it was you. I couldn't believe of all the people for you to fall in love with, it was Louis." Eloise reaches out and squeezes my hand. "The boy who feels like a son to me." I smile at her. "When he told us what Yves and Elisabeth had done, I told Victor I wasn't going to sit back and let these vile creatures try to destroy my child." A single tear falls down Emily's cheek. "So, Victor and I pulled every favor we had owing over the years to put those two away and get them out of the industry."

"You did that?" Emily asks.

"Of course, sweetie. I needed to make it all right. No one messes with my family."

Emily smiles. "We're sorry that the two of them got away,

but at least you're safe in knowing they won't be back in France," Victor adds.

"I had no idea, I thought you hated me. That you never wanted a family... that's what I was told all my life," Emily tells Eloise.

"No, sweetie, I wanted you more than anything."

"But they kept you away from me..." Emily becomes upset. "My own family."

"Emily, don't be mad. Your brother and sister were puppets for your father."

"I always felt like an outsider in my family. They were always close with Dad, but me, I was more like you than they were, and I think I reminded him of you, so he was always distant with me."

Eloise holds out her hand to Emily, who takes it. "I'm so sorry, sweetie, that I didn't fight harder, but I thought I was doing the right thing at the time. Had I known, I'd have done more," Eloise tells her.

Emily shakes her head. "I'm sorry I didn't come find you sooner. I kept you alive in my mind by keeping up my French, by doing art, but I had to do it all in secret because we were not allowed any of those things growing up, but for some reason, I had to. I needed to. It was an ingrained part of me."

Eloise looks at Emily sadly.

"I'm glad I am here now. Hopefully, we can have the type of relationship we should have always had."

"Yes. I'd love that." Eloise smiles through her tears.

"This is a cause for celebration," Victor announces. "We need champagne and lots of it. Where's chef? He needs to cook up something fantastic. I have gained a daughter today..." he claps me on the shoulder, "... and a son. Two of the hottest artists in the world at the moment."

45

LOUIS
SIX MONTHS LATER

"Can you believe we have an exhibition at the Centre Pompidou here in Paris?" Emily smiles widely.

"It's a dream, mon coeur."

This is our first substantial show together, something we have been working on day and night for months.

Each of us were locked away in our studio, lost in our own little world. Then, when we were hungry, we made our way to the kitchen where Gabriel had a delectable feast waiting for us. We sat and ate, both splattered in paint. We would talk about where we were with our paintings, discussing ideas.

This is what I have always wanted, what I now have with Emily. The perfect balance between love and art. She's brought me back to life, taught me to appreciate what I have and to take a moment to enjoy it.

And we certainly *enjoy* those moments.

Actually, we have moments *all* over the place.

We've had moments in the sunflower fields, in the pool, all over the house, and I wouldn't change a thing.

All the bullshit we have gone through to get to this point in our lives has made us stronger, has stripped both of us to the core, and shown us what's important in our life. That's why we named our latest exhibition 'Love in Color' because that sums us both up—each of us didn't realize how much we both lived in the darkness. On the outside, we both looked like we had it together, but really on the inside, we were both missing something, and we didn't know what it was until we found each other.

And now we live life in full color.

Tonight is a big deal. Emily's invited her girlfriends. Daniel is here. Victor and Eloise have been invited, and of course, my mother. The moment I introduced my mother to Emily, she fell in love. She told me she knew Emily was the one for me, and that she was far better suited than Elisabeth ever was.

And she's right.

What Emily and I have is easy.

Our love for each other is there, no need to showboat it, no need to fake it. We're quite simply one with each other.

Little does Emily know that tonight is not only going to be a huge exhibition for her paintings, but I also have a surprise in store for her too.

THERE'S a small after-party with our nearest and dearest. I hired a boat to cruise along the Seine to celebrate a successful exhibition. The champagne is flowing, and everyone is enjoying themselves.

I stand at the head of the table. Everyone stops what they're doing and turns to look at me. The sparkling lights of Paris are lit up behind me, and the famous Parisian monuments we pass along the way as we cruise down the Seine.

This is the moment.

"I just want to say a couple of words." Everyone goes quiet. "First, I want to thank you all for making the journey to Paris to celebrate this special night with us. I know Emily and I are so happy that you did." I look around at all the smiling faces along the table. "Secondly, I'd like to thank Emily." I look down at my gorgeous partner. "I want to thank her for making me fall in love with art again, for pulling me, kicking and screaming, out of the darkness and back into the light... back into the real world. I know for a fact that I'd not be where I am at this moment in my life and career if it wasn't for her."

Emily's bright green eyes well with tears.

"'Love in Color' was the name of our exhibition, and that's what Emily has done to me. She makes all the colors in my life more vibrant. Emily makes me stop and take the time to appreciate the small things... like the fields of sunflowers or a delicious meal. She's my right-hand woman in love, life, and business, and I can't see my life without her. And so that's why I want to ask her..." I turn to face her directly, "...if she would like to spend the rest of her life with me. Taking time to stop and smell the flowers together."

The table is silent as all attention is focused on Emily.

I move and fall to one knee pulling the red box that has been boring a hole in my jacket all night out and open it for her.

Emily's eyes widen. I know what I have bought is extravagant, but it's truly her. The emerald in the center reminds me of her eyes, the rubies on the left-hand side remind me of her lips, the yellow diamonds on the right side remind me of the sunflowers she loves so much. I know it may not be a traditional ring, but it's us. It's 'Love in Color.'

"Yes," Emily answers straight away. "Yes. Yes. Yes." She leaps into my arms, and we fall onto the wooden floor of the boat. She kisses me all over my face while our friends and family are all cheering out their congratulations.

"If you keep pressing yourself against me like this, I don't know if I'm going to be able to control myself, and I'm pretty sure this dinner didn't include an X-rated show." Emily bursts out laughing as she moves away from me. "Give me your hand." She holds it out as I pull the ring from its box then place it on her finger.

The perfect fit.

"It's so beautiful." She looks down at it dreamily. "I love it, and I love you." She reaches over and pulls me into a passionate kiss.

"You ready to spend the rest of your life with me?"

"Well, you're my favorite artist."

THE END

ACKNOWLEDGMENTS

Thank you once again for purchasing one of my books to read. Never in my wildest dreams did I ever expect to be doing what I love as a job and all because of **YOU**!

As always I have to thank my wonderful family who let me have peace and quiet when I am on deadline.

My amazingly supportive author friends who every single day help me navigate this business. Being an author is a lonely but having my girls right there with me makes the journey so much better.

Of course I can't forget to mention my amazing editor, fantastic designer, the most brilliant Beta and review team and all round supportive readers.

THANK YOU!

ABOUT THE AUTHOR

JA Low lives in the Australian Outback. When she's not writing steamy scenes and admiring hot cowboy's, she's tending to her husband and two sons, and dreaming up the next epic romance.

Come follow her

Facebook: www.facebook.com/jalowbooks
Twitter: www.twitter.com/jalowbooks
Instagram: www.instagram.com/jalowbooks
Pinterest: www.pinterest.com/jalowbooks
Website: www.jalowbooks.com
Goodreads: https://www.goodreads.com/author/show/14918059.J_A_Low
BookBub: https://www.bookbub.com/authors/ja-low

ABOUT THE AUTHOR

Come join JA Low's Block
www.facebook.com/groups/1682783088643205/

You can also subscribe to my newsletter via my website.

www.jalowbooks.com

You can send me an email anytime here

jalowbooks@gmail.com

ALSO BY JA LOW

<u>The Dirty Texas Box Set</u>

Five full length novels and Five Novellas included in the set.

One band. Five dirty talking rock stars and the women that bring them to their knees.

This collection includes:

Suddenly Dirty

He was everything she wasn't looking for.
She was everything he wasn't ready for.

A workplace romance with your celebrity hall pass.

Suddenly Together

She was everything he always wanted.
He was everything she could never have.

A best friend to lover's romance with the one man who's off limits.

Suddenly Bound

He was everything she could never have.
She was everything he couldn't possess.

An opposites attract romance with family loyalty tested to its limits.

Suddenly Trouble

She was everything he wasn't allowed to have.

He was everything she couldn't have.

A brother's best friend romance with a twist.

Suddenly Broken

He was everything she wasn't looking for.

She was everything he wasn't ready for.

A friend's with benefits romance that takes a wild ride.

One little taste can't hurt; can it?

If you like your rock stars dirty talking, alpha's with hearts of gold this series is for you.

ALSO BY JA LOW

The Paradise Club Series

Book 1 - <u>Paradise</u>

** *Spin off from the Dirty Texas Series* **

My name's Nate Lewis, owner of The Paradise Club.

I can bring every little dirty fantasy you have ever dreamed of to reality.

My business is your pleasure. I'm good at it.

So good it's made me a wealthy and powerful man.

I have one rule—never mix business and pleasure, and I've lived by it from day one.

Until her.

** WARNING: If you do not like your books with a lot of heat then do not read this book. **

ALSO BY JA LOW

Playboys of New York Series
Book 1 - Off Limits

Chloe Jones is trying to put the scandal of leaving her Super Bowl legend fiancé at the altar behind her. No better way to escape than to turn her island honeymoon into a much-needed vacation with her girls. What she wasn't expecting was to meet a hot stranger. Don't they say to get over somebody you need to get under someone else?

Chloe's ready for a fresh start, shame her vengeful ex is making it difficult for her. That is until she lands the job of her dreams.

What she wasn't expecting was to come face to face with the hot stranger from her island escape—Noah Stone, New York's biggest playboy, and her new boss.

Chloe can be professional even if all she can think about is those lips. And the way he fills out his suit pants.

He's totally off-limits, and she's signed the paperwork that says so.

INTERCONNECTING SERIES

Reading order for interconnected characters.

Dirty Texas Series

Suddenly Dirty

Suddenly Together

Suddenly Bound

Suddenly Trouble

Suddenly Broken

Paradise Club Series

Paradise

Playboys of New York

Off Limits

ALSO BY JA LOW

International Bad Boys Set

Book 1 - The Sexy Stranger

** Was released as Fate's Plan a novella. This is now a full length standalone Novel **

Lilly

This is not how I saw my life panning out. Flying halfway across the world, leaving my dream job behind me all because my fiancé couldn't keep it in his pants. Coming home to my family is the exact cure I need for my broken heart.

What I wasn't expecting to see in my living room is a hot, naked, Italian man.

Did I mention, naked. I really shouldn't be looking at his...

Luca

I've always lived by my family's rules, but where has that gotten me? A cheating fiancée. A scandal that will be national news by morning.

I need to get away and plan my next move. A remote cottage in the middle of Scotland seems the right place.

That is until an awkwardly cute brunette stumbles into my cottage in the middle of a snowstorm where I'm standing. Naked.

She can't take her eyes off of my... I should go and put some pants on... shouldn't I?

ALSO BY JA LOW

Bratva Jewels Duet Box Set

SAPPHIRE - BOOK 1

An unconventional love is tested to its limits.

Mateo is used to being in the spotlight, he craves it in everything he does... except when it comes to his love life - that is firmly in the closet.

Tomas shuns the spotlight, the one he was born into, he wants nothing to do with it or his high-flying family who now reject him for his choices in love.

But Tomas' and Mateo's carefully constructed lives are turned inside out when they discover a beautiful, battered woman on their doorstep. The woman with the sapphire eyes has no memory of who she is or how she got there. She doesn't know about the Bratva Jewels - the Russian mafia's most desired escorts - or how her story intersects with theirs. Can Tomas and Mateo help her remember before the men who are after her find her first?

DIAMOND - BOOK 2

Round 2 with the Devil begins.

Grace thought she had left the nightmare of the Bratva Jewels behind her. Her days spent as one of the Russian Mafia's most desired escorts were some of the darkest of her life, but she was safe now. Or so she thought.

When Russian mobster Dmitri seeks revenge, he gets it, and Grace knows she must call on every ounce of inner strength she has to withstand what he has in store for her. What she didn't expect was to meet someone like Maxim...

Maxim is one of the Bratva's most skilled, and most feared, assassins. But his relationship to the Bratva is a complicated one. And when he meets Grace, suddenly everything becomes clear.

INTERCONNECTING SERIES

Reading order for Interconnecting Series

Bratva Jewels Series

The Sexy Stranger

Manufactured by Amazon.ca
Bolton, ON